SILVER MOON CRIES

THE WOLVES OF SHADOW GROVE, BOOK TWO

LEAH COPELAND

Title page

Silver Moon Cries

The Wolves of Shadow Grove, Book 2

By Leah Copeland ©2022

1st Edition

Covers by Design by Definition and Getcovers.

❀ Created with Vellum

To say tonight had been a living hell was an understatement, and it wasn't even over yet.

The energy in the room made my spine tingle. Aiden wouldn't sit down. He paced the creaking floors with his bare feet, the hem of his ripped jeans trailing the wood. "I should have taken the knife."

"You didn't know," I said, glaring at the silver bullet wound in his chest and fumbling with my Gigi's red jeweled necklace.

"But Fran warned me. He warned me and I didn't listen." Aiden dragged his palms from his disheveled charcoal hair down to his worn square jaw. "This is all my fault."

Ugh. Hearing Fran's name sent a vile shiver down my back, especially knowing he had Aiden contracted to do twenty-four hours of dirty work. "Why would you have? That guy was a dirtbag."

"I know, but he wasn't lying. I shouldn't have chalked it up to just a rumor. Now Dorian could be on his way, and until we confirm that, every person on this mountain is at risk."

I clenched my fist. How could this be happening? Dorian, one of the oldest werewolves in existence, coming for Aiden?

Ryan barged in through the front door wearing nothing but shorts and his usual scowl. "Everyone's getting ready and heading to their posts now."

Aiden stopped pacing. "What's the plan?"

"Half the pack will be at stations, and the other half will scope things out here. You and I will head down to the bridge to keep things isolated there. If there's an attack, I want to keep it away from the houses and the most vulnerable members."

Aiden wiped his hand down the back of his neck. "Okay. Sydney, I'm sorry, but…"

I stopped fidgeting with my necklace and leaned forward on the couch. "I know. We have to split up."

He nodded. "We need to get you out of here. We can have someone get you back to Havenport."

"It's too late for that." Ryan planted his dirt-covered feet in a dominant stance and balled his fists.

"It might not be," Aiden argued. "She needs to be as far away from here as possible."

"And this is why humans are a liability. It puts other pack members in danger to watch out for her when you can't."

I clenched my jaw shut. I hated how Ryan talked about me, like being a human was a freaking disease.

"Even if she got out of here, those hunters could have Dorian's army track *her* scent." Ryan looked down his long nose at me. "They could capture her and hold her for ransom. Then I'd have to babysit *you* to keep you from making a stupid decision."

My eyes widened. I hadn't even thought about that. Not that Liv would ever give my scent out, because I wasn't sure she would. But her brothers might. And he was right—Aiden

2

might come after me. Probably getting himself or someone else killed.

"I agree with that," I said, interrupting whatever Aiden was about to counter with.

His mouth dropped open, and he snapped his face in my direction. "What?"

Ryan stared at me with equal surprise.

"You're right," I repeated. "Making a run for it would be a dumb thing to do."

Ryan's gray eyebrows crinkled. "Okay. It's settled. Pete will be here any minute to take you to the shelter." He looked at Aiden. "You and I need to go. Now. I'll be waiting out back."

Without another word between us, he stomped into the hallway toward the kitchen.

I looked up at Aiden, my stomach clenching. Lavender circles hung under his eyes, and his sharp cheekbones softened as he held his turquoise eyes on mine. I didn't want us to split up, but it made sense.

It was the only way right now.

I stood up and wrapped my arms around him. In turn, he pulled my uninjured cheek against his warm chest. The meta-bond flowed from skin to skin, and I breathed in the scent of pine and day-old cologne.

From the corner of my eye, his bullet wound looked worse. The spindly black veins stretched down to his diaphragm, and my body felt the need to jump back into action to protect him.

I pressed my palm to his chest. "What about Cora? She hasn't come to heal you yet. You can't fight like this."

"I don't have a choice. Hopefully she doesn't show up in the middle of this mess, but I have to push through."

That wasn't good enough for me. Two things threatened his life right now, and there was nothing I could do about it.

"But what if it gets worse? What if something happens to you? What if—"

"Syd." Aiden reached up to my chin and traced his thumb along my lip. "It'll be okay. I'll be okay."

Would he, though?

Aiden raised his head as the rumble of a motorcycle billowed up the driveway. "That's Pete."

Heaviness settled in my chest, and I turned toward the window, but Aiden's fingers gently pulled my face back to his. Then he kissed me. Warmth flooded through me, briefly calming the nerves that tightened like a fist around my heart.

The front door opened, and Pete's footsteps shuffled inside. "Ryan told me to come get Sydney."

Breaking the contact of Aiden's fingers on my chin, I turned to see Pete standing there in the same clothes from earlier, a t-shirt and khaki shorts. His hair looked windblown, and he held a red motorcycle helmet under his arm that sheened under the recessed lights.

I shifted my gaze back to Aiden, trying to push away any thought of losing him. "Please, be careful."

His calloused fingers gently slid up my cheeks, and he searched my face one more time. "I'll make it back to you. I promise."

"Don't make promises you can't keep."

"I don't." He pressed his lips to mine, kissing me harder than before.

My pulse shot up, not because of the bond bolting through me, but because of the way he kissed me. Like he might not get to again.

That almost broke me.

"Time to go," Pete said.

I hesitantly took the red metallic helmet he held out for me. "We're taking your motorcycle?"

"It's the fastest way, unless I shifted and you rode my back, but I don't think Aiden would be a fan of that."

"Damn right." Aiden smirked. "Thank you. I gotta go. Please be safe." He pulled away from my grasp until I held nothing but cold air in my hands.

"We will," Pete replied. "Stay alive."

Aiden turned and headed down the hallway. Every part of me wanted to stop him, or at least kiss him one more time. That couldn't be the last time. Sobs crawled their way up my throat, but I swallowed them back as soon as Pete's footsteps headed to the door.

"Let's go, shall we?"

"Coming." I hobbled behind, my ankle raging with pain as we stepped off the porch and onto the driveway where his motorcycle stalled. It was covered in jagged red and black accents, oozing with speed and agility.

Pete swung his leg over and revved the ear-splitting engine. "Come on. Your seat's right behind me."

I went as fast as I could to the growling bike. It was almost too tall for me, but I climbed over and balanced on the ankle that wasn't the size of an orange.

Without hesitation, Pete snatched the helmet out of my hand and slid it over my head. "I know you're hurt, but we gotta hurry."

"Thanks," I said, my voice bouncing back at me under the visor.

"Hold on to me," he called out over the engine. He leaned forward, hands loose and relaxed around the handlebars.

I wrapped my arms around his rock-hard waist and we took off. Pete's hair whipped back in the sharp pine air, and I clenched my mouth shut to keep from screaming. When we veered off into the woods, I clutched my arms tighter.

We jostled and bounced through the darkness. The trees

were like scraggly monsters that wanted to reach out and grab us. I could barely see a thing between the visor and the branches blocking out any light. I almost tried to ask Pete how he could tell where he was going, but then I remembered werewolves had perfect night vision.

Brush and sticks snapped beneath the tires, and we leaned sideways into a turn, skidding against the dirt around a wide tree. Pete shoved his heel into the ground, sharpening the turn effortlessly and plowing through a narrow set of bushes until we sailed onto a thin trail.

Arms shaking and blood pumping, I kept my eyes peeled for any shadows that shouldn't be moving.

We broke free from the woods, probably a couple miles away from Aiden's house. A white, two-story home came into view at the top of a hill. Pete leaned forward, gearing the bike up through the grass. I went with it, clinging to him as my body vibrated with the power of the engine.

And then a shadow darted from around the house.

I gasped, and Pete jerked the bike to a stop. He threw his foot into the ground to keep us from tipping over and scanned the grassy hill.

The shadow was gone, but only for a second.

It appeared on our right again. A snow-white wolf with glowing red eyes.

Ice drenched my veins, and I held onto a scream as four more wolves closed in around us.

Pete revved the engine again, kicking the bike in full high gear just as the shadows began gunning toward us. He swerved to a stop, tires screeching on the paved driveway right outside the white house.

"Get inside! Go," Pete yelled.

We jumped off the bike, and I lunged for the back door, my ankle giving out as I gripped the handle. Just then, more red eyes appeared on my left. They were like lasers zeroing in on me.

In a panic, I yanked the door open and jumped inside, slamming it shut in time to see Pete punch the wolf sideways into the motorcycle. The wolf howled and the bike crunched against the asphalt, but it gave Pete time to shift.

His clothes fell to pieces on the driveway, and he stalked around the other wolf as they rolled to their feet. Two more barreled out from the woods, launching at him. Fangs at the ready, Pete dug his paws into the ground, his eyes flaming as he braced against the attack.

My hands shook uncontrollably, and I pulled the helmet off to get a better view. But I almost screamed again when two chilly hands touched my arm. I whirled around to see Tabitha.

She stood at the entrance of a wood-paneled hallway. Her hair was a much duller red in the dim lighting and long shadows cast down her pointed cheeks. "Everyone's downstairs. We have to go."

"But Pete's out there alone," I protested. "He needs help!"

She pursed her thin lips and shook her head. "Julius is out there too."

But a sharp cry erupted outside, causing both our gazes to snap in that direction. A storm of fur and gnashing teeth rolled around in the driveway.

"I'll help him once you're downstairs," Tabitha said, linking her hand around my arm. She tugged me down the hall, bringing me to a metal door that didn't look like it belonged among the dark walls. She whipped it open and gently shoved me onto the landing. "Help keep the children calm."

I stared down the metal staircase into the darkness at the bottom.

"Tell Theresa I'm fighting, and no matter what happens, do *not* open any of these doors until I come back."

Reaching my trembling fingers toward the cold steel railing, I took one last look at Tabitha before she slammed the door shut and ground the lock in place.

2

---

*a*nother metal door stood in my way when I got to the bottom of the murky stairs. I knocked, the sound echoing against the concrete that surrounded me.

It squeaked open, and a sliver of a woman I vaguely recognized appeared. It was Theresa, Nat's mom. She clasped her fingers around the edge of the door, her blue diamond eyes looking me up and down with suspicion. But she seemed to remember me too. She grabbed my wrist and pulled me inside, slamming the door shut behind us.

We were in a boxy room. Under the dim lights, about fifteen children sat against the far wall. They varied in age, some looking as young as four and others as old as twelve. All of them stared at me with bold blue eyes, but none of them gave me the sensation like needles jamming into my neck the way Becca's glare did.

She leaned against the wall, one leg crossed over the other in her skinny jeans and short boots. Her sleek arms folded across her dirt-smudged tank top, and her mocha hair flowed in graceful waves past her perfect shoulders.

I wanted to fade away under her piercing glare. She was

9

the type that made me feel like my brown eyes and loose black curls were plain. But instead of folding, I forced myself to stand up taller.

I couldn't compare myself to her. I was a dancer from the ordinary world, and she was a badass werewolf, probably hardened by the necessity of defending her pack.

"Sydney, right?" Theresa asked from behind me.

I turned, glad for the distraction from Becca. "Yeah. You're Theresa?" I tried to keep my vocal cords from wobbling, but my nerves were almost shot after this never-ending night. "Tabitha told me to tell you she's fighting."

"Good to know. Thanks."

A crash above made us all look up at the concrete ceiling. Gasps from the children bounced off the walls.

"It's okay," Becca said in a soothing voice. "Just stay quiet. Okay?"

For a second, I almost believed she could be nice.

There was a long scraping sound, like furniture moving across the hard floor above us. Then a clattering and banging that seemed to come from everywhere. I cringed at each noise, especially when the scritch-scratching of claws slid across the house.

Seconds later, everything went eerily silent.

Theresa let out a soft exhale as the tension in the room seemed to soften with the quiet.

Still shaken, I made my way to the wall opposite of Becca and sat down. The cold cement made my skin jump, but also kept me grounded. I pulled my knees into my chest and said a silent prayer for Aiden, Pete, and Tabitha. I even said one for Ryan, although he was kind of an Alpha Douche.

Nat stood up out of the sea of children to my left and waded over to me. She sat her small body down beside me, still in her red pajamas from earlier. "Hi," she whispered.

"Hi," I said, trying to keep my voice low. "Have you been down here long?"

"No." She shook her head shyly, almost hiding her face under her sleek chin-length hair. "Mom told me Aiden woke up."

I gave her a small smile. "Thank you for your help."

"You're welcome." She stared ahead and tightened her lips like she wanted to say something else. "Are you and Aiden dating?"

My face flushed as everyone's attention turned to me. "Um…"

"Nat. Mind your own business," Theresa scolded from the doorway.

Nat folded her arms and after another minute, she asked, "Did you know I healed you after your car accident?"

I smiled again. "Yeah. Thank you for that. I owe you."

"Nah." She waved her hand. "It was nothing."

"It was something."

She stared at my face for a long moment before pointing to my cheek. "Does that hurt?"

"Oh." Reaching up to the cut I got when I jumped out of Liv's window, I fought back a wince against the puffy skin. "It's okay."

Without another word, she extended her fingers up to my face and began humming softly. My shoulders went rigid, unsure what to do as I felt all eyes on me again.

Her fingers grew warmer against my cheek, and within seconds, she pulled her hand away. "All better."

"Whoa." I touched where the bruise had been, but all that remained was a dull soreness. The torn flesh had been renewed, and the swelling was almost gone. "Thanks."

"You're welcome. Are you hurt anywhere else? I can help with anything."

My eyes landed on my ankle, which bulged out over the

11

top of my Converse shoe, but the last thing I wanted was to zap any more of her energy. After each round of healing Aiden last night, she looked more and more drained. "I'm okay, but thanks. You're sweet for checking on me."

"I just like to help people," she said casually, leaning back against the wall.

Another thump hit our ceiling, followed by a series of crashes and shatters.

My stomach rolled, twisting at the reminder of what was happening outside.

"Everyone stay where you are and be quiet." Becca pressed her finger to her mouth and turned toward Theresa.

Something sounding like a rock slide landed above us and Theresa staggered her feet defensively.

"What the hell?" Becca asked, scanning the ceiling.

Then it happened again. Over and over, until the children started screaming and a couple of the older ones shifted.

A *thunk* hit the floor, then traveled until it picked back up on the metal door at the top of the stairs.

Theresa's eyes bulged and she stepped back. We all watched our door, listening to the constant jarring pounds coming at a steady rate from upstairs.

I stood up and reached for the comfort of the cement wall against my back. My palms sweat more with every sound, and my muscles threatened to turn into a puddle of mush.

"Are they trying to smash through the door?" Becca asked, moving up by Theresa.

"I think so." Theresa's voice shook over the clanging metal echoing down to us.

Then a screeching erupted from the top of the stairs, and in less than a second, something rammed *hard* against our door.

Becca swore, kneeling down and drawing a knife out from her boot. The blade gleamed under the corner lights, and I could tell from how it shined that it was silver. She dashed over to me faster than I could track and held out the engraved handle. "Take this and stay with the kids. The littles can't shift yet, but they can run fast."

I nodded, my fingers trembling as I took the blade.

Jolting echoes boomed through the room. Theresa slammed her palms against the metal door, leaning into it as the middle began protruding.

"Scoot back," Becca instructed the children. They moved against the wall, uncovering another metal door in the floor.

With a grunt, she pulled a small lever and thrust it open, letting the door fall backward onto the floor. "Everyone go. Run! Go!"

One by one, the kids jumped into the dark doorway. I waited my turn, watching in shock at how this night was unraveling.

"I can't keep them back," Theresa yelled from the door. Her body jolted against each hit from the other side.

"Go!" Becca yelled at me when the last kid jumped.

I peered over the edge and dropped the knife first. The last thing I needed was to accidentally stab myself on the way down. It clunked against a hard surface, and I stepped off the ledge. The drop was only a few feet, but it was enough to make me lose my balance, and my shoulder met the cold shock of the cement floor.

The door above me slammed shut. The echo traveled down the surrounding tunnel, bringing me back to what I needed to do. *Run.*

I swiped the blade up and jammed it into my back pocket. The tip was so sharp, it cut right through the denim, poking out like a crappy makeshift holster. But it worked.

My feet clumsily followed after the kids. They were way ahead of me, even the smallest ones, like tiny specks under the sporadic floodlights.

How was I supposed to keep these kids safe if they were so much faster than me?

The last kid disappeared at the entrance. I had to keep up or I wouldn't know where to go. I pumped my arms, rekindling the adrenaline I needed to erase the pain firing through my ankle.

When I made it to the door, the humid air hit my lungs and the morning light peeked over the trees. I almost got a sense of calm, but then I came face to face with a dusky brown wolf.

My heart stopped just before my feet did, and I reached for the knife. This wolf was smaller than the others. Familiar, even. It was their pale blue eyes. They were like the ones I'd just made eye contact with inside the shelter.

"Nat?"

She dipped her head down and flicked her tail, as if saying *yes*.

Relieved, I dropped my hand from the knife. "Let's go. You need to run ahead. I can't keep up."

I picked up my feet again, pushing through the unstable grass and tree roots. We were already in the woods, mostly shielded by the green of the trees.

"Nat, go!" I yelled at her through winded breaths, but she stayed by my side, visibly going slower than she could have.

Pitchy howls erupted somewhere behind us, and I picked up the pace. My muscles burned, and my feet felt like a million pounds, but I kept going.

Heavy bounding footsteps crashed through the brush behind us. I prayed it was Pete or Aiden, really anyone from Ryan's pack, but when I glanced back, nausea punched through my stomach.

Red eyes followed us, gaining quickly as the gray wolf they belonged to took a massive leap off the hill and collided right into Nat.

It happened so fast. It was a blur.

Everything twisted inside me watching Nat get taken out and slammed into a tree. Her yelp rang out, and I skidded to a halt, swearing from the stabbing in my ankle.

Her small body hit a tree and she rolled to her feet like a cat. She bared her teeth, her eyes penetrating through the other wolf as it stalked around her, completely ignoring me.

The wolf's paws were almost the size of Nat's midsection, and it smacked its huge claws at her again.

I watched in horror as the wolf kept swiping at her, growling with intent. When it tore a gash along her shoulder, something snapped inside me.

I rushed at the wolf, the knife already in my hand, high above my head. Coming up onto its hind parts, I slammed the blade into its hip. "Nat, run!"

The beast's gray head reared back, and a piercing, ragged howl broke free from its mouth.

More pained howls sounded in the distance. I left the knife in the wolf's hip and turned to run, but something slammed against my back. Wind swept through my hair and then a furious blow rattled through my skull as I hit the base of a tree.

I blinked, trying to clear the stars in my vision, but they strung together like a black veil over my eyes.

Something heavy jumped on me. My lungs struggled under the pressure, suppressing the scream bubbling in my throat. Thick needles dug into my skin, threatening to break through the surface. I opened my eyes in time to see white jagged teeth coming at my face and threw my hands up under the wolf's neck. Every ounce of my blood ran cold as those devil-red irises glared down at me.

I couldn't hold it much longer.

Would this be how I died? Getting eaten by a werewolf?

My arms shook, and the air ran like hot coals down my

throat, spreading fire through my constricted lungs. Hot breaths beat against my face. Vicious snarls vibrated through the furry throat in my hands.

This was it. My arm gave out, and I jammed my other elbow up, but I was too tired—

A blur of amber eyes and ash-brown fur sailed into my vision, hurtling the gray wolf off me.

Pete.

The stabbing air whooshed back through me, and I propped up on my elbows.

Twigs snapped and vicious growls echoed as Pete and the other wolf rolled through the trees. Nat rushed at them both and latched her mouth just under the silver knife sticking out of the gray wolf's hip. She bit down hard. The wolf's shriek cut through the air, washing a chill down my back as Pete seized its neck.

Bones snapped sickeningly, and I looked away until there was a crash on the ground and everything went quiet.

When I turned back, the wolf lay in the grass, its red eyes now a shade of dull blue, and its head rotated in an unnatural way.

Pete's and Nat's gazes rested on me again, both staring at me with a human gleam in their eyes. Pete glanced at Nat, like he was sending a message to her, and then she howled before bounding off in the direction of the other children.

"Thanks," I choked out, scooting up against the tree and digging my fingers into the bark. My attacker's body had now formed back into a human. A woman with steel-gray hair. Her eyes were a dull blue now, not red like before. And they were empty. All life drained.

Had she known what she was doing?

Aiden had told me before that Dorian could control wolves if he absorbed their Alpha. Did that mean all these wolves were his *puppets*, under mindless compulsion?

The thought ate at me, tearing me to pieces. I turned away, refusing to look at her anymore. I gradually pulled myself to my feet and leaned against the tree. Every part of me shook in protest.

Something wasn't right.

Pete whined, then disappeared in a blur. The sounds of his paws hit the ground farther away until they stopped behind a tree somewhere.

My knees quaked, and suddenly my body felt like it was on fire. I grabbed the lowest branch to keep myself upright. What was going on? Why did I feel this way?

Then I saw the jagged marks on my arm.

They burned red, skidding the width of my forearm angrily.

Pete appeared again, wearing ripped khaki shorts and dried blood streaks across his chest. Without missing a beat, he moved right in front of me and reached for my arm.

My breaths shallowed as I followed his line of sight to the cuts. By now it felt like someone had poured gasoline in them and lit a match.

"She bit you."

I shook my head, trying to make sense of his words, but it only made my vision swim. "It's just a scratch," I mumbled.

"No, it's not," he said harshly, his fingers turning my forearm back and forth. "A scratch wouldn't blister up like that. She got you with a fang."

I gasped when I looked down again. The small red tears had already swelled into welts, and sweat beaded down my arms. It was so hot all of a sudden. All I wanted was to jump into arctic waters.

"No," I whispered, but the ground wavered, and I reached for Pete's shoulder. "I'm fine…just a little shaken."

"You're not fine, Sydney."

17

I wanted to argue, but I couldn't breathe. My feet faltered even though I wasn't walking. "What's happening?"

"It's the venom." Pete's hands reached out to me as the world spun and turned upside down. His arms curled under me and the next thing I knew, he was running back toward the houses.

"Venom?" I asked, my voice getting carried away with the wind.

"Werewolf venom," he answered.

Werewolf venom.

I wanted to say something, but I couldn't get the words out. My heartbeats sledgehammered, speeding up and slowing down at random. Every drop of blood in my veins was like molten lava trying to burst through my pores.

Pete tightened his grip around me. "I know it hurts like hell, but you're almost through the initial pain."

Hurts like hell didn't even come close to what this was. I kept my eyes on the pink and orange smudges of the sunrise, fighting to stay awake.

"Am I..." I wanted to finish my sentence, but my words got lost in my head.

Pete looked down at me as if understanding what I couldn't say. "Yeah. You're going to turn."

a deep sigh skated across my face.

"Did you find Aiden before bringing her here?" Tabitha's soft voice came from right beside me.

"No," Pete said from somewhere nearby. "I wasn't sure the best way to tell him."

A cool hand settled over my forehead, and I cracked my eyes open, almost regretting it when the sunlight burst into my retinas.

Tabitha knelt on the floor by me, her eyelids creasing in the corners with worry. "How are you feeling?"

I blinked away the fuzziness in my vision. We were back in Ryan's and Tabitha's living room. Their house was a mess, but at least it was still standing. A gaping hole had been torn through the jagged drywall, allowing the pine breeze to waft inside, cooling my aching skin.

Pete and Becca stood on the other side of the room. Pete's jaw clenched tight; his arms folded across his hard, bare chest. Becca stood beside him in leggings and a loose shirt, a deep scowl resting on her striking face.

"Where's Aiden?" I asked, hardly recognizing my throaty voice.

"He should be here soon," Tabitha answered. "Everything went a lot longer than we thought. Dorian's army was…"

"Insane," Pete said. "I don't know how we pulled that off."

"It all came down to the other packs stepping in," Becca said.

My body sank into the couch cushions. Knowing Aiden was okay was all I cared about—not that everything down to my hair follicles throbbed.

But then my stomach turned, and a wave of shivers washed through my bones. My hands started shaking, and I pulled my arms in toward myself, preserving as much body heat as possible.

Tabitha reached behind me and pulled a blanket across my shoulders. It was a nice gesture, but it didn't really help.

"How are you holding up?" she asked.

I opened my mouth to answer, but all my stomach acid decided to work its way up my throat. I was totally going to hurl.

When I twisted onto my side, Tabitha already had a trash can ready for me. Her cool hands swept my curls back, gliding over the slippery sheen of sweat on the back of my neck.

And then it happened.

Coughing against the leftover burning in my mouth, I collapsed back on the couch. "Am I dying?"

"No, honey. It's the transition starting. You'll feel better soon."

The *transition*?

I wanted to ask what she meant, but Aiden's voice cut me off.

"What's going on?" he asked. He stepped in through the broken wall, now wearing basketball shorts. The wound in

20

his chest had stretched farther, too, sending another rush of panic through me.

We needed to get that witch over here to heal him.

"Aiden," Tabitha spoke gently as he took in the mess of drywall and splintered wood. But she didn't have time to say anything else before he saw me.

His eyebrows slammed together, and he was beside me in a second. "What happened?"

"They broke into the cellar," Tabitha answered. "Everyone had to evacuate."

Aiden whipped his head around to look at her. "Where are the kids? Are they okay?"

"They all made it to the warehouse," Becca said. "They're okay. Theresa's bringing them back."

"Good." The wrinkle between Aiden's brows smoothed a little, and he reached for my hand under the blanket. The fabric shifted off my forearm, revealing the searing scratches, and his eyes snagged on them. "Please don't tell me that's—"

"Nat was in trouble," I whispered, finally finding my voice through the brain fog. "There was another wolf. I stabbed her, and she turned on me."

Revulsion crossed his face.

"By the time I got over there and took the wolf down, it had already happened," Pete said.

"When?" Aiden demanded. "When did this happen?"

I had no idea how long it had been. I looked past Aiden's shoulder to Tabitha and Pete, trying to ignore the look of disdain on Becca's face.

"About an hour ago," Pete answered.

Aiden stood and whirled on him in one fluid motion. "An *hour* ago? Why didn't you come find me? We could have tried to do something!"

Everyone in the room flinched at his shouting, but Pete didn't waver.

"There's nothing we can do. I know you don't want to believe that, but this isn't the first transition you've seen."

Aiden paced the room, his back muscles rippling up both sides of his spine. "Cora's supposed to come here."

"Can she help?" I asked, hoping that Aiden wasn't just grasping at false hope.

"We'll find out," he answered, his footsteps getting heavier across the dirty wooden floor. "She has to be able to do something."

Pete stepped forward. "You have to be honest with her."

"I *am* being honest with her."

"Then you have to be honest with yourself. The venom has already traveled through her body. It's done. It's permanent."

My insides twisted. Something about the way Pete said "permanent" made me almost vomit again.

I didn't want this. Aiden clearly didn't want it for me either. He seemed terrified, even though I was the one whose life was about to change forever.

This was so much more than getting thrown into his world. This was his world branding me with a new set of genetics. This was his world becoming *mine*.

"Are you sure we can't do anything?" I asked, begging one more time for some kind of hope.

The only one who would look me in the eye was Pete. He crossed the room and sat down on what was left of the couch by my feet. "This is going to happen. On the next full moon."

"When is that?" Aiden barked out. "A month?"

"Three weeks," Tabitha said. She stood beside Becca, her arms folded around herself, her face so wan she looked frail.

My fingers grew clammy around the edge of the blanket. "Does that mean I have three weeks until I…"

"Turn?" Pete said. "Ideally, yes."

"Ideally," Aiden scoffed. "There's no other option, and

three weeks isn't a lot of time." He sounded near-hysterical as he paced back and forth.

"What do you mean by *ideally*? Can something else happen?" I asked.

Pete opened his mouth to speak, but Aiden stopped him. "Don't. It doesn't matter."

"She needs to know the alternative."

"There's no point," Aiden argued, fury sparking off his tongue. "It's *not* going to happen like that. It can't happen like that."

"What are you talking about?" A shiver crawled over my skin again. "What's the alternative?"

Pete's eyes met Aiden's before he slowly turned to face me. "You'll turn...if you survive the transition."

A lead weight cannonballed into my stomach. My eyes shot to Aiden. He had one hand propped on his hip and the other raking through his hair.

"*If* I survive?"

Aiden came back to kneel by me once more, claiming my hands in a desperate grip. Our bond flowed like electricity up my arms. "You *will* survive. We're going to help you through it."

I stared at the creases around his frown and his stitched eyebrows. His mouth said one thing, but the grief in his eyes, the way he clung to me, the way he shook...all of that said something else.

Ryan's clunky bare feet stepped up into the living room next. He also wore a pair of shorts, along with a sleeveless shirt cut down the sides.

Tabitha reached for him, pulling him into an embrace and whispering something in his ear. He stiffened and leaned over to take in my state. Those bushy eyebrows rose, and he ran his knuckles over his stubble. "Son, maybe it's—"

"What?" Aiden spun around. "Maybe it's better this way?"

23

Tabitha's fair face creased as she looked up at Ryan. "This isn't the time."

"Well," Ryan huffed. "Maybe it is. It was going to happen at some point. She's with us now. Having a human around was too much of a liability, whether or not she saved your life."

"She saved Nat's life, too," Tabitha added, pursing her thin lips.

Ryan froze. "Is that how this happened?"

"Yes. That's how this happened," Aiden snapped. "Because a *human* stepped in and saved one of our lives again."

Everything went so quiet that I wanted to either shrink away or make as much noise as possible. Shrinking away probably would have been easier, since I felt like death.

"Thank you," Ryan said. It took me a moment to realize he was talking to me. "You've stepped up to protect this pack, more than some of our own members have. Thank you for your sacrifice."

Staring back at Ryan's hard expression, despite his soft words, I wasn't sure what to say. Before I got the chance to respond, he broke our eye contact and looked around at the others. "We should give them a few minutes. Everybody out."

Aiden gripped my hand again as everyone filed out of the room. "I know you don't want this. I'm so sorry."

I squeezed his fingers and cleared my rough throat. "What are the chances of death?"

He didn't answer, but his gaze ripped right through me.

"I need to know. You can't protect me from it, no matter how much you try."

He shook his head, leaning his forehead against our clasped hands.

"You gotta tell her, man," Pete said from the doorway. "You can't keep her in the dark. She's better off knowing everything."

The sleek muscles of Aiden's shoulders rose and fell in a tormented sigh. "You do it. I can't."

Pete took a careful step back into the room. "Once you get past your current symptoms, getting to the full moon is the easiest part. But when it comes up, the change conjures all your inner demons. The more you have, the harder it is to get through."

"What do you mean? Like, emotional baggage?"

Aiden finally looked up, his mouth set in a deep frown. "Yes."

"Okay? Why is that such a horrible thing?" I was so confused.

"Your body gets thrown into fight or flight. You'll have hallucinations of your fears and failures. The more fears and grudges, the harder it is to keep your heart rate from spasming out of control...until it just gives out. That's why so many adults don't survive the transition. They're filled with too much grief from life."

My face must have said it all, because Aiden spoke up. "We'll help you. You can do this. You're strong, and I've seen you pull through death itself. You're a survivor, Syd."

But I didn't feel like a survivor. I held my breath to keep from getting sick again as another wave of nausea flooded through me.

There was no way I could get through that. After Liv's betrayal, Dad leaving, and all the other things I'd gone through this summer...

How could I face them again?

I was so screwed.

4

My eyes fluttered open. Yellow light blinded me for a moment before I blinked fully awake.

I was in a cloud-soft bed with a navy-blue comforter pulled up to my shoulders. The light was coming from a bedside lamp behind me. The last thing I remembered was Ryan had called a meeting, and then so many voices filed into this secret back room of his house. Aiden had kissed me on the forehead and said he'd be back, that they needed to discuss Dorian and the hunters.

And then somehow, I made it here.

I sat up and peered around. To my right stood a tall wooden dresser and a closet door. Straight ahead was a TV, and on my left were double French doors that faced the lush trees outside.

"Hey." Aiden stood in the doorway and my heart almost stopped at how much he seemed like himself again. The coloring had fully returned to his tanned face, and his eyes were back to their vibrant blue. He'd also cleaned up and put on his usual black v-neck and jeans. Somehow, he made even the simplest outfit something stunning.

"Is this your room?" My voice was raspy, but stronger than it was earlier.

The corners of his mouth turned up slightly, and he strode toward me, taking a seat on the edge of the bed. "Yeah. I carried you over here after you fell asleep earlier. Figured it would be more comfortable."

"Wow. I was really out of it. I had no idea."

"How do you feel now?"

"Better. My face doesn't feel like it's going to melt off anymore."

"Good." He slipped his fingers under my palm. They were warm and slightly calloused, but I loved it. The zap of energy from our bond came through, filling me to the brim with emotions I couldn't really explain.

"How about you?" I asked. "Did Cora heal you?"

"She came during our meeting, after you were already asleep."

"Can I see?" I asked, reaching for the hem of his shirt to make sure his wound really was gone.

He took my hand before I could see anything. "Hold on. There's something you should know."

"Okay?" I ignored the flutter of panic building. "What is it?"

"Cora couldn't get everything."

The panic spiked like a hot poker in my chest. "What do you mean?"

"She got a lot of the poison pulled back into the wound, but it was laced with black magic. She doesn't have enough power to manipulate and remove black magic, so I'm stuck like this." Aiden slowly raised his shirt, revealing the sooty bullet hole. It was smaller and darker, like the silver poisoning had pooled in his skin.

I reached out, running my fingers over smooth flesh.

"What does this mean? Will it keep moving toward your heart?"

"It will if I don't take the drops she gave me." He lowered his shirt and pulled a small tincture bottle from his pocket. "I need to take two every couple days to keep it localized."

"What happens when you run out? Are you going to owe her something every time you need more?" My words came out rushed and frantic. She hadn't really fixed the problem; she'd just put a really fancy band-aid on it.

"Syd, calm down. She said she'll take actual money for it instead of favors."

"Oh." That seemed to take a small weight off my shoulders.

"Please, don't worry about it." He stuck the tincture bottle back in his pocket and took my hand. "We have other pressing issues."

I frowned, remembering everything else that had happened during this weekend from hell. My sense of control over my life seemed to slip from my fingertips by the second. "How did the meeting go? I didn't even get to hear what happened at the bridge."

Aiden's face darkened, and he glanced away. "Dorian wasn't there. He just sent his army to come get me. They had already surrounded us by the time we got to the bridge."

A shudder rolled down my back, and I gripped his fingers tighter.

"I really wasn't sure if we were going to make it. They were *strong*. At one point, I think Dad was fighting off three at once. It wasn't until the other pack from West Virginia got here that things started looking up."

"I'm glad they showed." I scooted toward him, sliding my arms around him.

His hand slinked around my waist, and he planted a kiss

on my shoulder. The seconds passed in silence before he finally spoke again. "I asked Cora if there was anything she could do for you."

"And she can't?"

"No." I could see his mouth turn down out of the corner of my eye.

I winced at the sting as my last bit of hope drained away. Pete said it was permanent, but I'd still hoped Cora could do something. Anything. But if she couldn't heal Aiden, how could there have been any hope for me?

Now I was stuck on this path toward a future where I'd be completely different...if I had a future at all. And if I lived, would I join Aiden's pack? Would I have to stay here?

What would that mean for dance?

"Syd." Aiden leaned into my space, filling it with the scent of pine and soap. "I know you're scared, but I meant it earlier when I said you can do this."

"I don't really have a choice."

"Didn't you tell me once that there's always a choice?"

I vaguely recalled saying that to him after he made that deal with Fran. "Very funny."

"But it's true." His fingertips drew small circles into my palm. "Sometimes people don't make it through this because they give up. It's a battle, and a conscious effort to face your demons and choose survival. But you've done it before."

"When?"

"After your car accident. When I found you, you were still alive because you fought for it."

I shook my head, a heavy wave of defeat coming over me. "This is different."

"The circumstances are, but that's it. You have to believe you can do this."

The way he looked at me and held my hands made me

want to believe it, but this seemed so much bigger than just *choosing* survival. What would it be like to face my fears in hallucinations?

I shuddered and took a deep breath, forcing everything to calm inside me. There had to be a way to get through this.

The sky dimmed to a champagne orange through the French doors, and I suddenly realized it was late. "What time is it?"

"Almost eight."

"Crap. I slept all day? I never called Mom to let her know I was okay. She's probably freaking out and looking for me."

"Actually." Aiden stopped me as I threw the covers off my legs. "I bought you some time."

I froze. "What do you mean?"

His teeth scraped over his bottom lip in the guiltiest expression ever. "I talked to her while you were asleep."

"You talked to her—" Realization dawned on me. "Or you messed with her memories?"

"Uh...yes."

"Are you serious?" My eyes widened. "You know how that affected me before. Why would you think I'd be okay with you doing that to her?"

"I wasn't sure how much time you needed today. The last thing we want is a search party out on the town for you. Liv had already called your mom and made a mess...and I fixed it."

"Oh, no," I groaned. "Was it bad?"

"It's okay now," he said. "Your mom will probably think you went out for a bit while she was asleep."

I shook my head, completely mortified, but also a little relieved. Even if that made me feel like a horrible daughter. "Fine."

Finding fuel in my leftover anger, I jabbed my fist into his arm. It hurt my hand a little, but I did it again anyway.

He jumped back. "Okay, the first punch, I get. But what was that one for?"

"Because that was so stupid on your part. Liv or Donnie could have been at my house waiting for you."

"I brought back-up, and I wasn't there long. Two minutes, tops."

"Okay...does that mean I can go home?"

Aiden's chin tilted down, his eyes flicking over my face. "You could go home."

"But should I? Wouldn't that put Mom at risk, just like I worried about before? And now with this—" I peered down at the teeth marks on my arm, which had faded to pink. "This complicates things. What if Liv's family shows up later on? I don't think she'd do anything, but Donnie's an ass. I wouldn't put it past him to come knocking on my door and—"

A gaping hole ripped through my chest as I realized I couldn't stay with Mom much longer. There were too many dangers.

"You can go home," Aiden said again. "I'll make sure we have some pack members there to keep a lookout. You should spend a little time with your mom, if that's what you need right now."

"But I can't stay there for long." I swallowed down the rocky lump in my throat. "When I change—I can't go home after that. Even now, she's at risk if Dorian can track my scent, too."

"Syd. Take a breath." Aiden scooted closer and wound his arm around my waist, pulling me into his lap. He held me like a safety net, grasping me against his chest. All I wanted was to curl up and cry into his shoulder, but I needed to put my big-girl pants on and deal with it.

"We have to take things one day at a time right now. Dorian is still a major concern, but we don't know if he knows about you. And I called Omar today. He's bringing his pack over here for a while, and Cora agreed to help us out as much as she can. We're confident if we can spread the word about him, we'll be able to foresee the next attack."

Resting my arms on top of his, I relaxed a little. "Are you going to warn the other alphas you know?"

"Already have. Every pack along the East Coast should know about it by tomorrow. They'll spread the word, and packs will hopefully begin aligning with each other."

I let out a slow breath, leaning my forehead into the curve of his neck.

"All I want you to focus on right now is getting through this transition and figuring things out with your mom."

"But where will I go after I leave home?"

Aiden lifted his cheek off my head and tilted his gaze at me. "I kinda figured you'd stay with me."

"Oh." My stomach flipped. "Wouldn't that be weird for you? We've only been together for, like, a day, and I was unconscious for most of it. It might be moving too fast...and it could be for a long time." Maybe months—or years—if we lasted that long...

But Aiden, chill as ever, just chuckled. "True. We haven't been official that long, but we've already been through more life and death situations than the average relationship endures. So, when you think about it that way, it's like we've been together for years." He flashed a smile that made my heart spin and planted a kiss on my forehead.

"Seems like sound logic." I smiled, shoving down the fluttering worries that kept popping up.

Aiden leaned down further, brushing his lips on my cheek and working his way down to my mouth. My face heated against his, and I sank into him. I really didn't want to leave this spot on his lap, but my time was limited with Mom now, and I needed to be there for her.

"I need to go," I whispered.

"After you eat. Your dinner's in the kitchen."

The warmth that flooded my chest was almost as strong as the hunger pangs I finally felt. "You made me dinner?"

"Don't get too excited. It's just ramen."

But I was, because that was so...*normal*...and that was what I needed right now.

5

*D*usk settled in the sky like black smoke covering the moon. Aiden turned the truck down my street, passing the familiar houses and white fenced yards. A subtle smile pulled at my lips at the normalcy.

It felt so good to be back home.

If Aiden's memory thing really worked on Mom, she'd probably be at work, pulling a late shift with payroll. That meant I could walk into an empty house and crash in my own bed. I was so ready for that.

Right before we turned into the driveway, Becca's mocha-colored tail swished through the trees. She and Pete followed us here, although she'd made it pretty clear she didn't want to. She and I hadn't hit it off, for reasons I wasn't even sure of, but I was grateful she and Pete were here. I could sleep without worrying about unwelcome visitors tonight.

But as we pulled into the driveway, my stomach plummeted. All my hopes of a quiet evening broke apart.

Liv's car faced out toward us, and she sat on my front porch. She rose to her feet, clinging to the railing as Aiden slammed on the brakes.

"Stay here," he said.

Before I could say anything, he was out of his seat and crossing the front lawn toward her. His shoulders raised up, ready to shift out in the open, and Liv gunned it for him, her eyes slit with rage.

I jumped out of the truck, leaving the door wide open as I ran after Aiden, not nearly as fast as either of them.

"You son of a bitch," Liv yelled as she took a swing at him just before I thought they might collide with each other. He dodged it, ducking down and then coming back up, his shoulders broader than before. "My brother's in critical condition because of you!"

"You think I'd stand around and let him threaten Sydney?" He dodged another blow and hurtled his elbow into her jaw. I heard her teeth click as she stumbled back, catching herself on the porch railing.

"Liar!" She launched herself at him again, spinning into the first round-house kick I'd ever seen in real life. Aiden dodged it, following up with a swift punch that barely connected with her shoulder.

Liv moved with fury, matching Aiden's force as she sent her knee into his ribs. He grunted and grabbed her by the neck, shoving her down to the ground with bared teeth.

As she picked herself up, she whipped something out of her back pocket, and at the flick of her wrist, a blade flipped out. A rush of panic surged through me with flashbacks of Aiden getting stabbed again. She ran at him, but he didn't shy away.

"Stop!" I yelled, but nobody paid any attention to me.

Eyes glowing, Aiden stepped out of the way at the last second. Liv dug the heel of her canvas shoe into the dirt, pivoting toward him again and raising the blade. He grabbed her wrist, twisting it around and wrenching a scream from her as she crumpled down to her knees in the grass.

The blade fell to the ground, but Liv reached around with her other arm, linking her elbow around the back of Aiden's knee. He fell forward, landing on his shoulder beside her, and she grabbed the knife.

"Liv, stop!" I screamed at the top of my lungs.

Aiden sent his foot into her chest, knocking her backward before she had a chance to use her weapon, and suddenly he was on top of her, pinning the knife at her throat.

I stopped breathing, looking around to make sure nobody was watching.

A pair of amber and aqua eyes blared intently from the trees, waiting for Aiden to give a signal to intervene, but that was it. No neighbors.

"That's enough." I stormed over to Aiden and pulled him up by his shirt. "The last thing we need is a bloodbath in my front yard."

Liv's green eyes seared up at him as he backed away with me, holding the knife by his side. They both breathed heavily, and I swore I could hear the anger rattling from their bodies with each gasp.

Aiden and I stood a few feet back from Liv. After a few seconds, he tossed the knife into the grass beside her. "The next time you pull that out on me, it goes in your throat."

His words sent a shudder through me.

Liv scrambled to her feet, her hair a tangled ringlet mess from last night's party. She blew a strand out of her face and clenched the blade in her fingers. "Watch your back. And tell your furry friends hanging around to watch theirs too." Her voice was so icy it could have started a blizzard.

"You need to leave," I said, stepping in front of Aiden. So many emotions stormed through me, I almost felt myself spiraling out of control.

"Sydney, I'm trying to protect you." Her voice softened,

matching her expression as she looked at me. "The fact that you can't see that just shows how brainwashed he's got you."

"Brainwashed?" My anger burned like wildfire in a second. All I could think about was how much I wanted to hurt her. I wanted to make her pay for what she did to Aiden, and for using me. Her family was responsible for Dorian's attack, and this bite on my arm that changed my entire future.

I lunged toward her, but before I could take her down, Aiden's arm snagged around my waist. He pulled me back into his sturdy torso. His body was hot with rage, like being against a furnace, but he was somehow more level-headed than I was right now. "Go home, Liv!"

"I was doing my job," she said. "You just can't see how dangerous he is."

"Last I checked, we almost got killed because of you."

"My family was only out for him—never for you, Sydney. You were totally safe."

"Are you so out of the loop with your family that you don't even know what they're capable of?" I asked. "Chris said he was going to kill me! Did you know that? He shot his freaking gun at me!"

Liv scoffed. "He'd never do that. We're supposed to do what's necessary, but never at the risk of another human."

"You were doing what's *necessary*?" I gave a harsh laugh that echoed through the yard, hardly recognizing the sound or my own actions. "You *used* me, Liv. And I hate you for it!"

She snapped back a step like my words hit her in the face. Good. I'd hurt her.

"One day you'll see that what I did was for you. He should never have brought you into this mess. If you're going to hate someone for getting caught in this crap, hate him."

I tried to break free from Aiden's hold again, staggering

my feet into the dirt, but he only tightened his grip on me. "Let me go," I sneered.

"You'll either do something you'll regret or get hurt," he said in my ear. "Don't let her get to you—it's not worth it."

As if his words sobered me, I took a deep breath that burned its way out of my lungs.

"We should tell her," he added, his arms loosening a little from my waist. "She needs to know the result of her family's actions this weekend."

"You do it." I squeezed my jaw tight as Liv's daggered eyes shifted between us. "I don't know if I can."

"Tell me what?" She flipped the blade back inside the handle and stuck it in her back pocket. "Please. Enlighten me, dogface."

Aiden balled his fists, still holding on to me, maybe even to keep himself from going at her again. "Your family is working with an Ancient named Dorian."

"A what?" She crinkled her expression in bored disbelief.

"One of the oldest werewolves. Your family gave him my blood to track, and they attacked while Sydney was with us."

"More lies." She shook her head and folded her arms. "Syd looks fine—minus your slimy paws all over her. But not for long. I won't let you—"

"Don't," I said, my patience breaking under her smug attitude. "I'm so sick of your threats. I'm so sick of you never listening. If you'd freaking stopped to hear what I had to say last night—"

"What? I would have changed my mind about killing him?" She rolled her eyes. "Not possible."

"He was trying to save me from all this stuff!"

Liv laughed. It was a hollow, bitter sound that fed my anger. She would never believe she was in the wrong unless I admitted what happened today.

I had to face it. She needed to know that her best friend

wouldn't be there for her anymore, because we would soon be supernatural enemies.

I held up my arm, rotating it to show her the truth. "I got bitten because of you."

Liv's eyes shot to the fading bite marks. After a second's hesitation, she rushed toward me and reached out. Her fingertip grazed my arm before she jumped back like she'd touched a scalding surface. "No," she whispered. "You can't be…"

I waited, watching the wheels turning in her head as about ten shades of horror etched into her expression.

"Your dad and your brothers were working with Dorian," I said. "They sent him after Aiden. That's how this happened."

"No!" She faltered back another few steps. The way she bent her knees and arched her shoulders reminded me of a wild animal about to bolt.

All three of us stood there, our bodies tense, the air thick with silence.

Liv's eyes glossed as she stared at me. And then, without another word, she sprinted back to her car and left.

I stared after her taillights, unsure what to think as I blinked back stinging tears. It didn't really surprise me that she ran, but for some reason, a small part of me hoped for more.

Aiden held on to me and dropped his chin down to my shoulder, almost like he could sense my shock about what just happened. "I'm sorry, Syd."

I opened my mouth to say something, but nothing came. Instead, everything crashed down on my head.

Liv had been my friend for years. How had I not seen what she really was? How could our friendship have ended up like *this*?

And how was I going to make it through all of this without a best friend?

6

$\mathcal{I}$t had been three days since...everything. The bite mark on my arm was completely gone, and I'd holed myself up in my room. Mom thought I had the flu, which, after the wave of anxiety-induced sickness I went through yesterday, didn't feel too far from the truth.

I couldn't face it. I couldn't accept what my life had become, all in one night.

My phone buzzed on the bed next to me, jarring me out of my thoughts and lighting up the dark room. I glanced over at the screen to see Aiden's name right before it dimmed again. Part of me almost wished Liv hadn't returned my phone when she came here. It would have made things a little easier.

Syd, please call me, his text said.

An ache the size of the Grand Canyon filled my chest, and I curled my knees up, resting my forehead against them. He wouldn't understand what I was going through. He was born a wolf. This had always been his life.

But I never asked for this. I wasn't prepared to be a were-wolf—if I survived the change.

All I needed was some time to mourn my life as I knew it. Dance…my friends…Mom.

Everything was about to change.

A knock at my door made me jump and rock the entire bed. Mom poked her head in. "Hey, dinner's ready."

"I'm not hungry." I forced a smile as best I could.

She lingered at the door anyway. "Do you want a light on in here? I can barely see you."

"No. I'm good. I've been sleeping."

"Oh. Are you still sick?" She opened the door wider, letting the hallway light spill over me.

"I think I'm feeling better," I said, squinting against the brightness. "Just tired."

"Hmm. Well, would you be able to come down and keep me company while I eat? I miss you."

That broke my heart, and I blinked back tears that wouldn't normally have been there.

Aiden had told me my emotions would be heightened, but the fear of disappointing Mom, of leaving her in a couple weeks, was excruciating. I should have been soaking up every moment with her, not sulking in my room.

Finally, I nodded and slid off the bed.

"Could you put a shirt on, too?" Mom asked before heading back downstairs.

"Why? What's wrong with a sports bra?"

"It's not lady-like."

I rolled my eyes and grabbed my hoodie from the edge of the bed before heading downstairs. The fabric itched against my skin, and I shook my shoulders in an attempt to shrug the feeling off.

When I stepped down on the hard floor in the foyer, I shielded my eyes from the blinding light fixture from the dining room. "Did you change the lightbulb in here?" I asked, walking to the other side of the table and pulling up a chair.

The way it dragged across the floor made me cringe. It was like nails on a chalkboard.

"No." Mom sat down across from me. Her pot roast was already losing its wisps of steam, and the vinegar from her salad dressing burned my nose. "I haven't changed the light in here in months."

"It seems brighter. Does it seem brighter to you?"

She laid her napkin neatly in her lap and picked up her fork. "No, honey. I hope you're not getting a migraine or anything. Those always make me sensitive to light."

"Right." I wished it was from a migraine.

How did werewolves function like this? Aiden never acted like anything bothered him, but right now I felt like I was ten feet from the sun and wearing sandpaper.

"So, have you talked with Aiden recently?" Mom steered a crouton around her salad with her fork. "I know you said you weren't dating before—"

"We weren't."

"Right. But he gave you that ring that you haven't worn in a few days."

I stretched my empty fingers out, ignoring the small pang of hurt. The last time I saw that ring, Liv's brother ripped it off my finger right before...

I cleared my throat. "I lost it."

"And what about the one who gave it to you? Have you talked? I'm just curious."

I shifted in my seat. It wasn't like me to be super secretive about my friends or my life. I hated leaving Mom in the dark, but I wasn't sure how much to tell her. "Yeah. We've talked."

"Oh. If things go well with you two, maybe he'd like to come over for dinner sometime. I'd like to get to know him a little better."

I fumbled with the edge of my sleeve. Having Aiden over for dinner probably wasn't going to happen, but I needed to play it off like everything was fine. "Sure. We can work something out."

Mom nodded and took a bite of her salad, which sounded more like she was chewing rocks. She swallowed and gave me a sideways look. "Is something wrong? You look mad."

I concentrated on unclenching my fingers. "Still not feeling super great."

Mom sighed. "When you feel better, you should call Liv."

A sudden wave of heat spilled over me. "Why?"

She laughed, like this conversation was amusing. "Because you're friends, and you haven't seen each other in a few days."

"Well, I don't want anything to do with her right now."

Her smile fell. "Did something happen?"

"Yes, and I don't want to talk about it." I took a deep breath, counting backward like my counselor taught me, but it did nothing to keep my anger down. My insides were about to pop the longer I pictured Liv...how she looked at me the other day, and how she threatened Aiden...

"I'm sorry to hear that." Mom reached for the salt shaker slowly, watching me like she was afraid of making a wrong move. "Did she do or say something?"

My anger finally bubbled over, and I slammed my palms on the table. "Why do you always have to keep pushing it? I told you—I'm not talking about her, so can you stop prying into my relationships and let things go?"

My skin tightened and my hands shook. Liv's betrayal still ran through my blood like acid, but when I focused on Mom's face, my fury melted into sheer terror. Everything that I'd tried so hard to keep wrapped up inside started to fall apart.

Mortified at my outburst, I rushed around the table, bumping my hip into the chair at the end. I caught it before it toppled onto its side, then ran up the stairs.

When I got to my room, I slammed the door behind me and ripped my sweater off. My shoulders rose and fell in deep, furious breaths, and I glanced around the room.

In the corner, one of Liv's purses I'd borrowed months ago hung on the closet door. On my nightstand, a tube of her bubblegum-pink lipstick stood up beside my alarm clock. The list of things that used to be hers went on and on as I looked around.

Breathing as deeply as I could, I paced the room. My hands clenched over and over as raging fire burned through my veins.

I turned and leaned on the edge of the dresser, digging my fingernails into the grain of the wood until they left half-moon markings. My reflection in the mirror didn't even look like my own. Agony creased everything, and the circles under my eyes were deep brown against my bronzed skin.

My chest compressed, threatening to explode from the pressure. And then I snapped.

I let my fist fly through the glass with an animalistic scream, shattering the mirror into jagged pieces that rained down the edge of the dresser.

It was like a release. My rage calmed, and I felt like me again, minus the warm blood trickling from my knuckles. I stood back, staring at the aftermath of my outburst.

"Sydney?" Mom's muffled voice came from the other side of the door. "What was that noise?"

My head snapped up. "I dropped something, but I'm cleaning it up. Don't worry."

I shifted the broken glass away from the edges of the dresser, trying to get them in a neat little pile without stepping on any on the floor. When I shoved a big piece of silver glass from the top of my jewelry box, a glimmer of fiery orange light radiated through the room.

It was coming from Gigi's red pendant necklace.

45

The necklace was draped on top of my flat black jewelry box, and I stared at it in awe as the light pulsed out from the center of the jewel. I reached for it cautiously, lifting it by the slinky silver chain. A soft hum traveled up the chain and through my fingers, the glow fading in and out.

My lips parted as I watched it pulse. I'd never seen this necklace light up before in the years I'd had it.

"Sydney." Mom jarred me back to the present, flinging the door open and flicking on the light.

Startled, I dropped the necklace. It landed face-down by my feet, but the hum still reverberated through my toes.

"What happened?" Her mouth fell open as she stared at the reflecting shards of glass strewn everywhere. Then her eyes landed on my hand. Thin red streams dripped down my fingers and left tiny stains on the carpet. "What in the world? Did you punch your mirror?"

"Um...yeah." I frowned, clenching my throbbing hand. Tiny shards of mirror glittered in my skin, but it wasn't enough to take my attention completely away from the necklace on the floor. I needed to figure that out. The hum faded, and within a few seconds, the necklace returned to its normal dark red.

"Sydney! What in the world possessed you to do that?" Mom stared at the blood, her hand bracing the doorknob.

Meeting her gaze again, I realized there was no way around answering her question. It was pretty obvious. "I lost my temper. But I'm okay." Stepping around her out of my room, I turned left into the bathroom and grabbed the fuzzy pink hand towel by the sink. It stung and snagged on the glass in my hand, but I forced myself to apply pressure. "Everything's fine."

"How is this fine?" she asked from right behind me.

"It was an accident, but I'm okay. I'm just going to clean it up."

She grabbed my forearm and lifted the towel to take a better look. Her cheeks paled at the beads of glass sparkling through torn flesh. "We're going to get a real shirt for you, and then I'm taking you to the hospital." She went back into my room and returned with one of the tank tops from my closet. "Put this on."

Dread kicked through me. When she mentioned the *hospital*, all I could think about were those bright lights, all the smells and the needles—

"I don't want to go. Let me try to clean it up here."

Mom's eyes widened in a quiet rage. "Absolutely not. You probably need stitches…and some anger management. Now, put your shirt on and get in the car."

I sighed out a deep breath. I hated when she lowered her voice like that. It creeped me out.

"I'll see you downstairs in one minute," she said, turning and heading back down.

"Fine." I slipped the shirt on and carefully maneuvered my hand through the arm-hole. Then I went into my room to grab a book, since the ER could take a while, and my eyes caught on my necklace again.

I picked it up off the floor and set it back on the dresser, eyeing it for a minute.

Had it really glowed?

I was pretty sure it did. That couldn't have been my imagination, unless the venom was already causing hallucinations. But Pete said that wouldn't happen until the full moon.

Maybe it did glow. But why?

I needed to keep an eye on it. Maybe there was more to it than just being an heirloom.

7

*T*hankfully, nobody gave me any stitches, but letting the doctors clean the glass out of my flesh had been *real* fun. I had to call on some extreme willpower not to haul off and punch anybody. They were just doing their job, anyway.

After a short lecture from Mom and the promise that there'd be a longer lecture in the morning, I excused myself to my room.

The gauze on my hand waved in the corner of my vision as I took the stairs two at a time. At this point, I was desperate to get away from Mom's judging eyes and the rosemary lingering from her dinner. It was like a spice overload, even when I stepped into my room.

But then my stomach flopped again as soon as I faced the glass all over the floor.

Fudge nuggets.

I couldn't deal with that right now.

I hurried to the window and unlatched it, raising the pane with such ease that it slammed up to the frame.

Wow. Not only was I getting a major temper, but I was getting stronger.

I leaned my head out the window, breathing in the honeysuckle air. There was something else, too. Something musty. Not in a gross way, but in a way that made me think of the woods. Of freedom.

It was nice.

But the mess of glass called me to clean it up. I swiped the bathroom trash can and started picking up the glinting shards, avoiding their bladed edges. They clattered to the bottom of the plastic trash can just as I felt a familiar sweeping down the back of my neck.

"You know that's seven years of bad luck?" A deep voice filled the room behind me, and I whirled around, falling backward onto my butt when I saw Aiden leaning against the windowsill. He wore black shorts, and his abs rippled up into smooth broad muscle.

"Holy crap," I gasped. "How did you get up here?"

Aiden flicked his brows up and gave his dimple-popping smile. "You have that handy garden trellis right around the corner."

"Great. How am I going to sleep at night knowing anyone can climb that thing? I knew Mom shouldn't have put that there," I grumbled.

"Chill. Not everyone has my skills…and if anyone other than me ever tries, I'll kick their ass."

I couldn't help but smile at his confidence as I dropped a glass shard into the trash. Another *thunk* echoed right after mine, and I glanced over at Aiden. He was right beside me, helping me clean.

"So," he said casually. "You broke your mirror."

I nodded.

His eyes flashed to the gauze on my knuckles when I

dropped another piece of glass into our pile. "What happened to your hand?"

I answered with a slight irritation I couldn't hide. "The mirror."

Aiden looked over the mess again, realization settling in his dilating pupils. "So, you *punched* it."

Heat washed down my body. The fabric of my clothes felt like they were closing in over my pores. "If you're gonna get technical about it, sure."

He stopped cleaning and shifted to face me. "Why?"

"I don't know. I lost it. Like…I came unhinged."

"Is that why you've been avoiding me?"

I felt his stare on me as the guilt corkscrewed to the pit of my stomach. Before he left a couple days ago, he told me to call him, and I never did. I didn't really know what to say. It was like my mood sat on this pendulum that swung back and forth at its own accord.

With a shrug, I dropped another piece of glass into the trash.

"Syd, could you stop for a minute and talk to me?" He reached for my hand before I could pick up another section of mirror.

When his fingers touched mine, the bond rushed through my arm, clouding my head at first with confusion and anxiety. I'd been feeling all those things for a while, but it suddenly became overwhelming. I wasn't sure what to do with it as I sat back on my heels.

"You're shutting me out," he said, staring at our laced fingers. The same wrinkle from the bridge of his nose up to his forehead appeared again. His signature worried expression. "Did I do something wrong?"

"No…I needed some space. I needed to pretend like everything was normal and not have any reminders that it's all messed up."

"I know it is. If you need space, just tell me next time so I don't keep calling you, wondering if something terrible happened."

"Sorry. I figured whoever you had patrolling out here would update you that everything was fine."

"But it wasn't." He glanced at the white gauze taped to my hand. "Do you remember at Omar's when I told you I felt like something was wrong, and you were having that nightmare? I had that same feeling tonight. So I came here to check things out, but you and your mom were gone."

"She took me to get this taken care of." I waved my hand around and let it fall by my side.

"Right." Aiden raised his brows and stared at me like he was waiting for a response. "Do you get what I'm saying? I must have *felt* when you raged and broke the mirror."

I opened my mouth, thinking through the evening. The timing added up. "But how did you feel it?"

"I was in a meeting with my dad and some other alphas, and I felt this big wave of anxiety. Or anger. It's hard to explain, but my mind went straight to you, and I knew I had to get over here."

Another small spike of energy flowed from his hand into mine.

"Do you think it's the bond?"

"That's the only thing I can think of to explain it."

"What else do you think can happen because of this bond?"

"I don't know," he said with a sigh. "Pete never found much information about it besides how rare it is, and it can cause some major shifts between the natural and supernatural. That's pretty much it."

We sat there quietly for a moment, our fingers woven together. My gaze drifted up to the dresser, where Gigi's necklace lay. Should I tell Aiden about what happened? If I did, what would he be able to do about it?

Maybe waiting to bring it up was best. The last time we did anything related to jewelry, we went to Fran, and that was the last thing I wanted.

"I missed you," Aiden said, watching me like he was trying to break through an invisible wall.

"I missed you too," I said quietly. "Sorry I'm so bad at relationships."

His lips twitched. "What—you think I'm good at them?"

"I don't know. I don't even know how many girls you've dated before."

"One," he answered. "And it lasted a month."

"Oh." Slight jealousy prickled my shoulders, and I suddenly needed to change the subject. "What was your meeting about? Any news on Dorian?"

He shook his head. "We've asked other packs to let us know if they hear anything, but so many are afraid. They either won't help us search for him or they're going into hiding."

"Hiding isn't always the worst idea," I said. "Especially when you're not at your max strength."

"Hiding won't solve the problem."

I rolled my eyes and pointed to the silver poisoning lingering in his skin. "You're still vulnerable."

"This?" Aiden peered down at his wound as if he was just noticing it. "It's fine. We have it maintained. I can live with it."

I shook my head as another moment of silence filled the room, besides the lull from the TV downstairs. Aiden tugged at my hand and brought me up to my feet.

"You know what? I think I need a night." He crossed the room and switched off the light.

"A night for what?"

He landed on the bed right in front of me, and I could tell from the street light shining through the open window that he was scrunching up my pillow under his head. Then he reached out for my hand and pulled me toward him. "I need a night where we don't talk about the things ahead or the pressing issues. That's all we've dealt with the last couple weeks."

"I still need to clean up the glass."

"It can wait until tomorrow. Right now, I need you right here." He patted the empty spot on the mattress right beside him, and that was all the convincing I needed to forget about the mirror.

I slid down onto my side, wedging the other pillow under my head as Aiden slinked his arm around my waist. He pulled me against his chest, and I absorbed his body heat and calming presence.

The only other time we'd ever been this close was at Omar's, the night Aiden told me about his past. If anyone had told me then that we'd be doing that again in *my* bed, I wouldn't have believed them. And while our relationship so far had come with all sorts of crap, with him was the only place I wanted to be.

He rested his cheek against my forehead and slid his hand up my back, curling his fingers into the ends of my hair. Strands tussled against my shoulder, and his breath skated across my ear. I sank deeper into his arms, working my fingertips across the ridges of muscle around his waist. A dull fire built in my diaphragm, and my heart fluttered, sending my mind to places that made me blush as I traced up his abdomen.

"Syd." Aiden's deep chuckle rumbled through the quiet. "Your thoughts are heading into naughty territory."

"Hey, you're the one who got in *my* bed."

"Fair point. I won't complain. It feeds my ego a little."

"Shut up," I laughed, winding my leg around his and pulling him against me even more.

He smiled, and didn't fight the proximity.

His lips were so close to mine, I could feel their warmth. Every part of me flickered with the need to be near him, as if his touch woke me up from the inside out. It was like coming alive again, after three days of being numb. Three days where I couldn't see past all the problems.

But none of that mattered now.

I tilted my head up to bring my mouth closer to his. He leaned in, barely brushing his lips against mine. I let out a soft breath against the contact.

Then he kissed me. It was slow at first, like warm liquid pouring into me. He wound his arm around me in a safe, tight lock. My pulse climbed out of control, and my head spun as every breath became more difficult to hold on to.

I grasped his hip, bringing my leg up higher on his until I could almost wrap myself around him. He growled softly against me, tangling his hands deeper into my hair, but then he did the opposite of what I wanted.

He pulled away.

The adrenaline halted in my veins, and my chest expanded with a sobering rush of oxygen. "What's wrong?"

"Nothing," he said, smoothing his fingertips down my back. "I just don't want to move too fast."

"Too fast? You know that in a few weeks I could be—"

His finger landed over my mouth. "Don't remind me of the worst-case scenario."

"But—" My voice was muffled under his finger.

"It's not that I don't want things to happen, there's just a lot more to it than you know." He paused. "I want to make sure it's not totally in the midst of all the crazy things going on."

I frowned. "Crazy is the foundation of our relationship."

"I know, but I want a steadier pace with you. We deserve that. You're the one thing keeping me grounded right now, and I don't want to do anything to mess it up."

I sighed and ran my palm over his hip bone. Maybe he was right, even though I didn't want him to be.

I hadn't *been* with anyone before, and under normal circumstances, I would want us to take our time, too. But nothing would ever be normal again, and I didn't know how much time I had left with anyone I cared for.

"So you're not ready?" I asked.

He kissed the tip of my nose. "You'll be the first to know when I am."

"I would hope so."

He chuckled. "Let's get some sleep."

"You're staying for a while?"

"I'm not going anywhere." He pulled me back in.

Relaxing against him again, it only took a couple minutes before I felt the steady rise and fall of his chest. I looked up at his face. His eyes were closed, his lips slightly parted.

I took a mental picture of him sleeping before my mind wandered back to all the things threatening both of us.

Dorian. The full moon.

Liv. The look on her face when she touched my arm, and then the way she ran from me. It was pure shock and anger. She had no idea what her family was doing.

Then an idea occurred to me—one I wasn't a huge fan of, and Aiden definitely wouldn't be either—but it could work. I just wouldn't tell him what I was going to do.

Liv could be the key to taking down Dorian, and even though I hated her right now, I had to call her.

8

I sat at the small round table in *Books & Bakers*. The old exposed brick walls with the vanilla scent of books and coffee gave me the small sense of normalcy I'd been craving. It settled my nerves and made me feel at home, even though I was waiting for Liv.

The sunlight streamed over the two antique chairs in the front display window, stretching to the dark bookshelves lining the room. I flipped the hardcover of my book open and shut, listening to the espresso machine bubble and hiss on the counter behind me.

Through the window, Liv strolled down the sidewalk in a black crop top and leggings. Her dark blonde locks glistened in the sunlight, and she paused at the door like she was thinking about leaving. Then she flung it open, chiming the welcome bell as the door floated closed behind her.

Her face set in a serious stone expression when she saw me. She stiffened her shoulders as she walked to my table, scraping the chair across the floor and taking a seat.

My stomach rolled, and I let my book cover fall shut. "Hi."

Her gaze shot to my bandaged hand. "What happened?"

she asked in her tight, defensive voice. Her bright red lips set in distrust, and a small pang of grief struck my heart.

"Nothing. It's fine." It didn't hurt anymore. Besides the prickly corner of the tape poking into my skin occasionally, I'd almost forgotten about it.

"Right," she said, sitting back and folding her arms. "Why'd you call me if you say you hate me? What's this about?"

I tried to ignore her bitter tone and the desire to jump across the table to strangle her. Already acting like she was the victim here, as usual. "Before you get up and leave or have any smartass things to say, hear me out. I'm not your enemy, Liv. I know that right now I'm going through some changes—"

She scoffed and shook her head. "You make it sound like you're hitting puberty."

I pursed my lips, refraining from a detrimental eye roll. "As I was saying, this is all new to me. And before you say anything bad about Aiden, just remember that he never once used me—but you did. You hurt me, and I don't know how to deal with that. Seeing you right now is one of the last things I want to do—ever—but I'm here anyway, because I need to ask for your help."

Her brow arched. "You need *my* help?"

"Yes. This is *me* asking. Aiden doesn't know I'm here."

She leaned her elbows on the table. "Go on."

"I know you don't believe your dad is working with this Dorian guy, but I promise you, that's what I heard Donnie say. And by the time I found out Dorian was an Ancient, it was too late. He'd already traced Aiden's blood."

Liv tilted her head like she was bored with this conversation. "There's no way my dad is involved with an Ancient. He'd never do that. It goes against everything we believe in— it goes against who we are."

I flattened my palms on the table, lowering my voice so the clerk at the register wouldn't hear. "I know you don't want to believe it, but what I'm asking you to do is what you do best—snoop. You're one of the sneakiest people I've ever met."

"Well, that *is* true." She rested her chin in her palm.

"Then use your skills and prove to me your dad isn't up to something."

She frowned. "I don't have to prove anything to anyone."

"Then prove it to yourself." I knew I'd made a point when she blinked down at the table. "And when you do, call me. Aiden and I need your help. *I* need your help." I said the last sentence slowly, trying to hide some of my desperation. "Do this for your family. Dorian has an agenda, and it involves controlling werewolf packs…maybe something bigger. You know that's not a good thing for your family. And it's not good for me, either."

Liv bit her bottom lip and drummed her fingers along her arms.

The door chimed at the front again, and a man with short cropped hair and tattoo sleeves lining his arms walked in. The musky smell of cigarettes hit my nose as he gave the clerk at the cash register a nod and started meandering among the rows of books.

"So, what do you think?" I asked, giving my attention back to Liv. "Will you at least look into it?"

She tapped her fingertips on her arm one more time. "I'll think about it—but only because *you* asked. If your boytoy contacts me or asks me for a favor, I'm out. I'll never do anything to directly help him or his pack of mutts."

Her words dug painfully under my skin. I was going to be one of those 'mutts' if I survived the process. "Let me know what you decide by the end of the week."

Liv nodded and pushed her chair back. Without another

word, she took one last glance around the bookstore and barged out the door.

I let out a breath I'd been hanging on to. This whole thing was harder than I'd expected. But maybe if she saw the truth about her family, she could uncover Dorian's plans. All of that depended on her going against her family and finding out how much her father was really helping this Ancient though.

I grabbed my book and headed out the door, passing some of the other local shops along the sidewalk. When I reached Lucille's shop, I stopped. The lock was still broken from when Aiden and I had checked it out. Had she really disappeared, or did she leave?

Fran had said before that a Solstice Guardian prophesied an Ancient would come back...maybe Lucille went into hiding like some others did.

I lingered another few seconds, tempted to go inside and check it out again.

The distant chime of the bookstore door rang from down the street. Brisk footsteps rushed down the sidewalk in my direction.

My spine straightened, and my skin stung with apprehension, but before I could turn around to see who was running, a tattooed hand slammed down over my mouth.

Adrenaline burst through me, and my book hit the sidewalk. Flesh muffled out my scream as I was dragged sideways into the alley. I tried to break free, but my arms were pinned low under a strong grip.

I shoved my heels out, skidding the soles of my shoes against the asphalt to resist getting carried off, but my attacker pulled me deeper into the shadows.

My blood burned. I fought against the muscled wall enveloping me, and finally, my adrenaline turned to anger. I slammed my heel back onto the nearest ankle, getting a pained grunt in return. But the grip tightened around my waist. I tilted my head back, opening my mouth and biting down into his cigarette scented hand.

"Agh!" the man yelped as he yanked his hand away. "Good thing you haven't turned yet."

I jabbed my elbow back and shoved, mashing us both into the wall. He cursed again and flung me against the other concrete wall behind the dumpster. The wind knocked free from my lungs, sending a thick wave of nausea through me.

The man in front of me was the one who'd walked into the bookstore. His thin pierced lips pressed flat, and his icy hazel eyes sized me up.

"I expected you to be taller," he said, stalking toward me and stopping about five feet away.

"Who are you?" I yelled. "What do you want?"

"I've seen what you'll be." His tattooed fists curled by his sides. "I'm sorry for this, but I can't let Dorian get his hands on you."

He closed his eyes and started chanting, stretching both palms out toward me.

A heaviness came over my limbs, but I pushed against it and I swiped a broken beer bottle off the ground by my feet. I charged him faster than I'd ever moved before, slashing the jagged edges of glass at him. But I wasn't fast enough. At the flick of his wrist, an explosion of pain surged through my skull, and I dropped the bottle, immediately losing my bearings.

A shrieking ring pierced my eardrums, and I fell, cracking my knees on the pavement. I grabbed my ears, unable to hear anything. Unable to see as I doubled over. I couldn't even tell if I was screaming through the pressure trying to break through my skull.

Something warm and wet trickled from my nose, and I tried to open my eyes. The asphalt cutting into my palms was the only way to tell where I was, but even then, my senses grew fuzzy around the edges.

Then it all stopped.

The pain and the pressure relented, and I could hear again. Grunts and shuffling made me force my eyelids open. The man had been thrown sideways, catching himself on the crusty dumpster, and Liv stood where he'd been just seconds ago.

My chest unclenched, letting a relieving rush of air back into my system.

Liv moved in, swinging her hand around the back of his neck and vaulting her knee up into his stomach. The guy gasped and pulled his clenched fist up toward her, opening his fingers out like he was tossing something at her.

A cloud of dust hit her in the face, and she stumbled back with an angry scream. She squeezed her eyes shut, shaking her head furiously. "You are *so* gonna regret that!"

He turned back to me, and I braced myself against the brittle ground, my skin tightening, pulling like something was crawling all over me. Before he could reach me, Liv jumped on his back, roping her arm around him in a head-lock. She linked her legs around his waist and anchored herself higher on his shoulders. With a wicked smile, she jabbed her fingers into his neck and held down.

The man pulled at her arms, his face reddening deeper shades until his skin purpled. He dropped to his knees, swaying back and forth as his eyes rolled to the back of his head. Then he face-planted onto the asphalt with a soft thud.

Liv landed gracefully on her feet well before he hit the ground. She calmly dusted her hands off and then combed a tangle from her hair. "You good?"

I nodded, still staring at the guy.

"Are you sure? Your nose is bleeding a lot."

I swiped the back of my hand under my nose and looked

down. A deep red stream smeared across my skin, but the trickle had stopped. "I'm okay. It's not bleeding anymore."

"Okay." She knelt over the man and picked up his right hand. It hung limply from his wrist as she studied the silver band around his index finger. "I'll take that," she said, twisting it off and sliding it around her thumb.

"You're stealing his ring?"

"It's how he controls his magic. I've seen them on a few other witches. We're lucky this time; others can conjure the magic from their bodies instead of a piece of jewelry."

"Weird."

"Yeah. I'll be right back, okay?" She started walking toward the street. "Gotta grab some stuff from my car."

I watched her disappear around the corner and realized my purse was vibrating against my hip. Sliding my phone out, I moved away from the guy and saw Aiden had called me three times in the last two minutes. "Hello?"

"Syd? What's happening? Where are you?" he rushed out. I heard his truck engine grumbling in the background.

"This guy—this witch—he came out of nowhere." My head felt like it would float away, and I leaned back against the brick to steady myself. "I'm okay though. Liv was here. She knocked him out."

I winced at the silence he gave me.

"Where are you? I'm coming to you," he said.

"The alley by Lucille's shop."

"Okay. I'll be there soon." He hung up as Liv came back around the corner with two different bands of rope tossed over her shoulder and a wad of tissues.

"Here." She held out the tissues to me.

"Thanks." I took them and wiped the excess blood from my nose.

Liv straddled over the guy's hips and got to work, winding the rope around his wrists.

"You keep rope in your car?"

"Duh. You never know when something like this will happen," she answered, leveraging her foot on the man's back to pull the rope as tight as possible. Then she bound his feet and backed away, smiling with satisfaction at the knotting skills I hadn't known she possessed.

"What are you going to do with him now?"

She leaned back against the brick wall. "I'm assuming your boy is on his way, and his truck is more suitable than my car for towing this creep somewhere else."

"Yeah. How did you know to come through here? I thought you left."

"I did. I was all the way down the street when I realized where I'd seen that guy's tattoo before. So, I came back."

"Which one?" I asked, peering down at my attacker. He had a lot of tattoos. Mermaids with fangs, angels with fanned wings, and various curved symbols up his arms and neck.

"The one on the right side of his neck."

I tilted my head, taking a closer look. He had a waning crescent moon with an eye in the center right behind his ear, taking up almost the entire side down to his shoulder. "What does it mean?"

"I don't know. But it represents a coven, and he looked super out of place in that bookstore. Not that people with tattoos don't go to bookstores, obviously, but he wasn't even really looking at the books. Can't really blame him anyway, books are so—"

"Liv," I said sharply. "You're telling me he's a witch?"

"Oh. Yeah." She sounded so casual—so used to this world that had only begun to reveal itself to me a few weeks ago. It was hard for me to wrap my head around it all. She'd been living this badass double life for our entire friendship and never once let it slip.

That ticked me off.

"Why didn't you ever tell me about all this?"

"My life's purpose is to keep humans safe. Blissfully ignorant. After Mom died...it got easier to hide, because I wasn't allowed to do anything anymore." Her hand found its way to her hip, which I wouldn't have thought anything of if I hadn't been able to see the glint of a dagger under her shirt hem.

"Your mom wasn't in a car accident, was she?"

Liv's face hardened like steel and she slid the knife out of the black fabric holster on her hip. "No. And all I have left of her is this."

As she slid her thumb over a faint engraving on the handle, a sinking weight found its way down to my toes. "What happened?"

She stared at the blade a second longer and slipped it back into its safe place. "My parents went to meet with another hunter clan, and a couple packs ambushed them." She tilted her head back against the brick wall. "You know, the weird thing is, up until then, I thought this hunters-versus-wolves thing was stupid. I mean, I still felt the desire to kill them when I saw one or sensed one nearby, but I didn't really *want* to. I didn't have a reason to hate them back then." She shifted her eyes to me. "Not like I do now."

I swallowed the lump rising in my throat. "Killing wolves is an instinct?"

"Yeah. Some hunters say wolves used to be a lot more feral, and since nature always needs a balance, some humans were born with this hunter gene to keep the mutts tame. That way they don't kill everyone in sight."

"But they're *not*. And they're not *mutts*." From what I'd seen, Aiden's pack stayed secluded on purpose. He told me before they wanted to live peaceful lives.

"Maybe not all of them. But you still haven't seen everything yet."

I understood why Liv was so angry after her mother's

death. She had every right to be, but what if her dad hadn't told her the whole story?

I pushed that thought aside and anchored onto the small amount of sympathy for her loss. "I know I said this a long time ago, but I'm sorry about your mom."

"It is what it is. Her death was a wake-up call. That's why ever since then, I tried to protect you more, because..." Her words trailed off, but I could hear what she didn't say: *Because you're my family, too.*

But her actions contradicted her words, even the unspoken ones. "Liv, you haven't done anything but put me in danger lately. How do you justify that?"

She threw a sharp glare my way, but didn't say anything, which somehow fanned the fiery anger rooted inside me even more.

"You guys burned down the guitar shop—with me inside —remember that? And how about when you used me to get to Aiden? I got hurt, and now I'm stuck. I'm going to *change.* And he's stuck—" I snapped my mouth shut to keep myself from saying anything about the wound left in his chest. She couldn't be trusted with knowing any of his weaknesses.

"I didn't know my brothers would burn down the shop. All I did was tell them about it. I figured they'd follow the dogs home—that would've been the smart thing to do." She shook her head and muttered something under her breath. "And when you were at my house, I locked you in my room to keep you safe. I didn't think you'd jump out the window, but I should have known you'd be stupid enough to do it. You've always been a bleeding hearts and tiny violins kind of girl."

I clenched my jaw until my back molars threatened to fuse together. This girl was treading dangerous territory. "That's really what you're going to say to me? After everything we've been through?"

"I don't know *what* to say to you, Syd. If I'd known you were that into him, I would have taken more drastic measures to kill him weeks ago myself."

Rage bolted through me, and my fingers coiled into tight fists. My skin pulled and my bones ached, like my body was desperate to release the outrage. I wanted to hurt Liv again—so bad that everything ached as I held myself there. It was the same feeling I'd had when I punched my mirror.

She watched me, her features twisting into wide eyes as she stood up from the wall. "Sydney?"

"You'll never hurt him again," I growled, pulling in hard breaths and fighting every inch of my body from lashing out at her.

Aiden pulled up at the curb and jumped out of his truck in a whirlwind. He headed straight for me down the alley, not paying any attention to the witch passed out on the ground.

He clasped his hands around my face and bent down to my eye level. "Breathe."

"What's happening?" Liv asked from behind him.

"I don't know," he snapped. "Did you say something to piss her off?"

"I hate her," I said, spiraling into my hot fury.

He moved his hands down to my shoulders. They rolled back with concrete tension, and my hands shook as I reached for his shirt.

"Don't let whatever she said or did get to you. Fight it," he reminded me. "You control your thoughts and emotions, and she's not worth whatever could happen."

The bond swept down through me, threatening to untangle everything I'd tried too hard to harness in a tight ball. The more I tried to keep it all together, the harder it was.

As I held eye contact with Aiden, my hands slowed their

constant need to clench and straighten. He latched his hand around the back of my neck, slowly moving his thumbs over my jaw.

I let out a deep breath. It seemed to release the primal hate inside me, but suddenly I was exhausted. "This transition is going to kill me."

"No." He shook his head, his eyes softening. "You're going to be fine. See how you just calmed down? That's how you tackle it."

"Why does that happen? Why do I feel this way?"

"It's your body trying to shift under a threat, but it can't yet. Not without the energy from the full moon."

Loosening my grip on his shirt, I leaned my forehead into his shoulder. "I can't do this."

"Yes, you can. You don't have to do this alone. I'm here as much as you want me to be."

I nodded and breathed in the spice of his cologne.

"I hate to break up this moment for you guys," Liv called sarcastically from behind us, "but this dude might wake up soon, and we need to get him out of here."

Aiden rolled his eyes and turned, glaring down at the guy and then back to Liv. "What happened?"

"He showed up in the bookstore and made a move to kill your girlfriend while you were out running around on all fours," she said dryly.

His jaw squared off. "Did he say anything?"

"He said he couldn't let Dorian get to me," I said.

Liv's spine straightened, and her eyes turned to slits. "He said that?"

I nodded, my eyes skating over the guy's tattoos and the ropes binding his limbs. "He told me he's seen what I'll be. And then I felt like my head was going to explode. That's when you showed up."

Aiden cursed under his breath and bent down to study the same tattoo Liv noticed before.

"You know that symbol?" she asked.

Aiden nodded. "He's a Seer."

"A Seer?" My voice echoed through the alley.

"He can see the future."

Lucille must have been one, too. At least I figured out one thing on my own in this crazy world.

Aiden stood up. "I'll have to take him back to my pack for questioning."

"Hold on. You can't just come here and take over. I was the one who took him down—I should be the one to question him."

"And then what?" Aiden's voice deepened authoritatively. "He was here for Sydney *and* mentioned Dorian. I need to know everything he knows, and if you take him, I'll never hear another word about it."

"And if you take him, *I'll* never hear another word about it. What he has to say could affect my family, too."

"Fine. I'll pick the location, and you can follow us."

Liv tilted her head, humming in thought before letting her arms drop to her sides. "Fine. I guess that's the only way we're getting out of here."

Aiden moved around the guy and scooped him up over his shoulder like a sack of flour. As he turned and headed back toward his truck, he tossed Liv a glare. "Try to keep up. I drive fast."

9

Once we were in the truck and Liv's car had crawled up behind us, Aiden took off, swerving around the antique shop at the corner. I held on to the handle above the window, leveraging against it to keep my butt planted in the seat, and a small groan came from the Seer in the back.

"You want to tell me how you and Liv ended up at the same place, at the same time?" Aiden asked, taking up his normal driving posture. He leaned his elbow against the door and pursed his lips, like he was trying really hard not to be angry.

"I asked her if she'd work with us."

His eyes shifted over to me, and we blew right through a stop sign. "You did what?"

"It makes sense to ask. She really didn't know her family was working with Dorian. She could find some things out for us."

Aiden raked his fingers through his dark hair. "What did she say?"

"That she'd think about it. She still doesn't believe her

dad's involved, but I think I convinced her to start looking into it."

"How do you know? We can't trust her."

"I *don't* trust her, but we don't have much else to rely on unless another pack with better information agrees to help. Do you know of any?" I raised my brows at him, already knowing the answer, but I held my ground through the thick beats of silence.

The vein on the side of his neck still bulged, but his face began to soften. Finally, he responded. "All right. She could be useful."

"Thank you." I sat back against the seat. "Are you mad?"

He shrugged. "A little. Only because of what happened after your meeting." He turned at the four-way intersection by the high school, taking us under the old metal bridge. "I'm glad to see Liv still cares about you enough to defend you."

True. Liv could have left and let the guy take me out. It would have given her one less werewolf to worry about later, but she turned her car around for me. She came back.

Something tugged inside me, sending tears up to my ducts. I blinked them back and folded my arms. This transition was making me way more emotional. I had to keep my head on straight.

Liv may have come back for me this time, but it still didn't change much. She tried to kill Aiden, leaving him with a permanent weakness, and she was the reason I dreaded the full moon. Even if she found out the truth and helped us, we couldn't trust her.

We turned down the street known for the old warehouses where my classmates used to hang out and make questionable choices after school. Aiden parked the truck on the gravel lot behind the old paper factory. The rusty gray metal still held cracked windows, although the main double doors had been removed from their hinges, leaving a gaping square open in the center.

Aiden cut the engine, taking away the comfort of the air conditioning. He leaned his head back against the seat and closed his eyes for a second.

"Are you okay?" I asked, reaching for his hand. When I touched him, a zing of emotions traveled through my skin, forming an ache in my chest. I pulled away, startled by it, and within seconds, it was gone.

"I'm okay," he said. "I'm tired. Dad's been all over me about stuff."

"Which stuff?"

"The hunters…and you."

I sat up straighter. "Me?"

"Yeah. Stuff with your transition."

I tensed. Hearing him say it never got any easier. "What about the hunters? Do you think they'll find out I knew them?"

"I haven't said anything, and I'm keeping it that way."

"Okay," I whispered, studying the shadows under his eyes. "How are you feeling?"

My question seemed to wake him up. He shifted in his seat and leaned on his elbow over the middle console. "I'm okay. The stuff Cora gave me seems to work."

"Good." At least there was a bright spot somewhere.

Liv's car rolled to a rocky stop behind us, and Aiden craned his head up to peer in the rearview. She slammed her door and came around to my side of the truck, tapping her wrist like time was of the essence.

She could be so annoying sometimes.

"Let's get this over with." Aiden got out and hauled the Seer back over his shoulder. He led the way into the warehouse, carelessly jostling the witch back and forth.

Liv followed behind me into the dank, open space. Our

footsteps turned into soft echoes on the cement floor, and a faint dripping came from the interwoven ceiling pipes somewhere.

Aiden picked a spot along the concrete wall and dropped the guy down against it. The man's hands were still pinned behind his back as he reclined against the wall, still unconscious.

Aiden knelt in front of him and patted his cheek aggressively. "Wake up."

The witch cracked his eyes open, blinking until he focused on us, one at a time. When he saw me, he held his stare.

I wanted to get out of there. Anything he had to say couldn't be good.

Aiden followed the guy's line of sight over to me, then fixed his intense expression back on the witch. "Who are you working for?"

The man's hazel eyes shifted to Aiden, his lips turning up into a hateful smile that made one of his tattoos ripple. He didn't answer, and I could see Aiden's shoulders slowly bristle.

"You have five seconds to tell me," Aiden seethed.

Liv cupped her fingers around the knife handle on her hip. "You're being way too nice."

Aiden ignored her, rearing back his arm and thrusting his fist across the man's jaw with a sharp crack that made me wince. "Are you working by yourself? Why are you after her? What did you *see* about her?" Aiden's voice had already lost all patience. He sent his fist into the man's face again, effectively punching away the smile.

The witch grunted as blood trickled down from the corner of his mouth. "I wanted to get rid of a potential problem."

"What's that supposed to mean?"

The guy stared at me like I was under a creepy microscope.

"My turn. This is taking way too long." Liv yanked her knife out and stepped forward. Kneeling beside Aiden, she held the blade up to the guy's cheek. "You need to talk if you want to keep your face intact. I'm not as nice as this pup over here."

A low growl erupted from Aiden's throat as he shot Liv a dark look.

"Are you working for this Dorian guy," she asked. My stomach knotted as I watched her slowly glide the blade down his cheek. It didn't cut into his skin, but it scraped along his stubble.

Maybe it was her threat, or maybe it was mentioning Dorian that triggered something, but the man took in a sharp inhale. "I'd never work for an Ancient."

"Okay, but how is she involved in this? She's human."

"For now." The man's voice was rugged and deep. "I've seen what she can be. If he gets ahold of her, we're all dead."

Aiden and Liv glanced at each other and she pulled the blade away from the man's face. "Why? We're all on the same side here, but killing her isn't an option."

The guy looked at us all again, one at a time. "Either of her futures are equally possible. If the worst possible scenario occurs, we might as well give Dorian the world."

"If I die?" I asked, taking a step forward.

He let out a sharp laugh. "That would be the best-case scenario."

Aiden looked down at the floor, his jaw clenched so tight, I worried it might snap.

"If you live—if Dorian finds that kind of power—he'll come for you. He won't stop until he finds you."

"Did you see him come for her?" Liv asked.

The man shook his head slowly.

"Then why would you make a move to kill her when you haven't even seen that?" Aiden snapped. "You're spilling innocent blood for something that might not even happen."

"I'm doing my duty to protect my coven and the universe."

"Wow. How kind of you," Liv said dryly. "What is it that you saw her become? She's transitioning into a werewolf. They're not that powerful."

The witch tilted his head back against the wall, giving me a better look at his puffy lip. "To speak of that kind of Sight is sacred."

"Oh, please." Liv rolled her eyes and pointed the knife at him. "You Seers and your rules are what's gonna get you killed."

I was so confused, but I couldn't stay out of the conversation any more. There was something I had to know. "Is whatever you've seen going to happen? Will I survive the transition?"

"Both possibilities are equal. Your future hasn't been decided."

"What does that mean?" Aiden asked.

"There are two paths fighting for her," the Seer said impatiently.

That's what Lucille had said to me before. Two paths—two worlds—fought for me, but I thought she meant at that moment in time.

But she was a Seer, too.

Had she seen what I'd become? Did she send me to Aiden for answers, knowing that path would lead me to face death or the full moon?

After the witch refused to say anything else, Aiden took him back to the truck.

"Hey." Liv's hand landed on my arm, but she pulled away as soon as she touched me. "It's going to be okay, Syd."

That was easy for her to say. My stomach was still on the floor from everything he said.

She sheathed her knife back into her side pocket. "I know what he said sounded really bad, but I do know that free will and circumstances can always change the future. Seer's can only tell you what will happen based on the decisions made right now."

Nothing she said brought me any comfort though.

We walked out of the warehouse together and found Aiden waiting by the truck.

"I'm going to take him back to my pack for more questioning," he said. "If he talks, I'll let Sydney know and she can give you the information...if you want."

"Sure." Liv nodded and started walking toward her car. She paused when she got to her door. "If you really want Sydney to be able to protect herself, teach her some self-defense."

"Hey. I can handle things." Barely.

"You could take care of yourself *better* if you had some training. And it could help with your rage."

I shot her a glare. It was true that everyone in this new world seemed so much stronger with their magic and mystical genetics. But I hated knowing she saw me as weak and angry. "You don't know anything about what I'm going through right now."

"I know." She opened her car door. "Call me if you want someone to teach you how to fight."

Aiden and I watched her get in her car and drive away.

"I hate to say it, but she's right," he said.

"You're going to take her side? I'm not weak."

"I know you're strong. You're only getting stronger. But strength doesn't matter much if you don't know how to use it."

I chewed on the corner of my lip. That was true.

"We can start this week. How about tomorrow?"

Aiden was going to train me? This could either be really fun or really embarrassing. "I guess tomorrow works."

The truck rocked slightly behind Aiden, and the Seer yelled something indecipherable over the radio.

Aiden smacked his palm against the truck door to silence him. "This is going to be a fun ride home."

10

*A*fter Aiden took me back to Mom's car, I went home and braced myself for the lecture she'd promised last night. Today was her day off, so hopefully she was in a good mood.

I walked through the front door and dropped my purse on the foyer table. The scent of coffee filled the house, and I found Mom sitting at the kitchen island in her pajamas.

"Hey." I slid past her and opened the fridge door. "You slept late."

"I couldn't sleep." She set her mug down and cleared her throat. "Where were you?"

"I went to the bookstore." I forced myself to keep a light tone as I pulled out the orange juice and took a sip. It had an extra punch of sweet citrus that I wasn't expecting. It was like I could taste every single orange thrown into the mix.

"Are you sure?"

I paused, holding the carton halfway to my mouth. "Yeah?"

She pulled her hair off to one shoulder, and as she stared

into her coffee, the shade under her eyes became more apparent. "You didn't leave a note."

"Oh. I forgot." I moved toward her slowly and eased onto the stool beside her. "I'm sorry. I will next time."

She didn't look at me, but she nodded. "Did you get anything?"

"No." My mind flashed to the Seer attacking me and I felt like my head would spin again at all the things he said in the warehouse. Fighting a shudder, I took another sip of OJ.

"How's your hand? Have you changed the bandage yet today?" Mom asked, her brow wrinkled.

"No, but it feels a lot better." I started peeling off the sticky tape, unraveling the gauze from my knuckles. Mom turned in her chair, watching closely, and when I opened up the bandage, we both stared at healed flesh.

"How in the world—" Mom reached over, trailing her fingers across my knuckles. "How did you heal so fast?"

Clenching my hand, I watched the skin tighten around my fingers. No scars or bruises at all. "I don't know," I lied. "I guess that ointment at the hospital works miracles."

"Guess so," Mom said slowly, reaching for her coffee mug again. "That's…strange."

"Very." But I knew it was all part of this transition. At least there was one perk to it.

After a beat of silence, Mom said, "Listen, Sydney, we need to talk. You've been acting…different, lately. It's making me worry you might not be ready for college."

"What? All you've talked about for a year was me going to college. Now you're backing off just because I lost my temper and hit a mirror?"

Mom cleared her throat and crossed her legs, her pajama pants bunching around the knees as she turned to face me. "Honey, it might be a little too much to take on right now. You've been through a lot the last month with the car accident, and I want to make sure you're prepared and not too stressed out. You deserve to have the best college experience possible, and that includes taking studies and self-care seriously...starting with another counseling appointment."

"Mom." I set down the empty carton of juice. "With all due respect—not that I really want to go to college—you don't really know what you're talking about."

"Excuse me?" Her thin eyebrows slammed together. "You want to try that again?"

I bit down on my lip until it tasted like metal. My skin started tingling, itching against the drafty air as my temper flared again. "You don't know what you're talking about," I said deliberately, trying to keep my tone down, but it gradually rose anyway. "You don't know *all* the things that happened to me in the last month, or all the crap I've had to work through—what I'm working through right now. But it doesn't affect whether I'll be a good student or not. My GPA was almost perfect, even when you and Dad went through your divorce. I'm more than capable of doing well in school."

"Sydney, you need to mind your tone." Mom's back straightened, and her lips pursed. "I'm telling you what I think is best, and I expect you to respect that."

"And I'm telling you that you're wrong. I've had a crappy summer, but I can't stop living just because of that."

But I'd been doing exactly that—I'd given up. I'd stopped living, except for today when I decided to do something with my time and contact Liv.

Mom stood up from the island and scooted her stool back in. "I think we need to talk about this when we're both in better spirits."

Without another word, she marched down the hallway and slammed her bedroom door shut.

Exhaling loudly, I backhanded the empty OJ carton off the island and into the cabinets. I wasn't really upset about not going to college, but it felt like another part of my future was getting ripped away from me.

But could I still go to college after turning?

Maybe. Pete and Aiden had jobs and something resembling a normal life before the guitar shop burned down.

Maybe there was some hope for me too, but it seemed like I was on my own to figure it out.

When I got out of the car, the familiar piney scent settled my muscles.

Mom and I hadn't spoken much since yesterday's spat. I hated it. I hated the silence. But now that I was at Aiden's, out in the woods, it all seemed very calming. Maybe that was a new wolf thing.

The car door slam echoed through the trees surrounding Aiden's cabin, and I already felt the bond whirring over my skin. He was close.

I took the little stone path between the flower beds leading to the front door, but stopped when the screaming grind of a saw came from around back. I headed around the house and found him in black shorts and sneakers, facing away from me as he cut beams of wood on a wide table. His shoulders coiled with concentration, and my gaze slid down his back. His sides rippled as he dropped a block of spare wood on the ground.

A smile formed on my lips, and as I stepped forward, his head snapped up before he turned to face me.

"Hey." He gave a wide grin and took his earbuds out as he moved in toward me. His arms wrapped around my waist, and he lifted me off my feet in a deep kiss that stole my breath. "You ready to kick some ass today?" he asked, setting me down on my feet.

I ran my fingers through the back of his silky hair. "I guess I'm ready to kick *yours*."

His dimples popped, and he leaned over me. "Not gonna lie, that would be kinda hot."

I laughed and hung my arms around his neck. "You didn't come over last night."

"Yeah. I spent most of the night questioning that Seer." The way his eyes shifted downward told me how unsuccessful it must have been. "I thought I could break him down, but he wouldn't talk. My last resort was torture, but that's not really my style." He slid his arms tighter around my back and lowered his voice. "I feel like I failed you."

"You didn't." I tightened my grip around his shoulders. The bond drifted down my arms like a soft vibration relaxing my cells. It seemed I was getting used to it, since I didn't even think about it anymore, but the longer we stood there, the more I felt this heaviness inside. It was like a mix of disappointment and fear, but I didn't really understand where it was coming from. Until Aiden let go of me and turned back to his table.

The heaviness faded with the break of contact.

Was I feeling what Aiden was feeling too?

"I know we have training today," he said, stacking short slabs of wood on top of each other. They clacked together like bricks as he set them off to the side. "But my dad called a last-minute meeting with the whole pack. He wants you there, too."

My heart skipped, tossing aside any realization I'd had about mine and Aiden's bond. "Your dad wants *me* to come?"

"You're going to be part of our pack when you turn, if that's what you want. You may as well start now."

A rush of emotions slammed through me, starting with panic. This was getting way too real.

As if he could tell what I was thinking, Aiden added, "I

know you don't believe me, but you're going to be fine. And I'm not just talking about the meeting today."

"I don't see how you can be so reassured about everything."

"Mindset is most of the battle. I'm less worried than you are because I've seen the things you can do. Forget about what that Seer said, and forget about the things my dad said. They don't matter."

I chewed on my bottom lip, standing eye level with the wound in Aiden's chest. It was like a bad omen, reminding me how messed up things were.

"We'll get through it together—today's meeting, and the full moon." He finished stacking his piles of wood and dusted his hands off. "Let's go. You'll get to see how we operate a little bit, and you can meet some of the others. We'll do our self-defense lesson after."

I nodded, still unsure about everything.

Aiden came up and took my hand, but stopped mid-step, staring at my knuckles. "Your hand's healed already?"

"Yeah. Super-fast, right?"

"Yeah. But we are only two weeks away from the full moon now. The closer we get, the more you'll see the changes."

"Does that mean my temper will get worse as we get closer?" 'Cause that's what I really needed right now—more tantrums.

"Probably."

I frowned. "Great."

We started walking up the small hill by the side of his house and veered left onto the dirt road. After a while, we came to a rickety dome bridge that I instantly recognized from the night of my accident. I'd escaped from Aiden, even though he'd been trying to help me, and that was where I came face to face with his pack.

But now it looked so normal. A few kids hung out on it, dangling their feet off the edge and over the stream. On the other side of it, Aiden's pack had already started gathering in the field.

I tensed with every hollow step leading over the bridge. There were so many people, and I could already feel several pairs of eyes on me before we made it across the grass to the cement fire pit.

"Don't be nervous," Aiden said. "Half the people here are from another pack anyway."

Easier for him to say.

Ryan stood by the fire pit and straightened when he saw Aiden. He stood taller and broadened his shoulders, signaling everyone to quiet down. "Thank you for coming," he said to the crowd. "I know you have questions about our attack a few days ago. Right now, we don't have a lot more information to give you. Many packs are too afraid to get involved in our cause against the Ancient, but we do have Omar Brinks' pack with us for a while as a precaution."

I scanned the unfamiliar faces until I spotted Omar. He leaned against a tree several yards away, standing well over six feet tall. His tight gray curls were a little shorter than when I saw him back in Charlotte, and he wore a white polo that made his eyes seem more vibrant. He gave me a friendly wave, which I returned, genuinely glad to see him again when he'd been so nice to me before.

"With their help, we have constant surveillance in case of another Ancient or hunter attack."

Guilt sparked in my chest when Ryan mentioned the hunters, and I folded my arms around myself. I saw Aiden's eyes shift to me, but otherwise, he held a stone-smooth face.

"Despite everything we've been through, we do have something to celebrate," Ryan continued. "In two weeks, my son turns twenty-one." Hollers and claps erupted around, and one guy behind us leaned forward and clasped his hand around Aiden's shoulder.

"Why didn't you tell me?" I whispered to Aiden. I knew his birthday would be soon, but I didn't realize it was that close.

He shrugged. "We've had other things to worry about."

"We are still moving forward with the birthday celebration—" Ryan said in the background.

"Ryan?" Theresa's hand went up among the crowd and she weaved her way to the front. "Sorry to interrupt, but some of us are worried about having the party when we should be on the lookout for threats."

Ryan considered her words for a moment as a few *'yeses'* and *'hmm's'* resounded around us. "I understand. I've asked Omar's pack to take watch that night so we can go on with our custom celebration. You all know twenty-first birthdays are the most important. It represents the year of leadership, when our children become equals with us. They no longer need us to guide them in their decisions, and it's something to hold in high esteem. And this one marks the year of a new Alpha." His eyes sharpened as he surveyed the crowd. "Since we have a strong pack for backup, who here still feels that we should cancel the birthday event?"

A few people raised their hands, including Theresa. Others shook their heads in protest.

"How many think we should still have it?" Ryan and most of the others raised their hands. "It's settled. We'll have the party. Manny, please get in touch with Cora so she can put up some protective wards around the field that evening."

"Will do," came a gruff voice. A man stepped forward whom I recognized from the night of my wreck. He'd been there when I'd woken up in the cell. He still held a stony expression, and his salt-and-pepper hair was cropped shorter now, making the scar down the side of his face appear deeper.

"Thank you," Ryan said, turning back to face us. "The birthday celebration will be two Saturdays from now, the night before the full moon." He scanned everyone's faces, hanging on me for a split-second before moving on.

My stomach churned at his subtle reminder that time was speeding toward my fate.

I glanced at Aiden. He stood tall, his chin raised with confidence as Ryan discussed the pack leadership. He studied his father fiercely, like he was ready to step up to the alpha role. That hadn't been the case when we first met, but it gave me hope that if his feelings could change toward his responsibility, maybe mine could change toward the full moon and what I was becoming.

But the fear still draped around my shoulders like bags of bricks.

After Ryan finished with a few other announcements, he dismissed us.

"Ready to go?" Aiden turned and pressed his palm against the small of my back. We turned to leave, following behind another family, but then Manny stepped in our way.

He held his eyes on me for a few seconds too long. I pushed back the leftover grudge I still had from when he'd kept me prisoner in Ryan's basement. It came back full-force anyway.

"Aiden, I'd like to have a word with you and your father. Pack customs."

Aiden hesitated, and his eyes darkened like storm clouds reflecting in the ocean. After a few seconds, he smiled faintly and nodded. "Sure."

"Thank you," Manny said. His gaze drifted back over to me and he dipped his chin in a curt nod before walking away.

"This shouldn't take long," Aiden said. "If you want to hang out at my cabin, I'll meet you there when we're finished. Help yourself to anything you want."

I looked around at the crowd dispersing. It would be awkward to wait here alone while the three of them talked, and I *was* kinda hungry. "Okay. I'll see you soon."

"Deal." He leaned down and kissed me on the cheek.

I turned to head back toward the bridge, passing a group of kids climbing trees in the distance. I recognized a few from the morning of Dorian's attack. A little boy halfway up the tree caught my attention. He smiled and waved before going back to pulling his tiny body up the trunk, and I couldn't help but smile back.

Maybe I could fit in with Aiden's pack. So far, lots of people seemed friendly, minus the obvious ones like Becca, and Ryan, but Ryan seemed like a grouch to everyone.

I made my way through the grass, but a pinprick radiated down my spine, stopping me in my tracks. My sixth sense was hardly ever wrong when I felt someone watching me.

I scanned the trees, but all of the kids were preoccupied.

Then I glanced over my shoulder at Aiden. He stood guarded; arms folded and shaking his head as his father lectured him about something. He seemed upset.

I breathed deep, trying to settle the butterflies gathering in the pit of my stomach. That was when I noticed Manny's steel blue eyes watching me.

He blinked away, focusing on Ryan and Aiden again, but an icy shiver still burst across my skin. It was enough to speed my steps toward the cabin.

Something about that guy didn't sit well with me.

11

I settled into the corner of Aiden's couch with a book from his shelf. The only options to pick from were guitar workbooks and Sci-Fi. Neither piqued my interest, but I wasn't really sure what else to do to pass the time.

Eating was out of the question now. I felt like I had rocks in my stomach after Manny's creepy stare.

I tried to shrug it off and made it a few pages through the first chapter of a space opera when the door opened behind me.

"Hey," Aiden said, clicking the door shut. He moved around the couch slowly, his expression somber.

"Hey." I set the book on the coffee table and turned to face him as he took the seat beside me. "Is everything okay?"

His jaw twitched, but it was so quick I almost missed it. "Everything's fine. Are you ready to train?"

"Sure, but are you sure everything's okay?" I reached over to him, and his skin almost sizzled as a shot of fiery anger burst through me. When I let go, it went away. "You're either really angry or—"

"I'm not angry. I ran over here and I'm ready to get started." As convincing as he sounded, his shoulder muscles were taut, like he was ready to punch somebody.

"Aiden, you can tell me if something happened."

He stood up and waited by the coffee table for me. "I know. Sorry. It was pack stuff Manny and my dad are trying to push on me, but I handled it. I promise, everything's okay. I just need to calm down."

"Okay," I drew out, unsure if I should press for more details.

"Getting some leisurely reading in?" He smirked down at the book on the coffee table, as if confirming I shouldn't ask more questions.

"Yeah. Sci-fi isn't really my thing, but it was better than nothing."

"Sci-fi is awesome. What are you talking about?"

I snatched my phone from my purse and stood up. "Classics are way better. They have everything—philosophy, mystery, romance—"

"Sounds boring."

I clasped my hands to my chest. "How dare you…take it back right now."

Aiden laughed softly and reached for my hand. His anger had settled, and so had his shoulders. "You should take this book home. Broaden your horizons a little."

"*Or…*" Excitement fluttered at my best idea yet. "We can do a book swap. I'll read this one and you read one of mine."

Aiden squinted his eyes at me for a few seconds. "All right. I can handle a book swap. You'll see how awesome space wars are and I'll see how *fun* whatever you pick will be."

Oh, my heart. "I would love nothing more. I can already think of five that will change your life."

He laughed and opened the front door. "Just find a good one. Something with war and killing."

"Sure." Just for that, I was going to pick the most romantic one I could find. I followed him out the door to the stone walkway. "So, where are we training?"

"By the lake. We should run. It would be a good warm-up."

Run? That was the worst.

"Better keep up." He strode past me down the walkway, breaking into a jog by the time he reached the end. "Let's go, Syd," he called over his shoulder, flashing a smile at me as he disappeared around the side of the cabin.

"Ugh." I picked up my feet, falling into a sprint after him. We passed his wood-working table, and I picked up my pace, clutching my phone tighter in my hand.

Aiden dodged between the trees, laying the path out for me so fast that he blew leaves back as he passed. He jumped over a fallen branch, his back muscles flexing with the movement. I followed his lead, pushing off the balls of my feet and pointing my toes as I went over. It almost made me feel like a dancer again.

Our footsteps cracked over the brittle sticks until we made it into the grassy clearing leading up to the lake. Aiden slowed to a walk and turned around, hardly out of breath. He raised his brows and gave a wide grin. "Good job. You're fast."

"Thanks," I said through my panting, clutching my aching side. "When will running be easier? You act like it's nothing."

"I run every day. After you turn, it'll be better. You're already keeping up. I wasn't even taking it easy on you."

I didn't know whether to call him a jerk or be glad about that, but I took a few deep breaths, letting the oxygen settle back into my chest.

"Before we start, I need to know how strong you are."

Aiden held his palm up, watching me drop my phone in the grass. "Give me your best punch."

My gaze shifted to his hand and I stifled a giggle.

"What's funny?"

"It just feels weird to punch your hand."

"At least it'll feel better than a mirror."

"Good point," I said, my ears heating with embarrassment. I tightened my ponytail on top of my head and shook out my shoulders.

"If it helps, just think about all the times you got really mad at me." He smirked, wiggling his fingers.

"You really want me to think about that?"

"If it helps."

"Whatever." I stepped forward about an arm's length from his palm and reared my fist back, throwing it as hard as I could into his hand. His fingers curled a little, cushioning the blow that wasn't really that powerful.

"Come on. You can do better than that, Syd," he teased. "Actually *try* this time."

"I was trying." I scowled.

"Hey, remember when I made that deal with Fran?" His smile faded. That question held so much weight, and he knew I was still ticked at him for that.

"Why would you even bring that up right now?"

"Because when I did that, you definitely wanted to punch me. Maybe you'll go harder this time. Just power through your hips a little more."

"Of all the things you could have used, you went for that one. I hate that guy. You know that." And his attempt to make me angry worked.

"Yup. Maybe we should talk it over." He acted so casual, holding his hand there, waiting for me to take the bait. "I owe him an entire day of my life now. Can you even imagine all the things he'll want me to do?"

My fury built until I brought my arm back and slammed it through the air, but I didn't go for his palm. I went right for his face.

With cat-like reflexes, his hand caught my fist just a few inches in front of his chin. "Nice," he said.

"You're an ass." I pulled my hand free from his grip, feeling a little better, but still irritated.

"But you're really strong." He shook his hand out. "That hurt."

"Good." I crossed my arms, narrowing my eyes at him. "Don't bait me like that again."

"I didn't know how else to get you to hit harder. You need to know what you can do in case someone else attacks you."

"But it doesn't do any good if they come up behind me. Right?" I cocked my hip out, giving him my best stink-eye.

"So the guy snuck up behind you?" Aiden frowned. His eyes glowed protectively for a split-second when I nodded, then he let out a deep exhale. "Turn around."

I crinkled my nose up. "What?"

"I'm going to show you a defense for when that happens. You'll get to practice on me."

"Okay?" I turned to face the trees and waited. Aiden's footsteps pattered up behind me in the grass, and then he curled his right arm around the front of my shoulders, pulling me back in a loose lock, like the Seer had done. But then his left hand found its way around my hip, and his movement slowed as he slid his fingers across my stomach. His pinky barely grazed below the hem of my shirt, leaving a streak of heat across my skin that made my irritation fade away.

"If someone comes around like this, lock your hands around their wrists." His breath skated over my cheek as he spoke.

"Um...the Seer's left hand was up higher, around my arms. I couldn't really move."

He secured his left arm around my ribcage and pulled me against him until his chest fit around my back like a wall. "Like this?" His words seemed to float into my ear, sending a chill down my neck.

I pulled in a shallow breath and tried not to think about how close our hips were. "Yeah."

"From here, you need to turn your head and drop your center of gravity."

I followed the instructions as best I could. My skin hot from our contact.

"Sweep your leg around behind mine. Then bring it in." Aiden tapped my left leg, keeping his tone detached as if this were a typical day.

I did what he said, successfully bringing his knee out from under him. He fell back, taking me with him, and I landed on top of him in the grass.

He raised his head up off the ground and smiled. "Easy, right?"

"For you, maybe." I'd been too focused on the spark of heat bouncing around in my stomach.

I started to push off him and stand, but in less than a second, he flipped me onto my back. A small shriek broke from my lungs through the unexpected movement, and then I was looking up into his glittering, sunlit eyes.

His full lips turned up into a half-grin as he leaned down and kissed me with a graceful, consuming force. I lost all inhibition in a matter of seconds.

I curled my fingers into his hair, pulling him against me until his body weight blanketed my torso. He cupped his hand around the back of my neck, pressing his mouth harder against mine. His scent saturated the air, and his breaths shallowed against my cheek.

A mix of emotions spilled into me—desire, thrill, and...*fear*. They were his at first, but as my heart pumped with adrenaline, I couldn't tell where they started or ended anymore.

And it didn't matter. Kissing Aiden was like an exhilarating sensory overload that I didn't want to stop.

I clenched his shoulders and tilted my chin back, but just like last time, he loosened his touch and pulled away.

"I'm not doing a good job at teaching you self-defense." He tugged at a tendril of hair that had fallen from my ponytail.

"Well, I've really enjoyed it so far," I teased, reaching up and kissing him again.

He laughed. "We need to focus."

"I know. But we could just call that a break."

"I could get on board with breaks like that." He smiled and stood up, pulling me up to my feet too. "All right. From the beginning."

We went over the same moves again. Once I got over the distractions, I hit faster and with purpose, tripping him up and knocking him over until his back was streaked with dirt. We paired the techniques with more offensive movements until we'd made a routine, and I believed I could win during a real threat.

"Good," he said. "I think that's enough for today. How do you feel about it?"

I pulled at the center of my shirt, fanning it back and forth. "Pretty good, but I want to learn more. Can we do this again?"

"Tomorrow, if you want. I won't go as easy on you as I did today, though." He flashed a bright white smile.

"Yeah, well, I think you're the one who needs to be prepared, because I crushed this lesson." I scrunched my nose up at him, matching my smile with his.

Aiden gave a subtle nod and folded his arms. "I think somebody's getting cocky."

I laughed, but before I knew what was happening, he zoomed up to me and threw me over his shoulder. "What are you doing?" I shrieked, dangling over his back. I kicked my legs, but his hand gripped behind both knees. "Put me down!"

"Nope." His laughter jostled me almost as much as his footsteps did as he carried me away. "I think I need to put you in your place."

"And *I* think if you don't put me down, I'm gonna place my foot up your—"

He picked up speed, his footsteps striking the narrow dock leading to the water. There was no question about what would happen next.

"Aiden! Don't you *dare—*"

One second, I felt the vibration of laughter through his shoulders. The next, I was flying—mostly flailing—through the air until my body splashed into the cool water.

12

I swam my way back to the top, gasping for breath and wiping my eyes just as another splash sloshed over my head. Aiden bobbed up to the surface and shook out his hair, spraying water droplets into my face. Much like a dog would after a bath.

"You jerk!" I shoved a wave at him. "My shoes will be drying for a week!"

"Sorry. You slipped out of my hands." He grinned boyishly and swam toward me.

I had every intention of dunking his head under water as payback, but I got distracted by the wet beads sliding down his dimples.

"You have to admit, that was kinda fun." He smirked, locking one arm around my waist.

"Never," I said coyly, trying to keep a smile from slipping free, but it was pointless with the flutters ricocheting down deep. I circled my arms around his shoulders and let him glide us back toward the dock with ease.

"You don't have to admit it for me to feel it."

I blinked away the water hanging from my lashes. "Wait—what do you mean?"

"It sounds weird, but I think I can feel what you feel. Without even having to smell it. It's been happening a lot lately."

I tightened my grip on his rigid shoulders and wrapped my legs around his waist. "Me too."

"Really?" He leaned back against the dock.

"I felt when you were angry earlier. And right now…" I focused on everything flowing through me. "I feel peaceful, and happy, but I know it's not just me. It's like two hearts beating inside me, except one is pure emotion I have no control over."

He searched my face. "I think it's the bond. I can sense when you're close by, and feel when something happens. Like when you broke the mirror or that Seer found you." His gaze sharpened, holding the same ferocity as the moments he went all Alpha-protective over me, but something else was there, too.

A hint of anxiety transferred through me that wasn't mine.

I traced my thumb down the side of his slick face. "What's wrong?"

"Nothing," he said gruffly. He blinked a couple droplets of water away before looking at me again. "I just started thinking about some things."

"Like what? I'm supposed to be the one worrying. You've been so chill about everything."

"I've been trying to be, for you. Sometimes it seems like things are piling up though."

"Why haven't you said anything?"

He flicked away a leaf drifting toward us on the lake's surface. "I didn't want to burden you. I'm going to be an

Alpha...Alpha's don't really talk about things. We're not supposed to let the pressure get to us."

"Says who? You can't do everything alone. You told me I couldn't, so you're not allowed to either."

He frowned. "I wish it were that simple. Sometimes things shouldn't be said until the right time. They can hurt people. They can hurt you, and the last thing you need right now is me dumping a bunch of stuff on you when the full moon is getting closer."

"Oh." I drew my finger down his chest, stopping just above the murky bullet wound that peeked out right above the surface of the water. "I don't really know what it's like to run a pack, but you should talk to me when something's bothering you. Our relationship can't be this one-way street where you do all the protecting and I spill my feelings all the time. That's so...lame."

He looked down. "I know. I'm just not good at talking about things out of nowhere."

"I'm not either, but we should start trying to do better."

His eyes slowly moved back up to mine, and an uneasy feeling slipped through me. It was like Aiden put this mask on that I'd only seen a few times before—when he'd kept my memories from me to protect me.

Was he hiding something now?

I wanted to ask more questions, but my phone ringtone cut through the stillness.

Aiden turned his head toward the annoying chiming, and suddenly, the mask disappeared. His face relaxed, and so did his shoulders. "You should probably get that."

"Right." I dragged myself up over the dock with Aiden following right behind. Water squished in the toes of my shoes as I ran over to my phone. When I picked it up, I had to do a double take at the screen. "It's Liv."

Aiden's eyes glimmered a blue hue as I tapped the green call button and put it on speaker phone. "Hello?"

"Hey. Any new info on the Seer?" Liv sounded guarded, just like yesterday.

"No. Nothing yet."

Liv sighed. "Let me guess—your boy toy's interrogation method is to sic a bunch of golden retrievers on him?"

Aiden's face burned a slight shade of pink. "Why don't you come over, and we'll give you a taste of what we've been doing?"

"Oh, I'm so scared," she taunted. "But seriously, time is of the essence here. We only have another couple of weeks before the full moon."

"I know, Liv," I snapped, releasing some of the anger building. "Is that all you wanted?"

"Actually, no." She paused long enough that I thought the call dropped. "I've decided to help you guys out...you know, out of the goodness of my heart."

Aiden and I rolled our eyes simultaneously, and he stepped forward, leaning toward the phone. "You're going to work *with* us?"

"Sure."

My stomach balled. "You found something, didn't you?" That was the only logical explanation for her deciding to help.

"I don't know. Maybe. You remember my audio recorder I used to take to school with me?"

"Yeah." I'd almost forgotten Liv used to take a digital recorder into her classes. She would listen to the lectures a lot that way, since reading the textbook took a lot of time with her dyslexia.

"I left it in my dad's office for a few days. At first, I didn't think I'd find anything. He's so boring sometimes. But he got a phone call a couple nights ago, and he was talking about a guy named Dorian."

My heart thudded heavily in my chest, and I looked at Aiden. He narrowed his eyes on the phone.

"And before you say anything like 'I told you so,' just remember my dad might not know who Dorian really is," Liv said.

"Why wouldn't he?" Aiden asked. "Hunters can sense other wolves, can't they?"

She went quiet for a few seconds. "What if he hasn't actually met this guy? What if this is a different Dorian?"

"Or…" Aiden shifted his weight to his other foot. "What if it's not?"

"Could you seriously be any more of a—"

"Liv." I cut her off, losing patience with both of them. "You know he has a point. But she also has a point," I said to Aiden.

He shrugged one shoulder up and let it fall carelessly.

"Fine. But my family would never work with an Ancient voluntarily. There's obviously a big misunderstanding."

"Right." I shook my head. She was in severe denial, but could I blame her? "Are you sure about working with us? You've thought about this?"

"Mostly."

"And you know you can't hurt or try to kill *anyone* in Aiden's pack. Your family can't either."

"I know." She sighed impatiently.

"And you know you're going behind your family's back in so many ways," I added, my nerves jumping up in my throat the more I thought about how this could go wrong. "You're betraying them, and if they find out—"

"They won't."

I looked at Aiden, and he nodded. "It's settled then. Keep us posted. I'll send you Aiden's number, just in case."

"Ew," Liv groaned. "Why?"

"Because I can't always be in the middle. And we don't know if I'll still be...around..." My words hung in the air between all of us until Liv finally broke the silence.

"Fine," she half-whispered. "Talk to you later."

When we hung up, I felt Aiden's gaze blaze on my face while I started a group text between the three of us. I refused to acknowledge what I'd said or apologize for it when I might not be here to see things with Dorian get resolved. It didn't mean that Aiden and Liv still couldn't work together though—as long as they didn't kill each other.

And as long as Liv didn't betray us.

New tension creeped into my shoulders. "Are you just as nervous as I am about this?"

Aiden searched my face for a long second. "Yes. We've never been able to work with a hunter before."

That definitely didn't make me feel any better.

13

*W*hen I parked the car at home, my phone had already blown up with snarky texts between Aiden and Liv. I could already tell my job was going to be a full-time referee.

But the more pressing issue was figuring out whose cherry-red Mustang was parked in our driveway.

I got out of the car and slowly approached it. The top was down, revealing an elaborate beige interior that still smelled of new leather, and shiny golf clubs across the backseat.

Turning my nose up at the old-man cologne wafting from the driver's side, I stopped running my finger along the sleek paint and took a step back.

There was a *man* inside my house. With my mom.

Fudge freakin' nuggets. Was Mom dating someone?

I followed the cologne scent up the sidewalk, ready to bust her as soon as I got through the front door, but when I peered into the living room, Mom sat with her arms folded on the couch.

Her expression was guarded. She stared blankly at

whoever sat in the recliner adjacent to her, but the chair was turned away from my view.

When she saw me, she stiffened and cut her eyes back over to her guest. "Oh, Sydney's back."

I stepped into the wide entryway to the living room, finally getting a look at the guy in my house. But all the air rushed out of me at once. "Dad," I sputtered, my blood turning acidic through the shock.

He looked exactly the same. Sandy hair parted to the side, gelled perfectly in place. A polo shirt and khakis that I'd always thought made him look like a frat boy wanna-be. A slight tint to his creamy complexion from too many hours playing golf.

I should have freaking known it was his car. His *new* car.

He locked his gray eyes with mine as he stood and came toward me with open arms. "Hi, sweetheart."

A sliver of panic wrapped around me as he hugged me. I thought of so many ways to dodge out of his embrace, but I couldn't recover from my shock fast enough to try any of them.

"How are you?" he asked, covering me with his balmy cologne. "And why are you all wet?"

"Long story," I answered, pulling away from him. "What are you doing here?"

He stepped back, his light eyebrows creasing with concern. "Is everything okay?"

"It's fine." I folded my arms, putting a little barrier between us. "Why are you here?"

A bright smile broke out across his face. It was the same one he gave me at Christmas when he promised he'd come to my graduation. "Can't I just stop by and see my girl?"

"Couldn't you have stopped by my graduation first? Or how about my eighteenth birthday?"

"I'm sorry, sweetheart. Didn't you get my check?"

His words made me cringe, and I had to go to the kitchen to keep from punching him. I crossed the tile floor, ignoring his sandaled steps behind me as I grabbed a glass from the cabinet.

"I did the best I could," he said. "I got your message a couple weeks ago and meant to call you back, but—"

"But, what? You lost signal on your Caribbean getaway?" I stared at him, flicking the faucet handle up and letting the water whoosh noisily into the sink.

"I was out of town on business. You know how my trips can get."

"Oh, yeah. I know." I filled the glass and drank some water before setting it on the counter noisily. I wanted Dad to know how irritated I was by his presence.

"Sydney." Mom spoke from the doorway between the kitchen and the dining room. "I called your father here."

What?

I whirled around, almost knocking the glass off the counter. It teetered back and forth, threatening to spill, until I steadied it. "You did what?"

Dad sighed. "Your mother is concerned, so I cancelled my trip and came here."

My anger burned deep in my chest. It was like she betrayed me. "I can't believe you."

"You know I always call him when something's going on," she said, tilting her brown eyes in an *I'm sorry* expression. "This has been a hard summer, and you've been acting different."

"Traitor," I muttered before taking another sip of water. When I set the glass down, I didn't realize how quickly I moved, or how heavy-handed I was this time. It cracked against the countertop before falling apart into a puddle of clear shards.

What was up with me and glass?

"Sydney!" Mom whisked past Dad, who watched me with wide eyes. "Be careful."

"Sorry." I grabbed the nearby towel from the counter and started sopping up the dripping water. "I got it, Mom. Let me do this." But she was already kneeling on the floor, picking up the big pieces.

"See, Ezra? This is what I'm talking about. Last week she broke her mirror—by *punching* it—and now this!"

Dad shoved his hands in his pockets, accentuating the slight weight gain in his stomach since the last time I saw him. His gaze swept over the kitchen, then back to me. The way his forehead wrinkled made him look ten years older. "I think I need to talk to Sydney alone."

Mom stopped collecting the mess and stared at Dad. "Why?"

"We can all talk right here," I said. "I'll start. How's Cindy?"

He stood up a little straighter. "She's doing good."

"Awesome. Good talk. I'll see you in six months when you stop by again." I wrung the towel out in the sink and then used it again to clean up the rest of the water on the counter, but all it did was spread it around.

"Sydney, I know I've missed some things," he said cautiously. "But I'm here now. I want to help."

"I don't need help with anything."

"You haven't been the same since the car accident." Mom dumped the glass in the trashcan and moved beside me again. She rested her hand gently on my elbow, but I pulled away. I couldn't let her think I was okay with her bringing Dad here.

"What car accident?" Dad asked.

"Ezra, I called you and left you a message about it a month ago. She was coming home from dance and swerved to miss a deer or something."

Dad frowned and moved around the counter, reaching his hand out toward me. I took a step away from him, and he stopped, letting his arm drop and dangle by his side. "I must not have gotten that message."

Yeah. Right.

"Consider this an intervention." Mom spoke quietly, like she was trying to calm a wild animal. "You're not yourself. I don't know what to do. You've been staying in your room all day and night, except for when you've seen Aiden. You've blatantly ignored my requests for you to come home at certain times. And you've been so...angry. You used to be happy."

"And you think calling Dad and ganging up on me is the answer?"

Her shoulders dropped. "I didn't know what else to do."

"Jenn, I need to talk to Sydney alone. Please." His tone had changed from when he requested that before. Both Mom and I locked eyes suspiciously. I was torn between wanting her to stay or not, but I nodded.

"It's fine. I'll hear whatever Dad has to say so he can go home." I looked back at Dad. He held his posture rigidly, staring at me like he could see to the depth of my soul.

Mom slowly left the kitchen, keeping the corner of her eye on him as she passed through the living room.

When we heard the TV turn on, Dad finally spoke. "When did you get bitten?"

My heart stopped. His words hit me like a semi-truck, stealing my breath and almost knocking me backwards. "*What?*"

He raised his brows, more earnest than I'd ever seen him. "When did it happen? The next full moon isn't too far away. You need to tell me everything so I can help you." The urgency in his voice sent panic searing through my blood.

"What do you know?" I stammered, taking a step back. "*How* do you know?"

"I felt it the moment I hugged you. I wasn't sure at first if that's what it was, but when your mother started talking about your temper and how you've been acting, it all added up."

I clutched my fingers to the edge of the counter behind me. "But how do you know about that stuff?"

His eyes drifted over my face like he was contemplating his answer, or maybe delaying the inevitable. "I'm half-witch."

And there it was—the truth-bomb that tilted my entire world off its axis.

His words seemed to echo in my head until my brain could finally grasp them. Even then, I wasn't sure I'd heard him right. "You're *what?*"

He swallowed and shifted his weight. "I'm half-witch."

This could *not* be happening. "But Mom's not—"

"Shh." He held his finger up to his mouth. "She doesn't know, and you can't say anything. I spent all of our marriage hiding it from her, and it was one of the hardest things I've ever had to do."

"So I'm..." My throat ran dry, and I thought about the necklace. I'd never tell Dad about it; he couldn't be trusted, but I had to know about Gigi. "Was Gigi a witch?"

He nodded.

My stomach flipped. "Why didn't you ever tell me? Why would you leave me alone with this?" My voice bounced off the cabinets and I was on the verge of grabbing him by the shirt to get answers out of him quicker.

"I didn't *leave you* with this," he said. "I made sure you'd be fine. When you were born, you didn't have enough magic to manipulate. It seemed...dormant, for lack of a better term."

"Dormant? Like, I have magic, but I can't use it?"

"Yes."

My head spun. I pulled up the chair at the island and slid onto it, rubbing my temples. "That means I've always been part of the supernatural world?"

Had Aiden and I gone through all that trouble this summer for nothing?

Dad shrugged. "I don't think so. I figured if your magic was dormant, you could stay in the natural world. So many people have traces of witch blood without ever encountering the supernatural."

"Well, guess what?" I snapped. "It happened to me. And you weren't there to help me with it. Aiden was."

"Who's Aiden?"

"My boyfriend. He's a werewolf."

Dad's eyes widened furiously and I cut him off again before he could go ballistic.

"He didn't bite me. He got me out of that car accident when I was almost dead. *I almost died*, Dad." The anger from before was back in full swing, like an axe trying to split through my chest. I needed him to really hear me. This could be the only chance I got to make him understand how much he missed. "Aiden brought me back to his pack and one of them healed me, but when I saw what they were, he tried to save me from *everything*. He risked his life for me. And then Liv—" I sucked in a sharp breath, holding back the tears trying to pry their way from my ducts.

"Liv what?" Dad's expression softened, and he reached for my forearm, but I dragged it back out of his reach.

"Liv's a hunter," I whispered. The scar she left was still so fresh, and saying all of this out loud was like rubbing salt in an open wound. "She found out who Aiden was and used me to get to him, and then an Ancient found his way to us. One of his followers bit me."

Dad's mouth opened, but I wasn't even sure he was breathing. "An Ancient? Are you sure?"

"I'm sure. This creepy gem dealer told us one of the Solstice witches had a prophecy, and then suddenly this Dorian guy showed up."

Dad cursed and wiped his hand over his face. "I'm so sorry, Sydney. For everything. I'm sorry I wasn't here for you —" His breath hitched, and for a second, his eyes glossed like he was going to cry.

I watched him, waiting to see what he would do. Dad never cried. He was always in his own la-la land, a *life is a permanent vacation,* kind of guy. Unless that was a mask to hide behind, but even then, I doubted he was that deep.

He looked down, shielding his face, and when he brought his eyes back up, they were free of any moisture. "I tried to keep you and your mother out of this, and when you were born, I thought it was my out."

"What do you mean?"

"I wanted out of this world," Dad admitted. "Your Gigi was the one who loved it. Not me. She made me practice magic when I was younger, but I didn't really want anything to do with it. I thought when you were born, I could move on, but then I worried all the time about yours and Jenn's safety—"

"But what about Cindy?" I blurted. "You're putting her in danger just as much—"

Dad shoved his hands in his pockets. "Cindy is a witch. She practices still, but not around me. She at least lets me pretend to be fully human, but it was too risky for you if I stayed."

I narrowed my eyes at him. "You can't say that's why you left. You can't make yourself out to be all noble."

"I wanted you to be safe."

"You *left.*" I mashed my palms against the counter,

pushing to my feet and standing almost as tall as him. "You hurt us, and you forgot about me. Do you know how many times I stayed awake at night wondering why Mom and I weren't enough for you? You stood us up, you didn't call us back, and you think you can make up for it with money? That's not love."

All that lingered in the air was the sound of the TV in the living room. Dad's gray eyes crinkled to his temples, and the corners of his mouth indented with tension, giving his face a sorrowful shadow.

I took a step back, halfway reveling in the pain crossing his face, but my triumph was quickly squashed down by the wringing guilt.

Hurting Dad wouldn't change the past. It wouldn't restore our family or mend mine or Mom's heart. The damage was already done, and holding on to the grudge would only cause more problems when I had to face my inner demons on the full moon.

But for some reason, I couldn't pry myself free. I couldn't let it go so easily.

"I'm so sorry," Dad said with a quiet edge. "I know I haven't been there for you. There are no excuses for it. I let my job consume my life, and I need to change that, but please, let me be there for you now. Let me help."

I shook my head. "You can't come back after all this time to save the day."

He raised his hands in surrender. "This is more important than you realize. Did your boyfriend tell you what could happen on the full moon?"

"That I could die?" My tongue sharpened again. "Yes. He told me."

"Right," he hesitated, like there was more. "But...witches cannot be wolves. Other witches have tried to turn before, but it never works. It's something about the magic clashing.

Witch magic and wolf magic are two different types. They're like oil and water—they can't mix."

My breath stalled. "So you're telling me I'm definitely going to die during my transition?"

"I don't know. You're not full-witch. I don't know how it will go for you, but I want to help you as much as possible. We can figure this out together." Dad reached for my hand again, and this time, I didn't pull away.

This time, everything was different, and if my family really had witch magic, I needed more help than even Aiden could offer.

14

To say Aiden was freaked about my witchy relatives was a ginormous understatement. He paced my living room, and I almost thought he'd tread a hole through the floor.

"You can't tell anyone, Syd. If my pack finds out, they'll think you've been lying this whole time."

I sat up straighter on the couch and crossed my legs. "Why? You guys work with witches."

"But we don't trust them. They take care of their own above everything else."

"Just like you do." I gave him a pointed look. "I'm not really a witch, though. I can't use magic. Dad said I only have traces in my blood."

He paused, facing me. "But that's where one side of your family is rooted, and I'm willing to bet all my money that whatever magic you have, started undoing my memory wipe before. That's why you had those visions and dreams."

I buried my face in my hands. Why couldn't this make more sense?

"Are you sure about letting your dad help?"

I shrugged. "I don't really have a choice. Unless you know a lot about magic?"

He frowned. "Not much."

"Should we tell him about the bond?"

Aiden sighed. "No. The less who know, the better."

He glanced at the door right before the doorbell rang. I moved past him to answer it and was greeted by Dad's wistful smile. His hand rested on a black suitcase handle that reached waist-height on his stocky stature.

"Um—I didn't realize you'd be staying with us," I said in a questioning tone.

"Oh, this? It's just some of my mother's things. I needed a good way to lug them all here." Dad clicked the handle up and rolled the case behind him into the foyer, stopping short when he came face-to-face with Aiden. They stared at each other, both wearing distrusting expressions.

"I said we should do this in private," Dad mumbled back to me. "We can't afford for you to be distracted."

I rolled my eyes and shut the door. "He's not a distraction. He's here to support me."

Aiden lifted his chin defiantly. "I'm Aiden. I would say it's nice to meet you, but…it's not."

Dad's scowl deepened, making his gray eyes seem smaller. "That makes two of us, seeing as you're the reason Sydney's in this mess."

"Dad, that's not fair," I countered, moving around him to stand beside Aiden. "Remember what I told you? If not for him, I'd be dead instead."

"Or if his pack had kept to themselves, like the others typically do—"

"Dad, stop. Please. He's here to stay."

He pursed his lips. "Fine. How much time do we have?"

"Mom won't get home from work for probably eight-ish hours. Is that enough time?"

He nodded and rolled the suitcase past us, letting it fall on its side next to the coffee table. He slid the zipper around, tossing the lid off and revealing the dusty leather-bound books and small knick-knacks at the top.

The smell of Gigi's strawberry perfume wafted off everything in the suitcase, and her handwriting scribbled over every book. I missed that smell. I missed her. My body filled with warmth, like her hot chamomile tea sliding down to my stomach all over again.

Dad pulled out the biggest book and flipped open the crinkled pages. "Gigi devoted her life to studying and perfecting her magic. She probably worked with wolves at some point. She might have something in here about transformations."

I glanced at Aiden. He sat in the recliner now, leaning forward on his knees with interest. I lowered to the floor and traced my finger over one of the brown jars in the suitcase labeled *Protection Salt*.

Underneath the other jars poked out a smaller hardback book. I slid it out and skimmed over the pages of diary entries. Gigi had drawn symbols and highlighted words in some other language—maybe Latin.

"I wish I'd known about this side of her," I said quietly. "I wish she were here."

Dad paused. "I know. Me too."

I flipped through several pages in Gigi's diary, and I came to one with a sketch of the necklace she gave me. There was nothing explaining it, just the picture of the stone.

Maybe it was time for me to bring it up. It might not have anything to do with this, but there had to have been a reason it glowed.

I cleared my throat. "Could the red pendant have anything to do with this?"

"What red pendant?" Dad didn't look up from the book

he had his nose stuck in, but Aiden watched me, waiting for me to answer.

"Gigi gave me a necklace when she got sick. She told me to wear it every day. I didn't really listen. I just thought it was sentimental—but a few nights ago when I got really angry and punched my mirror, it glowed."

Dad stopped turning the page, letting the book in his hand drop into his lap.

"Why didn't you say anything?" Aiden asked.

"I don't know." I bit down on my lip, their stares on the brink of burning through me. "Okay, I didn't trust you," I said to Dad.

"What?" He gasped, like I'd told him to go jump off the roof or something.

"You showed up out of nowhere. You can't seriously expect me to open up to you about everything."

"What about me?" Aiden wore his unreadable expression again. "You didn't tell me. I could have tried to find out more about it."

"Right." There was no avoiding it anymore. "I didn't want you to go to Fran or make another deal with anyone."

"Deals, huh?" Dad asked in a judge-y tone. "Bold. But stupid."

I shot him a look of warning. "I'm sorry I didn't tell you."

Aiden said nothing. He looked down at his clasped hands instead of at me.

"Okay, well, we need to get a move on." Dad put the book down in the suitcase. "Go get your necklace."

I hesitated, waiting to see if Aiden would say anything, but he didn't. Anxiety fluttered, but I forced myself on my feet and up the stairs, hurrying back down with the pendant.

Dad took it, admiring the ruby red gleam of it in the sunlit window. "I've never seen this before. When did she give it to you?"

"A few weeks before she died."

He dropped it into his other palm, closing his fingers over it for a moment. "There's magic inside, but I don't know what kind. It doesn't feel like Mom's magic, but anything's possible."

"Why would she put her magic in this?"

"To pass it down? Preserve it so it doesn't get lost? Those are my guesses." He picked up the book again and flipped the pages before setting the necklace in the paper's crease. Then he closed his eyes, chanting some kind of gibberish.

I clasped my fingers over my lips to hold back my rising nerves and giggles. Seeing Dad do this was so out of char-acter for him—or anyone, really. And it blew my mind that out of every other person in the world, it would be my dad helping me with this life-or-death situation.

Dad's chants grew louder, seeming to thicken the air in the room. I held my breath, waiting to see what would happen.

The book began to shake. My urge to laugh died as I watched the pendant rattle between the pages, reacting to Dad's words. As soon as he stopped chanting, the jewel stopped moving.

"What just happened?"

Dad picked up the necklace and held it out to me. "It has magic, but it's not Gigi's."

"How do you know?"

"Because her magic always felt like peace. This feels rest-less. Powerful. More than I can tell, but I can't get it unlocked to see what it is."

"What does that mean for Sydney?" Aiden asked.

"It means we need to figure out how to break into it."

"But what good would that do?" I asked, clasping the thin chain around my neck. "How would that help me transition?"

"This isn't your typical magic. This is something more. If

we can figure it out, this might be what helps you go from witch to werewolf."

Hope flickered, chased by a spurt of doubt. "I don't understand any of this. You said witches can't be wolves, but now you're telling me that this can help me be a wolf."

Dad stared at me solemnly for a long moment. "I hope so, but your Gigi apparently knew you would need this at some point. She spelled this to unlock, but I don't know how to open it yet."

"I want to believe that, but how can we know for sure? We have less than two weeks." Anxiety built until I felt like a door about to swing off its hinges. "Holy crap. We have less than two weeks. And then I'll be—" I didn't know whether to say dead or a werewolf.

I stood up, needing to get out of the house. The air staled, and my skin itched. When I turned to run for the front door, Dad slammed his book shut. "Stop. Look at your necklace."

Dipping my chin, I saw the faint red light pulse from the jewel again. It warmed against my skin like its own separate heartbeat, off and on, just like before.

"It's as if it's responding to your anger," Dad said.

"Maybe it's responding to the effects of the venom," Aiden offered.

Dad peered over at him. "You know what? You might be on to something."

15

Over the next couple days, Dad taught me some unlocking spells while Mom was at work. It was weird repeating phrases after him I didn't understand. Everything was so out of my element, but Dad and Aiden bared with my nervous giggles through it all.

The only problem was nothing worked. The necklace only glowed when my frustration got the best of me, and that wouldn't help me with the full moon. I was supposed to keep my cool and face my inner demons head-on.

"Why won't this work?" I wiped my hands down my face. "Why is it only responding when I get mad?"

"When your body goes into fight or flight, the venom triggers your wolf. That's your primal part coming alive to fight," Aiden said. He sat forward in the recliner, rocking the chair slightly. "But you don't have your wolf yet. Maybe that same energy is calling on the necklace."

I looked at Dad, hoping he'd have a simpler explanation.

He only shrugged. "What he said makes sense to me. Magic and the natural world always have a balance, even when we don't understand it."

My shoulders slumped and I pulled my knees to my chest, watching Dad pack up the books and stick them in the suitcase.

"You need to practice every chance you get," he said. "These spells might not work until the right time—whenever that is." He zipped up the suitcase and propped it beside him. "Before I go, I need to talk to you about something. You've probably realized you have to move out by the time the full moon occurs."

A sharp twinge hit my heart. There it was again, the reminder that I had to leave Mom. "I know."

Dad repositioned his grip on the suitcase handle. "I think you should move in with me and Cindy."

"What?" My voice pitched up on its own accord, and I shot to my feet. "Why would you ever think I'd do that?"

Even Aiden sat forward in alarm, his eyes shifting from me to my dad.

"I'm not living with you and Cindy, and I think you know why."

Dad's lips pursed, and he broke eye contact with me for a second, but when he looked at me again, it was deliberate. He'd thought about this, and he never liked taking no for an answer. "You really should consider it, unless you'd rather be stubborn and risk your mother's safety. I'd hate to get a phone call that something happened when it could have been prevented."

I took a step back, my gut turning inside out. Somehow, after all this time, his words still had a way of ripping my heart out. Why would he think I'd let that happen?

"You can't speak to her that way." Aiden stepped between Dad and I, hands clenched at his sides.

Dad slowly turned his head, as if just realizing Aiden was in the room. "Excuse me?"

"If you feel like you have to send Sydney on a guilt trip to get her to come live with you, you're out of line. You haven't been there for her. You don't know what she needs."

"You think *you* do? All that matters is that I'm here now. I'm trying to do better."

Aiden's posture stiffened, and even from a few feet away, I felt the heat rolling off his body. "That's not how it works. She hasn't told me much about you, but I can tell how much pain you've caused. You can't come back and say that the last however many months you've been gone don't matter. Slates don't get wiped clean that easily when a heart is that broken. For you to tell her if anything happened to her mom that it would be on her, you're even more of a coward than I thought."

My jaw fell. I'd never heard anyone speak to my dad on my behalf like that. Part of me panicked, since Dad's stare turned so red-hot, he might as well have lit his eyeballs on fire, but the other part of me wanted to cheer Aiden on.

"You think you can swoop in here and protect her?" Dad growled. "That you're what's best for her now? If it weren't for you, she wouldn't be halfway between who she was and something she doesn't even understand."

And my annoyance was officially back. "Listen, I don't need anyone protecting me."

Dad didn't pay attention to me. He inched toward Aiden, looking up at him by a few inches. Aiden broadened his shoulders in response.

"I've made mistakes," Dad said. "Believe me, I'm paying for them now when I see how she looks at me. But she's my daughter. I love her, and I will do anything it takes to make sure she lives a long, happy life."

"Staying with you won't be what she needs when it's time to shift. Did you think about that?" Aiden folded his arms. "What are you going to do for her when she'll be a risk to herself and anyone in her path? How will she be safe?"

Once I remembered to breathe, I stepped between them, wedging them apart with my elbows. Dad was the first to step back, but Aiden didn't budge, no matter how far I dug my elbow into his diaphragm. "I think we're done for the day. Dad, thanks for coming. Thanks for everything, but when I move out, I'll find my own place or stay with Aiden."

Dad blinked, breaking eye contact with Aiden finally. "Fine. Call me tomorrow. I'm leaving the supplies here. Make sure Jenn doesn't find them."

"Okay, great. Thanks." I threw my arm around him and guided him to the front door, leaving Aiden stewing in his temper.

"Practice. I mean it. I want you to memorize those spells in the next two days." Dad's hard stare penetrated my face as I opened the door. "And consider finding different company to keep."

"The best company for her is a wolf pack," Aiden called out from behind me. "Or have you forgotten, given your distance from your own world?"

Dad took a step forward like he was going to run back inside and take Aiden down...or get hurt trying, but I blocked his way.

"Bye, Dad."

He opened his mouth, but I shut the door before he could say anything. Then I whirled around to face Aiden.

He silently waited in the living room, his pissed-off expression fading the longer we held eye contact.

"Why?" was all I could think to say.

Dad was helping me through this unknown territory, and yeah—as a person, he sucked—but he was trying. He wasn't the person I would have chosen to help, but he was also connecting me back to Gigi in a way that gave me a sense of wholeness again. I didn't want to ruin that.

Aiden's chest expanded with a sigh. "I'm not apologizing for what I said."

"I didn't ask you to." I blazed past him to the suitcase, yanking it by the handle and rolling it behind me to the stairs. If I hadn't been a little stronger thanks to my pending werewolf form, the suitcase would have taken my arm off. "I appreciate what you said—I really do, but would it have killed you to not say anything?"

"Your dad can't get away with being a jerk to you like that." Aiden followed me around the corner and gently took hold of the suitcase, lifting it up the stairs like it weighed nothing.

"But what did that fight accomplish? Nothing." I padded up the stairs behind him. "You can put the suitcase in my closet."

Aiden disappeared into my room. I heard a clunk and then the closet door shut. He came back a second later and propped his forearm against the doorframe. "For the record, I wouldn't call that a fight, and it accomplished him having to rethink how he gets to treat his family."

He had a point, but I didn't need him taking on that battle for me. "Next time, let me handle it."

He frowned. "Okay."

"Thank you." I turned to head back down the stairs, but Aiden's voice stopped me from getting very far.

"Did you mean what you said about finding your own place?"

I paused, my foot on the top step. I *had* said that, and judging by his tone, it had hurt his feelings. "Maybe? I don't know." I turned to face him. "I wasn't sure if you still wanted me to move in with you."

"Why wouldn't I?" When I didn't say anything, he furrowed his brows. "Do you not trust me? You didn't tell me about the necklace, and now I feel like you don't want to stay at my place."

My palm turned clammy on the banister. "I trust you. I was just protecting you."

"From?"

"From yourself? From Fran? I didn't want you running back to him about the necklace when you already owe him."

"All right. Makes sense." He shrugged and glanced at his feet. "What about the part where you come stay with me?"

I didn't really know how to tell him the things I was worried about. So I went with the more obvious. "What will everyone else think? Your dad hasn't made me feel super welcome in your pack. Neither have a few others."

He tilted his head like he hadn't considered that. "I can see how my dad comes off that way, but who else?"

"Becca? Manny? They both stare at me like I'm a bug they want to squash."

He rolled his eyes. "Becca's harmless. She's high-strung, like Manny. It's probably in their genes to always have a wrench up their—"

I threw my hand up. "Hold on. Are Manny and Becca related?"

"Yeah. I figured Pete told you. Manny's their dad."

"Right." The more I got to know about this pack, the more tightly knit they seemed. Not that it was a bad thing, but it could make it more difficult for me to feel at home with them.

Aiden stepped out of the doorway and into the open hall. "You don't have to worry about them. The one that matters more is my dad, and he invited you to the last pack meeting. That should tell you he wants you to join us when you turn."

"I guess." But I wasn't totally convinced.

"What else?" Aiden asked, his eyes resting on me like he was trying to uncover my deepest secrets.

"What do you mean?"

"There's something you're not telling me. Your heartbeat is speeding up."

I rolled my eyes. "I really hate it when you use your wolf senses to read me."

"How else am I supposed to get some answers? You said the other day you wanted us to talk about things, but it feels like you're holding something back."

I bit down on my lip, fighting against the twisting, hypocritical guilt. I *was* holding back. I didn't want to admit the truth. It felt ugly, and kinda stupid, since we both had made it pretty clear we wanted to be together. But the future was unknown, and sometimes it felt like the only ending for us would be a brutal one.

I didn't know if I could take it.

But as his stare hung on my face, I cracked. "I'm scared, okay? I'm scared we're going to break up. It seems inevitable." As soon as I said it, I wished I could grab the words and swallow them back down.

Aiden's face smoothed, his jaw working back and forth. "You're afraid we're going to break up, or you think we will? There's a difference."

I swiped my hair behind my ear, my face starting to burn. "I'm trying to be realistic."

"Oh, so, *realistically*, we'll break up." He folded his arms and cocked his head.

"No. That's not what I meant."

"That's what it sounded like." His voice held an eerie calmness that didn't match his luminously sharp eyes.

I blew out a breath of frustration. "Look, this is my first relationship. Firsts don't usually work out, and the cards have always been stacked against us. We weren't even supposed to meet in the first place."

"That doesn't mean anything. You can't compare us to other relationships. Ours is nothing like anyone else's."

"I know, but the odds—"

"Screw the odds," he fumed, thrusting his hands out by his sides. "We've beaten them over and over."

"But what if there comes a time when we can't?" I shot back. My chest tightened, and my voice echoed over the wooden stairs and bare walls. "What if I'm a different person after the full moon? What if you change your mind about things?"

"Why would I change my mind?" His eyes pierced me, full of the anger I hadn't seen since he found out I'd gotten bitten.

"I don't know. I've only seen relationships where people change their mind about each other. We're not perfect. We don't know what will happen. I might die in a matter of days or you could…"

Or he could be taken. By Dorian.

Tears pricked at my eyes as everything surfaced again. All I wanted was for things to be normal for one minute, but it didn't seem like that would ever be an option for us.

"Syd…" Aiden moved into my space, reaching for my face and anchoring his palms under my jaw. His hands were warm, and the desperation that flooded through them wrenched through my gut. "It's okay to be afraid. It's normal. But what kind of life is it if we let it get in the way of what we want? Sometimes I'm afraid you'll decide you're better off without me."

I blinked the tears back, my heart thudding. "You are?"

"Yeah." He glanced down at my mouth and back up, speeding my pulse into a frenzy. "But just because we're afraid of things, doesn't mean they'll happen. I'm not going to let my fears stop me from fighting for you and what we have. You're worth everything to me."

Relief pried the iron grip off my heart. I reached up for his wrists, trying to still the hot and cold emotions pinballing around.

"If you're not ready to come stay with me, I guess I get it, but we need to figure something out so you and your mom will be safe."

Leaving Mom was the other part I didn't want to do, but this transition was coming, and the only constants in my life were her and Aiden. I needed to hold on to both of them, but I wasn't ready to move yet. "I need to think about it."

Aiden stroked his thumb down my cheek. "Yeah. Of course."

"Sorry…"

"It's okay," he said, giving me a sad smile. "Everything's changing. It's a lot. But I'm here, and I want to take the burden as much as I can. Don't worry about the living situation…I'll find a place for you if that's what you decide. Maybe Theresa and Nat have an extra room."

I felt guilty for asking him to do that, but maybe having a failsafe was good. "Thank you."

"Everything will be okay." He bent down, and as he kissed me, I wanted to believe that. More than anything.

But there would always be a part of me that couldn't.

*a*iden had stayed the night again. He'd insisted on climbing in through the window just to show off, but I wouldn't let him. It was way too weird.

We'd gotten pretty good about sneaking around. He'd move his truck down the street and wait for me in my room while I went through the awkward motions with Mom. Then I'd excuse myself to an 'early bedtime.'

Sometimes he'd have to leave before I woke up, but this time, he stayed. My heart somersaulted when I turned over to face him. He slept peacefully with one arm up above his head, his ridged chest rising and falling at a steady pace.

I liked seeing him this way.

"It's rude to stare, Syd."

I jumped at the sound of his voice, which was still rough with sleep.

"Sorry," I said. "Actually, no. I'm not."

He cracked one eye open, and one side of his mouth trailed up into a grin. "Then I'm not sorry."

"About what?"

"This." He twisted and shot his arm across me, pulling me

on top of him with the covers tangled halfway around my legs. A couple weeks ago, his movement would have looked blurred from his speed, but now I tracked with him, and I was ready. My palms pressed against his shoulders, and instead of gasping from shock, I laughed.

He grinned. "I guess I have to work on the element of surprise a little more now."

"I guess so." I rested my elbow on his chest and propped my chin in my hand. "So what are we doing today?"

"I vote we stay right here."

"That sounds fun, but really, what are we doing today?"

He hummed in thought. "Training, practicing spells…I have a guitar to build for a client."

"Well, do you want to get breakfast first?" I glanced at the clock. It was only nine, so that meant Mom was probably getting ready for her afternoon shift. "I'll let you sneak out the window this time."

Aiden laughed quietly and ran his hands up my back, finding a curl to wrap around his finger. "Sounds exciting. We could get donuts."

"Like reliving our first date?" I perked up and my mouth may have salivated a little, thinking about that cookie dough donut he'd gotten for me.

Aiden curled his lip up—not quite the reaction I'd expected. "You thought that was a date?"

"Wasn't it?"

"No. Not even close." He combed the rest of his fingers through my hair. "I want to take you on a real date. There's this family-owned Italian restaurant not too far from here. After your transition and everything has settled a little, I'll make a reservation."

"That sounds perfect." I melted into him, wishing we really could stay like this all day.

But my phone vibrated on the nightstand. I tried ignoring

it as Aiden played with my hair, but then it went off again...
four more times.

"Seriously?" I rolled over and sat up, swiping my phone
off the nightstand.

You and Fur Face. Bookstore. 30 min. Have news.

"Crap," I whispered, skimming the rest of Liv's bossy texts
to get my butt out of bed. "We gotta go."

When we got to the bookstore, Liv was already there, sitting
by the Coffee Corner where we'd met up last time. The smell
of fresh coffee grounds poured through the air as people
browsed the books and sipped their morning energy juice.

But not me. As much as I wanted to look at books, I
hoped Liv had something on Dorian.

Aiden's hand burned through the back of my shirt, and a
low growl exhaled up his throat when he laid eyes on Liv.

"Calm down," I whispered.

"I am calm," he insisted. "I just want to wring her neck
every time I see her."

Honestly, I wasn't so sure I'd stop him.

When we got to the little round table, Liv sat up
straighter and peeled her sunglasses off her head. Her blonde
locks poured down her jean-jacket shoulders, and she'd
donned her berry-red lipstick again. "Thanks for coming."
She shifted her gaze from me to Aiden. "You too, Mutt-Butt."

Aiden jerked, his fingers curling like he was about to
reach across the table. I stepped in front of him and shot Liv
a glare.

"What do you have for us?" I asked, taking the seat beside
her and patting the chair on my other side for Aiden.

He mechanically sat down, never taking his heated stare
off her.

She smiled, like getting under his skin was her newest hobby. It probably was. "First, any updates on your end? Has the Seer said anything else?"

I looked at Aiden. His jaw worked overtime. "He's not much of a talker."

She rolled her eyes. *"Witches."*

I felt Aiden's gaze jump to me, but I didn't react. I wasn't about to tell Liv about my family. "Anything new for you?"

"Well…" She happily propped her elbows on the table. "My dad's going on a trip next week."

Aiden leaned forward beside me, and my heart rate tripled as I dug my fingers into the chair. "Where?"

"D.C. He told me he's going on some lame fishing trip, but I went through his stuff yesterday and found hotel reservations." She smiled sweetly and batted her lashes.

"I hate to say it," Aiden said, "but, good work."

Liv raised a light brow skeptically. "Thanks. Anyway, I thought you guys should know, since that's our deal. I'll keep you posted on what I find out after I get back."

"Wait," I interrupted. "You're going?"

"We're all going," Aiden insisted.

"Uh—hold on." Liv held her hand up, like she was trying to keep her distance from us. "To answer your first question, yes, *I'm* going. Alone."

"No." Aiden shook his head. "We decided we'd do this together. That was our agreement. We're going too."

"Listen, Dog Breath…" Liv raised her voice, then quieted back down when she noticed the clerk glancing over at us. "That was not the agreement I made. We agreed to share information. Not go on missions together. You'd be a liability if we went anyway. You said Dorian could track you, right?"

Aiden's arm tensed against me. "I can't trust that you'll tell us everything."

"We don't even know who my dad is meeting with. It could be with some of his old buddies."

"But if this meeting is about Dorian, this could be our only chance to find out everything we need to stop him. We need to know what he looks like, what his plans are, who he's working with. Everything. How do we know you'll get all that information?"

"And how do we know you won't get caught?" I asked.

Liv folded her arms, reminding me of a little girl about to throw a tantrum.

"We need to go with you," I said. "If you say no, we'll follow you anyway."

Her green eyes narrowed at me, and after several tense seconds, she slouched her shoulders in defeat. "Fine, but it's me and Syd. You can tag along, but you have to stay out of sight."

Aiden opened his mouth to protest, but I grasped his knee under the table, interjecting before he could speak. "Deal. When do we leave?"

Liv stood up, and slid her sunglasses on her. "Monday. We can come back after or stay at a hotel. I'll tell my dad I'm going on a trip with Mike; he won't suspect anything."

I nodded. "We'll be in touch."

My anxiety had skyrocketed. As each day got closer to the full moon, my mood became unpredictable. Little things made me snap, and by Monday morning, I'd thrown my bedside lamp across the room, broken my alarm clock to pieces, and slammed the front door so hard that the windows cracked.

The only thing that seemed to help was training. Aiden ran with me until I was too tired to be angry about anything, but it was a temporary fix. I'd go out of control again hours later and my necklace would glow like a neon sign.

The more I was at home, the more Mom was at risk. That's why this trip to D.C. came at the perfect time. I'd rather dig out a hundred splinters from my skin than potentially face Dorian, but this gave me space to think about where I'd live next and prepare for what was to come.

I shoved another shirt into my bag and headed downstairs. The smell of burnt toast and coffee triggered my gag reflex, but I plastered on a faint smile anyway. It was the best I could do to act normal and go along with my alibi, which was that I was staying at Dad's house.

When I reached the landing, I shifted my bag over to my other shoulder and faced Mom.

She reclined on the couch in the pink fuzzy bathrobe I'd gotten her for Mother's Day two years ago, complete with matching slippers. Her mug steamed between her hands, and she had her hair piled on her head in a messy bun.

When she saw me, she set her mug down and stood up, but she didn't move closer. "Got everything? Toothbrush, underwear, books?"

"Yeah." I patted my bag. "Thanks."

She nodded, folding her arms around herself. "Okay then. Have fun." I knew she didn't mean to sound bitter, but her tone was deep and jagged.

"Mom—" I inched a step closer, but I stopped when the rumble of Aiden's truck sped up the driveway. "You know this could be good for us. You told me before that I should try to forgive Dad. Maybe this is a start."

Like that was going to happen any time soon.

"Right." Mom turned her head toward the snap of Aiden's truck door outside. "Well, Aiden's here. You shouldn't keep him waiting."

I chewed the inside of my cheek, wanting to close the gap

131

and throw my arms around her. I wanted to rest my head against her shoulder and tell her everything—what was happening to me, why I kept my distance—but I couldn't. I had to pretend I was still mad at her for her intervention.

Mom sat back down on the couch. "I'll see you soon."

When I stepped onto the porch and shut the door, Aiden was waiting at the bottom of the steps. He wore his usual dark jeans and black v-neck, this time under a red plaid shirt with rolled sleeves.

Despite the tension in his forehead and how his smile thinned, my heart skipped as I looked at him. This trip could be the worst thing we ever did, but at least I'd be with him.

"Hey beautiful," he said, reaching up across the steps for my bag.

I handed it over as I joined him on the sidewalk. He pulled me into his side, tilting his face down and kissing me gently. "You okay?"

"Yeah." Really, I felt like I was a mess waiting to spill. "Are you ready?"

He took my hand and walked beside me toward the truck. "I'm as ready as I can be."

I forced a smile. "Me too."

We didn't say anything else until we got to Shadow Grove. My fingers clenched tightly, my nails digging into my palms by the time we pulled into the parking lot where the charred brick of Pete's shop remained. Liv was already there, waiting in her car.

Aiden parked two spaces down from her, his shoulders rolling back as he cut the engine and glanced over at her.

Liv rolled her window down, staring at us through sunglasses that took up half her face. "You bitchachos ready to go?"

"Not two seconds in and she's annoying the hell out of me," Aiden said. He got out of the truck, and I followed his lead. "We're still waiting on my friend," he said to Liv. "He'll be here soon, and we'll take his car."

Her bright red lips turned down. "No. We're taking my car. I never said you could invite more of...you."

Aiden leaned against the truck and looked over at me. "She's crazy if she thinks I'm riding in that death trap for four hours."

I couldn't argue with that. Duct tape stuck out around the edges of her bumper, and the paint had peeled off most of the hood. Not to mention the rattling whenever she started the engine.

Liv must have heard him because she scoffed and rubbed her hands along the steering wheel. "Don't call Octavia a death trap. She's loyal. Right, Syd?" She raised her chin at me for support, but I shook my head.

"I'm with him on this one."

Liv stared at us for a moment behind her thick sunglasses. "Still, it's just us. Nobody else can come."

"We need back-up," Aiden said. "What if something happens to one of us?"

"Then we'll figure it out," she argued.

"Yeah. Because that's a solid plan."

"Okay," I said, clapping my hand over his mouth. "If you two are going to be like this the entire trip, we won't get anything done. Maybe it's for the best we have some more people come along, for our safety and *yours*." I gave Liv a pointed glance.

She worked her grip on the steering wheel like she was revving an engine, but she finally relented. "Fine."

She rolled her window back up and got out of her car, tilting her sunglasses on top of her head as she pulled her bag out of her trunk. And she looked like a total badass.

Her crop top stopped right above her belly button, and her tight black pants were tucked into short lace-up combat boots. On one hip she donned her mother's knife, and two more were strapped to her thighs. She had a few other gadgets sticking out of her boots that I really wanted to know about. One looked like a hand-held pepper spray bottle.

My mouth fell open. "How many knives do you have on you?"

She shrugged, like it was a normal thing to look so lethal. "A few."

The pump of a low bass came zooming around the corner as Pete pulled in. His recently washed silver SUV put Liv's car to shame, and by the way she folded her arms and stared at it, she knew it.

"Hey guys." Pete got out, smiling brightly at us in his gray t-shirt and khakis. He glimpsed at his shop, but turned away from it, acting like it wasn't even there. Then he approached Liv and extended his hand out. "Hi. I'm Pete."

She cut her eyes at me and hesitantly shook his hand. "I'm Liv."

Pete paused, his eyes quickly trailing down to her knives and boots. As I watched him study her, my stomach rolled. If he found out who or what she was, it wouldn't be good for her *or* me.

"You're not a wolf," he said, like it was more of a question.

Crap.

Liv shifted to her other foot, and leaned her elbow on top of her car. "Nope."

Pete crossed his arms suspiciously. "Are you a witch?"

"Close," Aiden said smugly. "One letter off."

Liv shot Aiden an icy glare and folded her arms to match Pete's stance. "I'm human."

Pete tossed his head back a little, throwing a few strands of hair out of his eyes. "*Human?* And you *know* about us?"

"Guess so."

"Sorry, but how?" Pete folded his arms, tracing his index finger down his chin. "If you don't mind me asking."

My pulse pounded, and I took in a deep breath to calm myself. Suddenly, Aiden's idea to bring Pete along was beyond disastrous.

I jabbed him in the ribs when Pete wasn't watching, and he jumped.

"Ouch. What was that for?"

"Why did you do this?" I mouthed the words to him while Pete eagerly engaged with Liv over how a human could be so involved in the supernatural and survive so easily.

"You know he could figure her out," I whispered harshly.

"Maybe Pete deserves to know," Aiden countered. "Don't forget she almost got us killed—*all* of us. Multiple times."

"But what if he blames me once he figures it out? What if he tells the pack I was the one who led her family here?" A burning welled up inside me, and I pivoted to face him, curling my fists. "Did you think about that?"

"Breathe," Aiden said. "He would never blame you or tell the pack about that. You didn't know what she was. You can trust him."

I stared at him, my shoulders rising and falling rigidly. It wasn't that I didn't trust Pete. I did...but he had his family to be loyal to.

"Syd, we need back-up anyway, and Pete's my best friend. If we find anything out about Dorian, he's the one I want with us."

More points I couldn't argue with. We really couldn't do this alone, but I didn't have to be okay with it.

"Fine." I opened the back door to the truck and pulled my bag out of the backseat. "Are we ready to go?"

Aiden reluctantly took it from my hand, giving me an apologetic look. "We're still waiting on Omar."

"You invited Omar, too?"

"More back-up."

Speechless, I pinched my lips together. Liv was going to be so pissed, and therefore, I was too.

"Don't worry." He bent down and kissed my cheek before carrying my bag to Pete's trunk. As he and Pete arranged the luggage in the back, Liv strutted over and yanked me aside, pulling me behind the tailgate where neither Pete or Aiden could really see us.

"This is the guy who owned this place, isn't it?" She pointed at what once was the *Six Strings* guitar shop. When I didn't answer, she groaned. "You have *got* to be kidding me. Seriously, I shouldn't have said anything to you guys about this trip. I should've done it myself."

I grabbed both her shoulders to face me completely, and they sharpened under my fingers. "Listen, we're all here for the same thing—to stop Dorian from whatever he's up to. I'm not super happy about all this either. Remember how you used me? If anyone finds out—" I waited for her to catch on. It didn't take long for her emerald eyes to widen with understanding. "Exactly. You'll survive one night with us. Just keep your ego in check."

A blue Charger drove into the parking lot, pulling up right behind Pete. Omar got out, and I noticed someone else in his car with him. A girl, maybe my age, I wasn't really sure with the glare on the windshield. She sat in the front seat, her eyes closed and her pink head of hair tilted back against the seat.

"Seriously?" Liv whispered. Her face burned red. "We're bringing more? Your boyfriend's out of control."

"I know, but he did it for our safety." I dropped my hands by my sides as my nerves sparked to my fingertips. Part of me was glad to have more back-up, but then there were more chances for Aiden's pack to find out about Liv.

I had to trust Aiden knew what he was doing though. He

always thought things through, and he wouldn't have invited Pete, Omar, and whoever this other girl was if he didn't think it was okay.

Maybe I was just letting my fear get the best of me. This trip was dangerous. We were voluntarily walking into a potential lion's den, and Aiden would be right there at Dorian's fingertips.

A lead weight slammed in my gut.

Liv seemed oblivious to my panic as she watched Aiden shut the trunk of Pete's car. She stepped back and forth, running her hand over her blonde ponytail. "This trip's going to suck. Like, epic proportions of suckage."

"I know." I let out a sigh and started walking to the car. "In so many ways."

17

*T*raffic and pedestrians congested the darkening D.C. streets.

Liv, Pete, Aiden and I waited on the rooftop of an eight-story building, overlooking the hotel where Liv's dad was supposed to be staying. Omar and the girl with the pink hair waited down on the street, hanging out at a coffee shop until we gave them the signal.

We were going to watch for her father and follow him to his meeting point. Then Liv and I would scope things out— by ourselves.

My stomach tumbled. I was totally going to hurl.

"Syd." Aiden stepped in closer beside me. "You don't have to do this."

"Yes, I do." My muscles tensed against that statement, but we had to do this. This mission was too important to wuss out on.

Aiden looked away, the dusky sky casting stern shadows across his face. "I wish there was another way."

"I know." I went back to watching Liv lean on the edge of the roof. Pieces of her ponytail drifted in the breeze as she

138

stared down at the hotel's glass lobby. Pete stood a few feet from her. He folded his arms, broadening his shoulders as he watched the noisy street below.

The hotel was nice—a sight that radiated luxury that Liv's family could never afford on their own. Whoever her dad was meeting with must have had a fat wallet, and maybe a lot of power, too.

Acid churned in my gut as I looked over the city lights. They twinkled like stars as the sun lowered. Time was moving too fast toward this meeting.

I looked at Aiden and how his temple muscle rolled. He must have been nervous, too.

"How do you do this all the time?" I asked.

He looked over, taken off guard. "Do what?"

"Live on the lookout for hunters and witches all the time."

He shrugged and pulled me in to his side. "It's not always like this. We stayed under the radar for a long time. But when trouble does show up, we have our pack. We support and protect each other. That's why I brought Pete and Omar. If something happens, I know they'll have our backs, and as much as Liv gives me heartburn, I know she'll have your back too."

I suppressed a smile at his comment, but I was still terrified to my core. Aiden's safety was my biggest priority. If Dorian really was here in this city, Aiden was within his reach and we didn't have the means to protect him.

This was so incredibly stupid.

Pete casually made his way over to us and leaned on the roof's edge beside me. "How does this girl know about all this, again? She was pretty vague." He peered over at Liv, who hadn't changed her stance at all in the last two hours.

I hesitated, my nerves sharpening even more. How was I supposed to answer that?

Pete raised his brows, looking between Aiden and me.

"There's a lot about her I don't know." That was true. Finding out that Liv was a hunter had been a total shock. There was no telling what else she lied about during our friendship.

Pete frowned, clearly not satisfied with my answer. "How is she alive if she knows so much about our world? Humans don't make it—besides your situation."

I looked at Aiden, but the dumbstruck expression on his face told me he'd be zero help.

"She's a spy," I answered. "For a witch."

"A spy?" Pete crinkled his nose. "I don't see how that could work unless she has some kind of insane protection spell."

"Yeah, maybe. That's the only logical answer."

Pete looked at me from the corner of his eye. "Are you sure?"

"He's out." Liv yelled, saving me from further questioning.

All three of us leaned over the cement edge, following her speared vision across the street. A slender, dark-blonde man in a black suit strode smoothly out of the whooshing hotel doors. There was no denying it was William McCallister.

He had the same military fade, thin lips, and judging green eyes as always. He came to a stop on the sidewalk with his shoulders back, clearly waiting for something. Pinning his hands behind his back, he scanned the streets until a black car pulled up along the curb.

My heart boomed in my chest, and as I watched him slide into the backseat of the car, my body stilled like cold steel replaced my bones.

"Go." Aiden didn't even look up. His face barely changed from the intensity he held, but Pete didn't need anything else to spring into action.

He jumped over the rooftop. A second later, his shoes clanged on the fire escape a few stories down.

Aiden rolled his shoulders back, peering over the edge of the building at a shadow on the street corner. "Omar. Now."

Omar's human shadow moved, zipping around a group of pedestrians and disappearing down an alley.

I clenched my hands to cope with the new adrenaline. This was actually happening. We didn't know what we would find out, and there was no going back.

Aiden turned to face me, looking into my eyes like he could see right through me. For a second, I felt like I could see through him, too. A crease of pain flickered down his face in the last of the sunlight.

"You can do this," he said, almost breathlessly. "You've been training. You're strong."

I nodded and reached for him as he plastered his lips against mine. A bolt of dread built up inside me. I clung to the edge of his shirt to keep myself together.

Why were we always getting separated when we promised to stay together?

What if this was a trap?

So many questions and unsaid things rushed through me, balling in my throat with nowhere to go. I tried tightening my hold on him, but he started backing away, dragging his hands down my forearms. Then he slipped from my grasp.

"I'll see you soon." His eyes glowed with a faint blue hue, and he turned around and sprinted to the edge of the roof. He sailed across to the next building, moving like a shadow in the direction of William's car.

In that moment, it was like my whole world left me behind.

"Let's go," Liv called to me from the rooftop door.

Snapping back to what I was supposed to be doing, I forced my feet to move toward her. Our footsteps thundered down the stairwell, and as we got closer to the bottom, we jumped the landings until we made it out to the street.

Tires squealed up to the street corner and the girl with pink hair rolled down the windows of Omar's blue charger. "Get in!"

We filed into the backseat, and I didn't even get the door all the way shut before she sped through the red light, almost pummeling over a pedestrian carrying a to-go bag. Horns blared and curses flew at us, but the girl didn't seem to care.

"I'm Sasha," she said over her shoulder. "I'm from Omar's pack. You're Sydney, and..."

"Liv," Liv said, leaning her head slightly out the window. The stuffy city air whipped against our faces as we plowed through another red-lit intersection.

"Cool." Sasha leaned forward and turned the headbanger music up, nodding along like this was an everyday road trip for her with two of her best friends. A small tattoo peeked out from her neck beneath her bobbed hair, and she almost had a doll-like quality to her features. Slanted cheekbones, a hoop nose ring, and big eyes that I assumed were blue.

But when she glanced over her shoulder at me, I jumped. Her eyes glowed gold, like Pete's. The mark of a human, turned wolf.

"You were bitten," I blurted out before I could stop myself.

"Yup." That was all she said as she jerked the steering wheel to propel us down another narrow street. I wanted to ask her about her change. I wanted to hear everything—to see what it was like for her. Pete and Aiden made it sound like humans turning to wolves was so rare, I probably wouldn't meet another like that, but this gave my heart a small beat of hope.

My cell phone rang, vibrating against my hip. It was Pete. "Hey," I said, putting him on speaker phone. Sasha turned the music down so we could hear him.

"He's going to an old abandoned church near North Hampshire Avenue. It's huge. You can't miss it."

"Got it," Sasha called over her shoulder, screeching our tires down another street. Up ahead, I caught a glimpse of Aiden's human silhouette on another rooftop. His silhouette was graceful, almost like a dancer floating through the sky at lightning speed. My pulse picked up, but dropped when he disappeared behind a taller building.

Sasha pulled down a dark alley, lurching the car to a stop between two brick buildings. I jammed my fist into the seat in front of me to keep from getting airborne, and by the time I got my bearings, I was the only one left in the car.

I got out and headed around the corner, following Liv and Sasha down the darker, emptier sidewalks. The church steeple poked up into the sky beyond another brick building, and my lungs stalled.

We were so close now.

Omar waited on the corner up ahead by the traffic light crossing, and Pete strode across from the other side. His footsteps were silent, but he moved with purpose.

"We've checked it out," Omar said. "One guy was waiting outside the church, but I took him down. He had red eyes."

"Crap," I said, losing the little oxygen I had left. One of Dorian's wolves. I glanced down at my arm, and even though there was no trace of the bite left, I remembered the burning and blistering of the venom like it was hours ago.

"The guy we followed here went inside through the sanctuary doors, so you should go in through the back," Omar suggested.

"Thanks," I said. "Here, take my phone. I don't want it to go off or fall out of my pocket while we're in there."

Omar studied me as he stuck my phone in his back pocket. "Are you sure this is a good idea? A human and an almost-werewolf going in there alone? If something happens—"

"We've got it," Liv interrupted sharply. "We're running out of time."

Omar's worried eyes slid between us before he glanced over at Pete and Sasha. "We're really letting them do this?"

Pete nodded and Sasha bumped her shoulder into Omar's side like old friends would.

"I say let them go," she said. "We'll hear the screams if something happens." She winked at me, like our deaths were a casual thing. Or maybe she had a strange sense of humor, but that still didn't sit well with me.

"Aiden says you need to go." Pete glanced up to the roof, but when I turned around, there was no one there.

"Let's go," I said to Liv, even though I really wanted to chicken out.

We all split off in different directions. Liv led me around to the back of the church where we hid behind a dumpster, watching the graffiti-stained door for a moment. No sign of anyone coming or going through the back.

"I don't sense a wolf nearby," she said. She started to sneak away, but I grabbed her shoulder.

"Wait. Can your dad sense me?"

She paused at the corner of the apartment building we hid behind. "No. You haven't turned yet. The only way to tell would be if he touched you, and we won't come that close to him."

"What about Dorian? What if he's in there? Could he tell if we were close?"

Liv shrugged, sliding her knife out. "No clue."

"Great."

With the little light from the dim lamppost over the lot, we crouched and hurried to the back door. Liv jiggled the handle and slowly opened it, letting me in first.

A rotten odor assaulted my nose right away, and I gagged, slamming my sweaty palm over my mouth to stay quiet.

My eyes watered against the smell, and I blinked, sharpening my heightened vision. There was no light, but everything in the church kitchen appeared in vague colors instead of darkness. It was like soft sunlight surrounded us.

But the sight in front of me was all but sunshine and rainbows. The metal tables glinted in the center of the room, and what rested on them disturbed me to my core. Four bodies lay there, covered in white sheets with their shoes sticking out from underneath.

A whispered curse came from Liv right behind me. She turned on her cell phone flashlight and held it up while covering her mouth and nose.

"What fresh hell is this?" She murmured, stepping forward and sliding one of the sheets back. She immediately dropped the fabric with a gasp.

My back froze to the wall. "What...what is it?" I didn't want to ask, but I knew she'd tell me anyway.

"You have to come see this for yourself. I can't even describe it."

I inched from the wall, coming slowly up behind her. I bit my lip as she moved to the side, revealing a man with such wrinkled skin and tight open lips that he didn't even look human. His hair was still black, youthful and thick, but his face was sunken. His turquoise eyes bulged with a permanent shocked appearance.

"*Holy crap.*" My insides coiled, and I gripped the edge of the table to keep my knees from buckling.

"He wasn't just a wolf," Liv said, her hand gently moving to his shoulder. She pulled back and curled her lip. "He was an Alpha."

18

*A*lphas. They were *all* alphas.

Aiden told me what Dorian could do, but I never imagined how horrible it could be until now. How he took alpha souls and left the bodies like freaking zombies. Hearing about it was one thing, but seeing it was a whole new level of messed-up I'd never imagined.

I turned away, doubling over and dry-heaving. Thankfully, I skipped lunch, or I'd totally toss my cookies right here.

"Syd." Liv placed her hand on my back. "Do you know what happened to them?"

I nodded, holding my hands on my thighs for support. "He absorbs alphas. He takes their life force or something. That's what he was going to do to Aiden."

A rod of rage stabbed through my center as I pictured him lying on that table. It was dizzying, tightening my skin to the point that I wanted to claw it off.

I stood, propping against the counter, my fingers clawing around the edge. "That's what he *will* do to Aiden...because of you."

Liv turned, her lips parting and eyes scanning over me as my chest expanded in hot breaths.

"Sydney, I'm sorry," she said. "I didn't know—"

"Don't act like you care." I spun and thrashed my arm out, smacking the phone out of her hand. It hit the floor with a clatter, the light shining up at the ceiling.

My insides scorched with venom and my mind tunneled on one thing—hurting Liv in all the ways she and her family had hurt *me*.

I stalked toward her with light, calculated steps.

"Sydney." She stepped back, bumping into the next table with a corpse on top. The body jostled with the impact. "We can't do this here. They'll hear us."

I didn't care. I lunged at her and threw my hands around her neck, squeezing as hard as I could with no remorse. She gasped and grabbed my wrists, thrusting them apart. Her knee sailed into my stomach, and she hurled me backward into the counter.

The fall was jarring to my bones as I hit the corner. Pain shot up my back, but it wasn't enough to keep me down.

"Sydney, I made a mistake, okay?" Liv moved backward, swiping her phone off the floor as I paced toward her. "I'm on your side now."

"No. You're on *your* side," I spat. "You only care about you. Not what I want. Not what makes me happy. If you did, you never would have told your family about Aiden."

Liv bumped against one of the stoves and stepped sideways, following the periphery of the kitchen. "I'm sorry. I didn't want to, but my brothers made me. I promise, I did it to protect you."

"Your apology is crap. It means nothing." Maybe she was lying, too. All I could see was her betrayal as I inched toward her.

She slid one of the empty metal tables between us,

backing toward the hallway. "We can't do this here. Let's just get through this, and I promise, when we get outside, you can beat the snot out of me all you want."

But her words evaporated by the time they reached my ears. I wanted to throttle her until she couldn't breathe anymore. I wanted to make her feel the pain I felt when I thought I was about to lose Aiden.

I jumped up and scaled the table in front of me. Pieces of my hair flew back as I soared through the air. My knees slammed into her chest, sending her to the floor, but she curled up underneath me and threw me over her head.

The room turned like a Ferris wheel as I rolled forward, my back slamming onto the cold tile floor. A breath whooshed out of my lungs on the impact, and in no time at all, she was on top of me, pinning me down. "Sydney, stop! You can't think clearly when you're angry. It's your wolf side trying to come out—it's not you." Her fingers pinched around my wrists, pressing them flat above my head.

I writhed against the floor, pounding my knees up against her, but her hips were planted firmly around my waist. "Get off me," I growled, barely recognizing my own voice. I could almost slip my wrist free to punch her in the face.

She snatched my hand back down and leaning forward over me. Then a soft glow of red light pulsed from my chest, and my necklace warmed against my skin.

"What the…" Liv's face glimmered in the light emanating from me. "What is that?"

I said nothing as I sucked in the foul air around us. My chest rose and fell heavily under her light body.

"Why is your necklace glowing?"

"Because," I seethed through my teeth. "I'm part witch."

"Witch?" Her jaw dropped. "You've known about this stuff your whole life?"

"No, dummy. I didn't know until I got freaking bitten—

thanks to you." I fought against her again, trying to leverage my arms up off the floor, but she was still stronger.

"Okay, we'll talk about that later. Right now, we're here to figure out what my dad is doing. Maybe with Dorian. Remember that, Sydney. *Dorian*." She said his name slower, trying to get through my blazing barrier of emotions. "He wants to kill the alphas. He has a plan that we need to figure out. If they hear us, they'll kill us, and then you'll never be able to protect Aiden. Do you understand me?"

As her words sank in, my necklace died down, along with my anger. It was like she doused cold water on a fire. I laid there, my breaths slowing as something released inside me. "I understand."

"Good," Liv said. "Nice moves, by the way. Fur Face taught you well."

"Don't." I turned my head, peering down the hall that had a small floodlight at the end. "You'll only piss me off again."

"Got it. Too soon. Okay. I'm going to get off you now. Stay calm."

"Fine," I breathed out, no longer feeling the absolute need to kill her.

But before Liv could move, a figure appeared at the end of the hallway, and a low growl filled my ears. A wolf with those same red eyes I saw before. It started running at us, and my heart jerked in my chest. "Liv, move!"

She sat up as the wolf connected with her and capsized off me into the metal tables. The table legs scraped the floor and the Alpha corpse rolled off, the sheet uncovering his haunting eyes again. A shudder filled me, and I jumped to my feet, rushing across the room and crashing my fist into the wolf's face before he could take a bite out of Liv.

It was like punching a brick wall, which *hurt*, but caught him by surprise. He shook off the daze and whirled around on me, lurching at me with spread claws. I twisted and whirled my elbow into his neck, but he still knocked me back, aiming his teeth at my throat. I held him at arm's length, just like I did the last time I had this kind of encounter, but this time, I was stronger. My muscles steadied, giving Liv time to smash her feet into his ribs and launch him into the wall. We heard a gross cracking sound as he collapsed lifelessly to the floor.

A tremor trailed down my back. The shadow of the body shifted back to human, but I didn't want to see what he looked like. He'd been under Dorian's mind control, and he probably didn't realize what he was doing.

"Come on. We have to go." Liv tugged at my arm and started down the hallway. As soon as we got to the end, there were more halls and doors leading to nothing. "This church is a maze. Which way should we go?"

"I don't know," I whispered. I've never been here."

"You don't have some kind of witchy vibe for any particular direction?"

I shrugged and waited for her to decide.

"Fine. Let's go this way." She crouched and took a left, staying close to the wall.

We passed empty classrooms, taking lefts and rights until muffled voices filled my ears. "Do you hear that?"

Liv turned, her questioning expression illuminated under the blue floodlight. "Hear what?"

"Voices." I focused, and then a distinct male voice I'd heard only a few times before came into focus. William.

"Don't tell me you're hearing dead people or something," Liv groaned.

"No. Your dad. Take a right at the end of this hall." I took the lead this time, turning the corner and stopping abruptly when we faced the outline of a man. He waited by another door, where the voices echoed on the other side. "We have to get past him."

Liv reached into her boot for the small can of mace and drew out her dagger, but instead of attacking the guy, she threw her dagger down the hall to our left. The blade hit the wall and clanged against the floor.

The man's head snapped up, and he started moving toward the sound, alert and looking around, his eyes glowing red. I clutched the wall as he got closer, unsure of what to do. As soon as he came up to the corner, Liv thrust her fist into his face, making him stumble sideways. He caught himself on the wall and turned toward us, but she sprayed him in the face with her mace.

He jerked backwards, clutching his throat and gagging. Then he dropped, falling face down to the floor.

I jumped back. "What the heck was that?"

"Wolfsbane." Liv stuck the tiny bottle back in her boot. "I got all sorts of tricks."

I nudged him with my foot. "Is he dead?"

"No. But he'll be out for a day or two. Come on."

I stepped over him carefully, following her to the door. We peered through the tiny window. We couldn't see much except someone's scaling shadow moving between the sanctuary aisles among gouts of candlelight.

"I'm running out of nearby alphas to supply. Wolf packs are scarcer these days." William said, his voice echoing against the cathedral style ceiling.

"We won't need them once the ritual's done." Another woman's voice trailed through the darkness.

"Syd, this way." Liv waved me over as she headed up a staircase to our right. We took it slow, easing into the creaks. When we reached the top, we slid behind the short balcony wall that overlooked the dusty red pews.

Four men lined the walls and doors on both sides of the sanctuary, and Liv's dad waited at the steps by the altar, facing someone underneath the balcony, out of our view.

William stood tall with his arms behind his back, and he turned, looking down at the object on the table between the candles. "And you only need five things for the ritual?"

"Yes," the woman said. "We need to complete the pentagram."

"And you're sure this is smart?" William picked up a knife, and I recognized the prongs jutting from the sides. That was the knife Donnie and Chris used against Aiden when I found him in the woods. It still had dark traces of his blood dried on the blade.

My fingers dug into the soft wood of the balcony to keep myself steady. They could still find him—he would never be safe until we got that knife back. Liv seemed to be thinking the same thing as she looked at me, her brows drawn tight over her eyes. At least, I hoped she thought the same thing.

"Are you giving me reason to question your allegiance to Dorian?" The woman's voice sharpened in the open space, and it was like a cold finger sliding down my neck at the mention of the Ancient's name.

"No," William said coolly. "But it *was* my understanding that he would be here for this meeting."

The woman finally slinked her way to the front, wearing a black, full-length dress that hugged her round curves. Her red hair pinched up in a curly bun, and she held a beaded chain in her hand. "He has agreed to meet by magic. I'll summon him if you're ready."

William nodded, tracing his finger over the edge of the blade like I'd seen Liv do with her knife before. He stepped aside, giving the redhead space to glide up to the altar and lay her beads on it.

I held my breath and glanced at Liv. We were about to see Dorian, and I wasn't sure either of us were ready for that.

19

I sat with wide eyes, staring from the balcony as the witch hovered her palms over the beaded chain and began chanting.

The atmosphere darkened, thickening the air until it laid like a heavy blanket on my shoulders. Strands of my hair blew back off my neck, and the candles sparked. The wind picked up just as the image of a man blinked in and out of existence over the altar.

He was young, with long blond hair that shimmered despite the dank sanctuary, and he wore a white shirt and black pants. The gusts of air died down slowly, but he still flickered in and out like a hologram until the witch stepped back and sat down on the first pew.

"William," the hologram said, his voice smooth and filled with authority. "Nice to see you again."

William nodded and set the knife down on the altar steps. "You as well, Dorian."

My heart thundered against my ribs, and Liv glanced down at the floor with such a pained expression, it made me ache for her. Her dad really was working with Dorian, and even though we both suspected it, it was still a shock.

"I was under the impression you would be here in person for our meeting," William said, shooting a glare at the redhead behind him.

"You'll learn soon that I do not stay in the same place for long," Dorian replied. His voice warbled, and then he slowly...*changed*. His body shrank down and re-stretched like putty, and an elderly woman in a white skirt stood in his place. "Much like I do not stay in the same figure for long."

"Holy crap," Liv whispered beside me. "Shapeshifter."

"Yes. I've noticed that. Just like I noticed your leftovers in the kitchen." William's tone was disapproving. "Were you going to take care of those bodies? Or are you really that careless about who is exposed to our world?"

Dang. Even though Dorian wasn't physically here, I didn't think I'd have the guts to speak to him the way Liv's dad did.

Dorian tilted his head back with an amused laugh, his hair floating down his back in long locks. "It's not my priority to keep humans safe. Do with them what you want."

William looked down at the knife on the altar steps. "I understand. Now, tell me—why did you have Anika bring the knife back? Did you find that Alpha?"

That Alpha?

I re-gripped the balcony wood, threatening to break through the fibers with the fury rising inside me. Liv reached over and touched my hand, mouthing the words *calm down*, but I couldn't. Not when they were talking about Aiden.

Dorian shifted again, remolding into a young girl with long black hair and a white dress. "Not yet. I'm saving him for last, for when my army is stronger. He needs to know in the end that he can't win. For now, I need you to take the knife to Lucille."

I stifled a gasp, unsure I heard him correctly.

"Did he say Lucille?" I whispered as softly as I could to Liv. She nodded, the fear on her face so clear, even in the dim light.

I shook my head, thinking back to the day I met Lucille. She'd given me that reading and seemed like a nice person. Like she was on my side. When Aiden told me not to trust her before, I brushed it off.

I wished I hadn't.

She was on Dorian's side, and I had my answer. Lucille had purposefully led me down this path. But why?

My hold on the balcony splintered under my fingertips, and I slowed my breaths to concentrate on what was happening. I needed to pay attention.

"We still need the Eye of the Moon," little-girl-Dorian said. "I need you and Anika to hunt it down for me."

"What else do you need?"

"Besides the Alpha?" The little girl smiled sweetly, making my stomach queasy. "I'll need a witch and a hunter to sacrifice."

William nodded slowly and rubbed his chin. "Isn't there an easier way? Are you sure this Eye of the Moon exists?"

"Oh, William…always so inquisitive." Dorian shifted again, growing taller and broader until he became a burly man towering over Liv's dad. He moved forward, dropping to the altar steps, dimming in and out again. His turquoise eyes glowed with disdain. "Anika? Please show William how little I enjoy his questions."

Suddenly, William dropped to his knees, mouth open and gasping for air. I cringed, watching his back arch like an invisible string pulled him upward by his chest. Liv went rigid beside me, and without another thought, I touched her shoulder to keep her grounded.

"May I remind you that your job is to take orders without question? Your doubt only makes me angry, and I don't have the energy to waste on that right now. The only loophole to completing the entire pentagram is if we had a hybrid. Do you know where we can find one of those?" His tone mocked, and the way his eyes glowered over William's pained face made my insides twist.

The air turned colder around me. For a second, I thought I was imagining it, but then I saw the empty space where Liv had been sitting.

Crap. She was gone.

Adrenaline spiked through my blood, and I looked back down at William and Dorian. The witch was standing by William now, her curled fingers turned up toward the ceiling as she smiled down at him, inflicting pain.

"Even if we *had* a hybrid, we'd still need a sacrifice and the Eye," Dorian hissed. "I suggest, for your family's sake, you find it. You have until a week before the eclipse."

Suddenly, a knife shot right through the witch's hand. She let out a loud screech, causing chaos to erupt through the sanctuary. Dorian blinked out of existence, and the men guarding the perimeter of the sanctuary snapped into defensive positions.

William traced his line of sight back down the aisle where the knife came. His eyelids flew open and he jumped to his feet. "Livvie?"

Dammit, Liv.

"You brought others?" Anika roared at William.

He shook his head furiously and whirled around as the red-eyed men swarmed down the aisle toward Liv. Two of them grabbed William by the arms. He jerked against them, watching as all hell broke loose on Liv's side of the room.

I couldn't see her though. I had to get down there.

My heart thrummed as I pulled a silver knife from my boot that Aiden had given me earlier. When I stood up, I made eye contact with one of the men holding William's arms. He looked straight at me, his eyes blaring like he was inviting me to the fight.

As if by instinct, I jumped over the balcony, landing on my feet on the pew underneath, but it wasn't stable enough. The wood splintered with a loud crack, sending me rolling onto the stone floor and smashing my forehead into the leg of another bench.

I yelled out a curse. The headache splitting through my skull only made me angry, and I came to my hands and knees.

Growls echoed around as wolves were thrown back and shouts erupted. Tattered clothes confettied the floor, and my necklace hummed against me, sensing my pending rampage. I crawled to my feet, my hand empty and the knife somewhere on the floor.

Liv kicked back a cream-colored wolf, smashing him into a pew and breaking it to pieces. She had things under control, so I whirled around to face the witch and William. His eyes penetrated through me with a mix of confusion and anger. But I didn't care about him right now.

What I cared about was getting the knife that still held Aiden's blood.

I darted toward the front as the witch grabbed her beaded chain from the table and turned around. Making eye contact with me, she yelled someone's name. In less than a second, something tackled me from behind.

Sharp claws slid down my arms like razors. With a harsh swipe of a paw, I was knocked into another pew and onto the cold floor. A sharp bolt of pain ran through my ribs, and I sucked in a quick breath as I reached for a loose stone from the floor.

My fingers clenched around its rough edges, prying it out as a rumbling growl skated over my neck like a cold chill. Another smack from a heavy paw sent me onto my back, and

I thrust my arm over, smashing the rock into the wolf's eye with a sickening thud.

He yelped and stumbled sideways, right into Aiden's sweeping fist.

My pulse surged with anger and I grappled to my feet. Hot blood ran down my face, but I didn't have time to wipe it off. Aiden was there with the others, shifting and fighting Dorian's wolves. They rolled and crashed through the aisles, shattering stained glass windows and breaking through walls until there wasn't much sanctuary left.

A humid breeze rushed over my skin like something whispering to turn around. When I did, William and Anika were gone.

I darted over to the altar steps and cursed. The knife was gone too.

Ignoring the chaos behind me, I sprinted out the open sanctuary door, scanning the sidewalks for any sign of movement. The night was almost like daylight with all the streetlamps, and two blocks down I saw the swish of a black dress turn the corner.

Pumping my arms, I ran as fast as I could down the street. My feet pounded the pavement, burning up my muscles and stealing my breath, but it wasn't as tiring as usual. I pushed harder, skidding my feet against the pavement to cut through an alley. I had to get that knife back.

Coming out the other side, Anika and William crossed the street, both going in separate directions. Anika held up her dress, but William was already out of view.

Taking my chances on her, I headed down the sidewalk, paralleling her. I whipped my head back and forth as I ran, watching her and what was ahead of me. Cars whooshed by, but when there was a quick break, I swerved across the street and followed her down another alley.

My necklace bounced against my chest with each step.

The red light radiated in all directions. With one more big step, I launched forward, grabbing Anika's legs on my way down to the ground.

The pavement burned against my skin when I landed. My arms tightened around Anika's legs as she pulled herself forward. Her hand groped the ground, reaching for something metal and shiny in the far-off glow of the streetlight.

The knife!

I gasped and pushed off the ground, lunging for it just as she snagged it back and stood up. She pointed it at me like she was ready to use it. Breathless and sweaty, we stared at each other, waiting for the other to attack.

"Give me the knife," I sneered, peering at her through the straying pieces of hair around my face.

Her sharp eyes narrowed, then caught on my pendant. The red glow brightened, casting out its light on the witch's porcelain skin, reddening her hair even more.

"The Maiden's Stone," she whispered, sounding more like a hissing cat. "Where did you get that?"

"What are you talking about?" I asked, careful to keep my gaze on her. The longer we stood there, the more my fingers itched for the knife.

A black car swerved around, coming to a screeching stop at the end of the alley. Anika looked over, and I took that chance to go after it.

Running toward her and closing the few feet of space between us, I slammed my palms into her shoulders, shoving her against the brick wall. The knife clattered to the ground, but before I could do anything else, she flicked her wrist and sent me flying backward.

My back hit the opposite wall before I crashed to the ground again. An aching pressure erupted through my chest, and my skin stung like needles where I'd skidded against the pavement.

As I pushed back to my hands and knees, I swiped a stream of blood from the corner of my lip, ready to go at Anika again. She stood by the other wall still, sliding the knife into the bosom of her sleek dress.

"You're coming with me," she said, curling her index finger at me, eyes falling on my necklace again.

"Heck no," I spat, climbing to my feet clumsily. Any strength I had before this was evaporating, leaving my muscles shaky.

"Fine," she said. "Be that way."

Something snaked around my neck, curling and squeezing, pulling my body forward. My throat closed, refusing to give air to my lungs as I grabbed at whatever was around me.

But my fingers clawed at nothing but skin. It was like an invisible python coiling around me and dragging me toward the car.

I ground my heels in front of me to keep from getting pulled forward, but they kept sliding against the asphalt. Anika walked in front of me, heading to the car and opening the door.

Dancing black dots filled my vision, and my arms lost their strength to keep pulling at the nothingness controlling me. I couldn't fight her magic much longer.

Far behind me, a low growl filled the alley, and the soft vibration of the bond slid down my skin.

Anika turned, her eyes widening as a herd of paws stampeded down the alley behind me. Then she jumped in the car and slammed the door, speeding down the street and out of sight.

The invisible snake choking me dissipated, and I collapsed onto my hands and knees. I coughed, dragging in the gravelly air as my necklace flickered out.

"No," I whispered, staring down the street where the

black car vanished. I debated running after it, but by now, it was long gone.

That was my only chance at getting the knife back. My one chance of freeing Aiden from Dorian.

And I lost it.

The haunting picture of the dead alphas returned to my mind, and I slammed my palms against the pavement. There was no way I could let anything like that happen to Aiden. I had to protect him, just like he'd been protecting me. Because that was what love was.

Love...

I *loved* Aiden.

How did it take me until now to realize that?

My stomach fluttered, and I looked up to see his bright blue wolf eyes staring into mine. He whimpered softly, nudging my throbbing forehead with his nose, and I reached my fingers into his black fur.

Even in his wolf form, the bond was strong between us. I couldn't let anything take that away. Not Dorian. Not my fear. Not the full moon.

I needed to fight through it. Enough whining about the unknown and the things that could happen. I needed to take control and make sure I survived, so I could make sure Aiden did, too.

20

I filled everyone in on what happened when we met back up outside the church.

We all had scrapes and bruises, and we left the sanctuary a complete wreck, but at least we knew what Dorian was looking for...and that Liv's father was really working with him. But for Liv's sake, I left that detail out.

Omar and his crew went back to Shadow Grove so Ryan wouldn't suspect anything, and Pete got the four of us a hotel room from a place with a broken sign and a door that wouldn't lock.

The funky, stale air hit me in the face as soon as I stepped onto the stained carpet, but I didn't care. There was a bathroom with a sink where I could wash the blood off my face.

The water ran pink at first, and I dried my face with a stiff towel. Looking into the mirror, I took in the purple bruises splotching my complexion, especially my right eye. The bruise reached all the way over to my cheekbone, and even my lip was puffy.

I looked like I'd gone right back through my car accident from last month.

Combing my fingers through my hair, I let it fall over my shoulders to cover some of the bruises. At least it would mostly be healed by tomorrow.

My body ached all over, and I went out to the main room, ready to crash. But instead of an empty bed, I found Aiden waiting for me, seated on the edge of the mattress. He stood up when I turned the light off in the bathroom.

His expression shifted to shock, and then slowly to rage as he took in my face. "Are you sure you're okay?" He reached for my hand, and the spark of energy hit me, filling me with his worry. I nodded, but he tilted his chin down, meeting me at eye-level. "You don't have to pretend."

"I know." I leaned into him, sinking into his chest as his arms wrapped around me. "I'm okay."

"What happened in the alley?"

I took in a sharp breath, recalling starving for oxygen and being dragged toward the car. "I wanted to get the knife back. I went after the witch...her name was Anika. She saw my necklace, and called it the Maiden's Stone...then she tried to take me."

Aiden's heartbeat jumped, and his hands pulled against me until I was flat against him. "Why would she try to take you?"

"I don't know. She didn't act like that until she saw my pendant."

"My question is, what's the Maiden's Stone?" Pete asked from the far corner of the room.

I pulled back, peering around Aiden's shoulder at him. He'd been so quiet, I hadn't even noticed he was with us. He sat at the corner table, his brown hair swept back from his face. His eyes glimmered, pinpointing both Aiden and I suspiciously.

"We need to start looking into that tomorrow," Aiden

said. He raised his brows, and I figured he meant I should call my dad about it.

I nodded and glanced around the room again just to be sure it was only the three of us. "Where's Liv?"

"Outside. She dropped her bag and ran out without saying anything."

"Right." As much as I wanted to give in to the fatigue weighing me down, I needed to make sure she was okay. The shock of finding out her dad was working with Dorian was probably too much to deal with alone, and I guess...maybe I actually cared a little. "I should check on her."

"Is she okay?" Pete asked, folding his arms and tipping back in his chair.

I shrugged, starting to step around Aiden. "I guess I'll find out."

"You know what I'd like to find out," Pete continued, "is what she is."

My muscles froze, and Aiden's arm tensed beside me.

"What do you mean?" I asked.

Pete let his chair back down on all four legs, his stare bouncing between Aiden and I. "Liv. She's not human. But you already knew that." When I didn't say anything, Pete nodded, the only sign of his anger a flutter of muscle in his jaw. "You both knew?"

The room was silent, my guilt coursing hot through my blood. I felt myself cracking under the pressure. But before I could break, the sound of Liv puking in the middle of the parking lot pulled our stares apart.

"Gross," Aiden whispered. I jabbed him in the side with my elbow and turned my attention back to Pete.

"I told you...she's a spy." Even I had started to believe that lie by now, but it was kinda true. Liv *was* spying on her family for us.

"Sure," Pete said. "I might believe that, but she is way too strong to be human. She threw a werewolf off herself tonight. That tells me she's a hunter."

"Look, man, there's a lot to this that you don't know," Aiden said.

"Right," Pete drew out the word. "I thought I was your second. I thought you trusted me with this kind of information, but *you two* lied. I thought you were my friends."

His words daggered through me. "We are, but it's complicated."

"I'm sure I can keep up." He raised his brows expectantly. "Does she have anything to do with the hunter attacks on our pack?"

And that was the heavy shoe I was waiting to drop. I shot a glare at Aiden. "See what you did?"

He rolled his eyes. "Fine. You're right. She's a hunter."

I closed my eyes and let out a heavy exhale. I didn't think he'd admit that so fast. This entire day had been emotionally exhausting—starting with Mom, then that meeting, and now this.

"What about my shop?"

Aiden broke eye contact with Pete. "I'm sorry."

At first, nothing happened, and I thought the silence would drown me to death. Then Pete stood up, slamming his chair back and cracking the drywall. In no time, he was out of the room, having left the door wide open.

A strangled scream erupted from the parking lot, jolting my feet into movement. Aiden was right behind me as I burst out the door and bolted between the cars. It only took me two seconds to find Pete and Liv. He held her against a van, his fingers clenched around her shoulders.

"Do you have any idea what you've done?" Pete yelled, towering over her. I'd never seen him so angry before. I could almost see the rage cascade down his back.

I expected Liv to fight back or at least deny that her

family burned down Pete's shop, but she didn't. All she did was stare up at him with fear and reach for his wrists.

"Say something!" Pete's voice erupted through the lot, probably loud enough for all of D.C. to hear him.

"I—I'm sorry." Liv's words came out weak, which only seemed to make Pete angrier.

His eyes burned like two suns, and he stood there for a few seconds longer until his hands released her shoulders. He curled his fingers at his sides and stood up taller. "My shop was everything to me."

Liv stood up off the van and stepped toward Pete. "I didn't—"

"What?" Pete raised his chin, balling his fists so tightly, his veins and tendons nearly broke through the skin. "You didn't do it?"

"I didn't know my brothers would do that," Liv pleaded.

"Did you expect anything less from hunters?" He held up his hand, silencing whatever she was going to say next. "The shop was my dream ever since I was a kid. My family loved music. My dad—my *real* dad—taught me everything I know about guitars. It was all that connected me back to...to being *human*." His eyes flashed like hot embers and he lowered his voice to a dark, stormy place that sent shivers down my spine. "And it's gone. Every piece of it is gone."

Liv's bottom lip quivered and her eyes glossed with tears. "I'm so sorry. I wish I could take it all back. I wish—"

"Save it." Pete stepped back, his icy gaze frosting over all of us one at a time. He held Aiden's eye contact the longest before turning around and storming off. Several cars down, we heard the lurch of metal and then a car alarm wail.

Liv stared after him, and for the first time since this entire mess started, real remorse flickered in her expression. She turned toward me and Aiden, chewing on the inside of her lips. "I really am sorry."

"I'll, uh…I'll go talk to him," Aiden said to both of us. He passed Liv and followed after Pete, disappearing around the side of the hotel.

Liv stared at her feet for a few seconds until I spoke first. "Let's go sit down."

She nodded, her mouth turning down and a round of sobs breaking free. I put my hand on her back and guided her over to the sidewalk right outside our hotel room.

"He's going to kill me in my sleep, isn't he?" She swiped the back of her hand under her nose.

I couldn't help but let out a small laugh. "No. He won't. We'll make sure of it. We've all been through a lot lately and we're all feeling some pressure."

"Uh, yeah," she responded shakily.

We took a seat on the edge of the curb and she rubbed the last bit of moisture from her cheeks. Her eyes held a blank expression now as she looked out at the road. I'd seen that expression before—mostly in the months following her mom's death. She'd check out to process things—to grieve, to rage, to question why things happened. And now she was doing the same with her father's betrayal.

"I know tonight was probably a shock for you…with your dad and all."

"Seriously. I can't believe this. All of it." A few seconds passed and she forced an exhale before raising her voice. "My family is actually working with that monster. Dad freaking offered another hunter as a sacrifice. Why would he do that?"

"Sometimes people do things out of desperation. Maybe Dorian or Anika got to your dad somehow." I was reaching for anything to make sense of it all, but William did seem way too calm and collected before everything happened.

"But he would never…" Her words trailed off, then she peered over at my face. "I know what happened tonight was my fault. Actually, a lot of things are my fault—not just tonight. But when we were in there, that *witch* was hurting my dad, and I couldn't handle it. I'm sorry you got hurt."

Despite trying to strangle her just a couple hours ago, I slipped my arm around her shoulders. "If it were my mom or dad, I might have done the same thing."

"But your face. I know you probably got hurt in other places."

I winced at my potentially cracked rib. "I heal fast now."

"Right." Her lips twitched, almost like she was about to give me a disapproving look before changing her mind. "I'm sorry. For everything. I get why you all think I'm the worst person ever now."

I laughed, the outer layer of my heart seeming to soften a little. "Maybe not ever."

Light footsteps trailed down the sidewalk toward us, grabbing our attention. Aiden hesitated at first when he reached our hotel door, but then changed his mind about going inside. He stuck his hands deep in his pockets and moseyed over to us on the curb instead.

"Is Pete okay?" I asked, taking in his solemn expression.

"Um…" Aiden twisted his lips. "He needs some time to cool down."

Something told me he was severely downplaying that.

"What should I do?" Liv leaned forward and peered at Aiden. "I really am sorry. He needs to know that."

"Does he?" Aiden asked. "I'm pretty sure you'll make it worse."

"Yeah. You're right. I should give him some time."

"Give it a few years," Aiden said. "Maybe a few decades before speaking to him again."

Liv's chin trembled again before another river of tears streamed down her face. "Why is everything so messy? What happened to my life?"

I squeezed my arm gently around her. "I think you're just finding things aren't so black and white anymore."

She gave a forced laugh before going into another fit of sobs. "I'm sorry…to all of you."

Aiden raised his brows, but neither of us said anything. We were too shocked at Liv's remorse.

"I didn't know what Dorian did to alphas," she said. "And Aiden, I did want you dead before, but I thought you had some sort of agenda. I blamed you for getting Sydney into this stuff. I still do, but I see how much you care about her." She slowly lifted her gaze to him. "I'm sorry."

Aiden sat frozen, his nostrils flaring.

"And Syd." Liv placed her hand on my arm. "I'm sorry for using you before. I hope you can forgive me eventually."

A heavy silence fell between all of us, like we were waiting for pigs to fly or the sound barrier to crack open. I never in a million lifetimes would've expected a sincere apology from Liv like that, and for the first time since her family attacked us, some of my anger faded. Maybe I was being naive, but I believed her.

I still didn't trust her, though.

"Thanks, Liv," I said quietly.

She sniffled and ran her palms under her eyes. "I guess I'll have to find another place to stay."

I sighed. "Yeah. Your dad saw you. It's not safe to go home anymore. I would tell you to go stay with my mom, but I'm trying to keep her out of this, too."

"Well, maybe I'll find a nice cardboard box to camp out in for a while." She hugged her knees to her chest.

I looked up at Aiden, asking him with my eyes if maybe we could do something, but he shook his head. He was right. Most of the people he knew were all werewolves, and to plant Liv right in the middle of that was too much of a risk, especially now that Pete knew she had everything to do with his shop.

Then I had an idea—one she probably wouldn't like, but it was worth a shot. "What about my dad and Cindy? You could stay with them. I'll make the call. Dad owes me."

Liv frowned. "I can't do that. That's so weird."

"But it's your only option right now."

She looked out over the desolate parking lot. "I'll think about it."

"I'll call him tomorrow," I said, pulling my arm back to myself.

"Fine. Thank you. Even when you're mad at me, you still help me. I don't deserve you."

A small smile crept onto my lips.

"Well." Liv stood up, brushing her hands down her pants. "This just got super awkward, and you know how much I hate awkward. I'm going to take a walk and clear my head." She got up and started walking past our door, but Aiden stopped her.

"I wouldn't go that way. Pete's out back. Avoid him at all cost right now."

"Got it," she whispered, heading the other direction.

Aiden and I both watched her walk away, and he moved to the curb.

"Did she mean it? Her apology?" I asked.

"Surprisingly, yes." He rubbed his hand down the back of his neck. "I didn't sense any lies. At all. I guess she's coming around."

I let that sink in. Was Liv finally on our side? Did we really have an ally in this?

"You didn't tell me everything that happened tonight," Aiden said. "I felt you freaking out twice. Not just when we heard everything going on in the sanctuary. What happened?"

"Oh. I lost my temper." I bit my lip and looked away. "And I tried to kill Liv."

Hearing myself say that out loud made me feel about a foot tall. Seeing his mouth hanging open at my admission only made it worse. But I told him everything that happened in that church kitchen. When I finished, his wide eyes glowed like they were electrically charged.

"I know, it was stupid," I said.

"And dark. I never would have thought—" He paused, choosing his words carefully. "I'm shocked, is all."

"We got caught by one of Dorian's guys. It could have been so much worse. I feel so...out of control."

"Uh, yeah." He snatched me against his side protectively, leaning into my space and turning my head toward his. "I should never have let you go in there with her. Next time, we go together or not at all."

"But we did it. We got useful information, and now Liv's on our side. I don't regret going in there, even though I came out looking like a blueberry."

He smirked and lightly pressed his hand to my bruised cheek. "A beautiful blueberry."

I laughed and leaned my forehead against his, soaking up the relief that we were back together and tonight was behind us.

"Promise you won't go after anyone alone again, okay?" He slid both hands down the sides of my face, holding at my jawline. "You could have gotten killed, or taken, and I wouldn't have been able to handle that."

I reached for him, latching my hands around his shoulders in response to the edge of pain in his words, but I couldn't make that promise. He was too important. "If I get another opportunity to keep you safe, I'm taking it."

A few heartbeats passed and he let out something between a growl and a groan.

"I know you don't like it," I said. "But you would have done the same thing for me."

"Yeah." He looked down. His fanned lashes cast soft shadows down his cheeks. "I know."

"Then you can't ask me not to do that for you."

"I guess that's...fair."

"I'm not sure it's about what's fair, but about how far we'll go for each other. And for you, I'll go as far as it takes."

Aiden glanced back at me, tilting his gaze like he was analyzing my words. "I get it. You know I would for you—no questions asked. I'll never change my mind about that."

I took in a quick breath of musty air, trying to still the rush of everything I felt for him. As his eyes held on me, my realization from before climbed its way back up my throat in the form of three words.

Those words *scared* me. I'd never said them to anyone except family, and even then, they were thrown around carelessly sometimes.

When my dad walked out, I told myself I'd never say them to anyone unless I truly meant them. Their permanence weighed on my tongue, reaching for the edge of my lips. If I said them to Aiden, I could never take them back—and I didn't want to.

"I love you," I sputtered out.

Aiden stilled, making my stomach dip and my heart sprint. He stared at me, lips parted and eyes tense, like he was waiting for me to say I was joking.

Had my delivery been too blunt? Should I have said it differently?

Oh crap. What if it was too soon or he didn't feel the same way?

A scalding tsunami of panic washed down my back, and I almost let it get the best of me, but his mouth slowly tipped up in a smile that spread into a cheesy grin.

I shoved him in the shoulder. "Would you freaking say something already?"

His grin widened and he pulled my lips against his, pouring warm elation into me wherever we touched. I tightened my grip on his shoulders, and he pulled me into his lap to face him. My legs curled around his waist, and he secured his strong arms around me, spreading his fingers over my back in a safety net I never wanted to be free from.

He grazed his lips to the corner of my mouth, leaving the cool air to rush to the rest of my lips. "I love you too. I've been wanting to say that since you tried to punch me in the face at our first training session."

"What?" I laughed and brushed my fingertips through his soft hair. "That's a really weird time to want to say something like that."

"I don't think it is. I love that you're a fighter, and that you want to protect me. You make me feel like I'm enough, Syd. Whether I'm Alpha or not. You make me feel *human,* and...real."

My chest swelled like a balloon about to pop, and I thought I loved him even more. All I knew now was that I was ready to fight for my life—for us—so I could be there for him. Nobody else mattered in this equation except me and him.

"I don't know if you've asked Theresa yet about me staying with her and Nat, but I was wondering if your offer was still on the table. If you still have room at your place. I don't think it's safe for me to stay at home anymore after losing control tonight."

He tilted his head back to look at me. "You want to stay with me?"

"If you're okay with it."

"Yes. I'm more than okay with it." He leaned in and kissed me again, surprising me with the force behind his lips.

"There's plenty of room, and I promise to keep the fridge stocked with cookie dough."

I smiled, taking in his disheveled charcoal strands, and the flickering blue shades in his eyes. "Careful. I might never leave on those terms."

His perfect smile brightened. "That's what I'm hoping for."

21

*W*e all made it back to the guitar shop in one piece. Aiden had been the one to keep the peace between Pete and Liv until we split up again. It was almost as if he'd had a change of heart toward her since she apologized.

I guess I'd had a slight change of heart too, but I still hadn't forgiven her. At least my thoughts didn't skip to fantasies about killing her anymore.

I didn't even mind calling Dad and forcing him to agree to letting Liv stay with him. He didn't like the idea, but she needed a place, and we needed someone to make sure she stayed aligned with us.

But I couldn't think about any of that until I officially moved out. Aiden took me home to pack. By nightfall, my closets were bare, and I had a full suitcase of books, including the one with Gigi's stuff.

Now all I had to do was tell Mom. She'd been at work all day, and my stomach twisted in so many knots, I swore ulcers were forming.

I laid on my suitcase in the middle of my room, struggling

to zip the bursting edges. Mom would be off work in ten minutes, and I wanted the truck packed by then for fear of changing my mind.

Then my ears picked up footsteps tapping up the porch. My heart lurched as the front door opened downstairs.

"Syd?" Aiden's voice echoed up to my room. Within three seconds, he stood in my doorway, gawking at my sprawled body. "Wow. That is one full suitcase." He tilted his head, his eyes flaring as they scanned down my back. "And one nice—"

"Instead of taking in the view, how about a little help?" I jammed my elbow into the corner of the bag, tugging on the zipper again. "This thing always gets stuck."

Aiden strode over and bent down, putting his weight into the corner. He brushed my hand away and smirked at me as he effortlessly zipped it up. "I see a new set of luggage somewhere in your future."

I laughed weakly and grabbed my duffel bag. "Let's get it outside before Mom gets here."

"Got it." He leaned over and picked up the larger bags like they were one-pound dumbbells, following me down the stairs and out the front door.

As soon as I stepped onto the sidewalk, Mom's headlights appeared at the end of the driveway.

My insides did all sorts of twists and turns. "Crap. She's early."

"It's okay." Aiden paused beside me, watching as Mom parked the car next to his truck. "Remember, you're doing this for her."

I bit my lip as Mom shut her car door and headed toward us on the sidewalk. She gave a faint smile, which turned down sharply when her eyes landed on the suitcases in Aiden's hands.

"Hi," she said. "I thought you got back earlier. I got a text from you...or so I thought." She reached into her purse, digging around and pulling out her phone.

"I did," I said. "I got back this morning."

She let her hand fall by her side. "Then what's going on?"

My mouth opened, but nothing came out. How would I tell her?

"I'll give you two a few minutes," Aiden whispered, stepping around us and crossing through the grass.

Mom's dark eyes followed him until he passed her shoulder, and then she raised her brows at me. "Sydney?"

The guilt ate through me. There was no way to do this without hurting her, and that killed me. "I'm going to live with Dad."

I cringed at my blunt delivery. I hated lying, but telling her the truth—that I was going to stay with Aiden—would literally be catastrophic for this entire side of the planet.

"You're what?" She faltered back half a step. "You go stay with him for one night and come back just to move out?" When I couldn't say anything, she added, "I don't understand. A few days ago, you couldn't stand being around him and now you want to *live* with him?"

"No, but things have been really hard lately. We need some space. Real space. Not just one night away. I need to deal with some things."

"Are things really that bad here that you would rather go live with him?"

"No." I cleared my throat in an attempt to steady my voice. "I don't know. But me being here isn't good for you." That was at least true.

Mom pressed her fingers to her temples, her shoulders jumping at the slam of Aiden's truck door. He stared down at the driveway, waiting for me with one hand propped on the edge of the truck bed and the other in his pocket.

"What's this really about?" Mom's voice pitched up,

ringing through the night air. "Is this because I wanted you to go to college before? Or because I told you that you shouldn't?"

"Neither," I answered, my hand clenching my bag. I took a small step toward her, but something stopped me. My chest constricted with this need to tell her what I had wanted to on the night of my accident, before my missed audition. This could be the only chance I'd ever get, and I had to take it. "Mom, do you know why I wanted to pursue dance instead of college? I thought if I made it big, I could afford to help you with the mortgage and the things we struggled to pay for. College only drains your bank account, but I was good enough to dance. Ms. Felicity said so. I wanted to follow my dream and save you from having to work so much to provide for us. That's why I didn't tell you about the audition before. I knew you'd say no, but I wanted *so badly* to make a difference for you and prove to myself that I could do it too."

"Sydney," Mom whispered, her eyes glossing with a sullen agony that cut through the edges of my heart. "It's not your responsibility to take care of things like that."

"I know. But it was what I wanted. Because I love you."

Mom's face blurred in my teary vision, and we stared at each other for what seemed like an eternity. She opened her mouth, but closed it right away, seeming to solidify this void between us, and as much as I hated it, that was my moment to leave. If I waited, I wouldn't be strong enough to go.

I moved in, wrapping my arms around her in a brief hug that I wanted to prolong until the end of time. Her hands barely touched me as she held onto me.

"I'll talk to you soon," I said into her ear.

Then I let go, and my feet reluctantly carried me away.

"If you need me to be more supportive, I can do that." Her words rushed out behind me. "We can work things out. We can talk about this."

The anguish in her voice nearly sent me over the edge, and I turned around to look at her one more time. Even under the faint porch light, her brown skin splotched with pink grief as she held herself back from crying.

That's all it took to unravel me. Everything I'd tried so hard to keep together broke like a dam. The pain washed through me, dragging the tears down my cheeks.

I wanted to stay. I wished I could tell her that, but I had to do everything possible to make sure she knew I couldn't be swayed.

"That's not what I need right now," I said.

Mom stared at me for several hammering heartbeats. She raised her chin, seeming to put on her brave mask that I'd seen in our more intense arguments. "Well, you're eighteen. I can't stop you. Let me know if you change your mind."

I nodded, trying to suppress the lump forming in the back of my throat.

She spun on her heel and hurried up the stairs, slamming the front door behind her. It jarred through me, but what followed was the worst sound I'd ever heard—Mom's wailing sobs. Ones she didn't want me to see and didn't know I could hear.

Each mourning cry was like another dagger in the heart.

We couldn't leave things off this way. This couldn't be the last time I saw her. Mom needed me, and I needed her, but if something worse than shifting happened to me on the full moon—

My tears plowed through my ducts like a hot torrential storm, and I lost my grip on my bag, letting it clunk onto the sidewalk. Knees sagging, I crumpled down onto the warm concrete.

I was the worst daughter ever.

Tear after tear spilled. They dripped onto the fabric of my leggings, seeping through to my skin. Aiden knelt beside me and turned my body to face him. I couldn't look up at him, but he wrapped his arms around me.

We sat there silently while I cried into his shirt and wished things could be different.

The spells still hadn't worked. Maybe it was the guilt from leaving Mom like that, but as the full moon got closer, I was on the verge of a nervous breakdown.

Nothing was working and my necklace hadn't even glowed. Not since the other night when Anika tried to take me in the alley.

She'd called it the Maiden's Stone, but none of us knew why. Dad didn't have any clue either. I hoped to find something about it in a book or in Gigi's journal, but so far, nothing.

It was like being back at square one.

"You're not trying hard enough," Dad said through my phone screen. "Just because I'm not there with you doesn't mean you can slack your way through this."

I opened my eyes and matched his pixeled frown. "I *am* trying," I insisted, crossing one leg over the other on Aiden's bedroom floor. We'd been practicing for two hours, and any minute I would have been grateful for reception to cut out so I could have a break.

"No, you're not. You're not focusing. Start the calming spell from the top," Dad barked.

I drew in a deep breath, letting my shoulders roll down away from my ears. Chanting the Latin words out loud, I really tried harder this time.

After a few minutes, the words flowed from my mouth fluidly, almost like I'd spoken them my whole life.

"Good," Dad said, much to my surprise. "Now try one of the unlocking spells."

"Quick question. If this necklace only responds when my emotions are high, then why am I supposed to calm myself? If there's something inside it to help me, wouldn't it work better if I let the transition take over?" A shudder rolled down my back. Everything about that question scared me.

"No." Dad frowned. "You're trying to make peace with your demons now, so you have fewer to deal with later. If we can lessen the height of your emotions, the stone might unlock faster because your threshold will be lower."

"Oh. I guess that makes sense. If I lessen the extent of my anger, I won't have to wait until I get all stabby-stabby to see if something happens?"

Dad pressed his lips together. "Stabby-stabby?"

"Y'know, murderous."

"Right." He wasn't amused. "Ready?" He closed his eyes again.

"Dad, what if all of this is for nothing?"

He sighed and leaned toward the camera. "Listen, Gigi gave you this necklace for a reason. She knew what she was doing. It's clearly something special, more than we realize if another witch called it by a name. It's time to believe this is going to help...and believe in yourself, too."

"What does believing in myself have to do with anything? I told you I'm dedicated now. I'm trying. I have to survive." Frustration rose, and I took a deep breath to push it back down.

"Believing it has more to do with it than you know. That's the first thing my mother taught me when I started learning magic. Your doubt will only get you in trouble. Now let's go. Again."

As much as I wanted to believe that, I couldn't. What he said seemed too much like a fairytale.

No. What I needed to do was memorize these spells, train, and learn. That's it.

When Dad and I ended our video chat, my phone vibrated in the tripod within about five seconds. It was a text from Liv.

Your dad is a total buzzkill. No rap music allowed? It's a prison.

Yeah. She wasn't wrong. He typically wasn't much fun and loved to enforce absurd house rules.

Were you waiting for us to be done just to tell me that? I responded.

Obviously, she said. *I miss my house. My bed. Parties. Danger.* She sent me a pouty picture of her hand draped across her forehead dramatically. *At least he has Die Hard. Watched it four times already.*

I snorted and shook my head. *I'll send you some books.*

To that, she sent a series of green vomiting emojis. *No thanks. Have fun living it up with Fur Face while I die of boredom.*

I sent her back a quick '*Sorry, not sorry*' and headed into the living room.

Tattered books covered the coffee table and floor, and I swore there was a haze of dust coating the air.

Aiden's head popped up over one of the stacks when I stopped by the stuffed chair. "Hey, you. How was your call?"

"Good." I plopped into the chair, sinking into the cloud-soft cushions. "How's it going here?"

"We haven't found much," Pete said, flipping a crusty yellow page.

"He means we haven't found *anything*," Aiden added.

"Not true. We figured out this eclipse Dorian referred to is probably the Total Solar Eclipse, which is eight months away." Pete pulled his eyebrows together, strands of his brown hair framing his cheekbones.

"And we could have found that out by looking online," Aiden said, closing a book and setting it on the coffee table.

"True." Pete shrugged. "I'll have to call Naomi. She says her pack has a huge library. We could go over there after the meeting."

"What meeting?" I asked, trying not to sound irritated at being left out of the loop.

Aiden leaned forward onto the edge of the couch cushion. "I called a meeting with my dad tonight to fill him in on everything."

"Oh." My stomach flopped. "You're going to tell him *everything*?"

"No. Just the stuff about Dorian."

"What about Liv?" I asked quietly.

"He doesn't need to know about our alliance with her right now, or that she even exists. Right?" He glanced at Pete, who pursed his lips and snapped his book shut.

"I don't know if I'd call it an alliance when we can't trust her." Pete shoved the book onto the coffee table like it had majorly offended him.

"I never said I trusted her," Aiden said. "Sydney doesn't either, but she's already gotten us closer to figuring some things out we wouldn't have been able to solve on our own."

Pete leaned forward and grabbed another book from the floor. "Sure. And since we're still using her, I agree that nobody needs to know about her or how evil she is. Yet."

"Good. Now that we have that settled, Dad should know what we know about the Ancient." Aiden looked at me again. "The more hands on deck to help look for this Eye of the Moon, the better."

I nodded, but my insides still twisted at the possibility of someone mentioning Liv. If Pete figured out she was a hunter, someone else could have too.

"Are you okay?" Aiden asked, watching me with his intense ocean eyes.

"Overwhelmed." That was the only answer I could give.

The full moon was only four days away, and I still wasn't sure I could get through it.

"I got you something that might help you feel better for at least a minute." He got up off the couch and flashed me a winning smile on his way to the fridge. He pulled something out, then tossed it across the room to me.

I caught it and couldn't hide the stupid smile beaming on my face. "You got me cookie dough?"

"And I resisted the urge to bake it."

Pete looked up and crinkled his nose. "But you *are* going to bake it, right?"

"No way." I started tearing through the cold tube of goodness.

"Before you destroy the packaging, read the label first." Aiden gave me a smug grin.

I pieced together the fold I'd already ripped off and skimmed the front. "*Safe to eat raw*. You got me weak cookie dough?"

"I got you *safe* cookie dough, because salmonella *is* a real thing."

"Whatever." I smirked and rolled my eyes. "Thanks for looking out for me." I broke off a chunk of dough. It bounced off my taste buds, bringing me back to life a little. "You're the best," I sighed out.

"I know," Aiden said, folding his arms.

"I was talking to the cookie dough," I said through another mouthful. "But you're pretty great too."

His smile faded. "I'm glad to know where I stand."

"Can you guys go back to not being weird?" Pete asked, snapping another book shut.

Aiden made his way back to the couch and handed me a book. "Now that you're all fueled up, you can help us look through these."

"Can't wait," I said dryly.

I set the cookie dough down and took the book. The pages were brittle and the edges frayed, like it would fall to pieces between my fingers. I skimmed through the first part, which was in an entirely different language. Not helpful at all.

I was about to close it when I finally came to a series of sketches. The first page was the moon cycle, labeled in the same language as the first half of the book. I turned the page to find more, but these were humans and wolves.

Someone had documented their shift, but I couldn't tell if it was a born-werewolf or a human who had turned.

The man in the book was drawn with harsh lines and a grotesque face. Each phase grew darker and hairier, with fangs and claws that looked like they could reach out of the pages.

It was horrifying.

That was going to happen to me? Just like that?

My lungs burned with the need for air, and I slammed the book shut so hard, Aiden and Pete jumped in their seats.

"What's wrong?" Aiden asked, shoulders stiff, like he was ready to get up and fight somebody.

"I think I came across a werewolf's diary, complete with entries about shifting." I sat back and took a deep breath, pushing away mental pictures of me looking like that sketched man.

But Aiden didn't look like that when he shifted. He was a beautiful black wolf.

"Let me see." He moved around the coffee table and took a seat on the armrest. When he opened the book, his eyes went wide. "Whoa."

"What?" Pete asked, sitting up and peering over at the pages.

"This is…" Aiden flicked the pages over. The pictures only

became more graphic, leading to a wolf tearing apart a human.

"Horrible," I whispered.

"And not accurate." Aiden tossed the book into a messy pile on the floor. "That might have been how wolves were at first, but we've evolved. So has our venom."

"Some are still violent though," Pete countered.

Aiden shook his head. "Everyone's shift is different."

"But what if I get out of control?" I asked. "What if I hurt somebody?"

"No." Aiden leaned over and combed his fingers through my hair. "I told you, we'll keep you safe until we know you're okay. You'll still be you."

"Well…" Pete set his book down on the cushion beside him. "You'll mostly be you."

My heart rate jumped. "What do you mean?"

"It's one of the hardest things you'll ever go through. You're facing fears and things you hate. Your body will literally break, and then you'll have a new side of yourself that wasn't there before. That changes people."

I shuddered and closed my eyes, tightening my arms around myself. "Can you tell me what your first shift was like?"

Pete's features darkened and Aiden gently squeezed my shoulder.

"Do you really want to know?"

I didn't really, but I couldn't stop myself from nodding. Maybe hearing someone else's story would help. It couldn't be worse than what I saw in that book. "Tell me."

"Okay." Pete's mouth tightened, and he sat up straighter. "I went camping one night with a buddy and his family. We were playing flashlight tag, and I wandered too far away from our game. When I tried to find my way back, I crossed paths with a wolf. I guess I got in his or her way. It bit me, and I passed out like you did. When I woke up a day later, I'd been found by a couple park rangers. They got me to the hospital, but by then the bite had already healed. Nobody believed me about the wolf. They all said it had been a nightmare from dehydration or something. So, I accepted that. Until the full moon came."

I found myself clenching my teeth, my body tense as I listened.

"I went to bed that night with a fever. Mom thought I'd come down with the flu, but I woke up in so much pain. Everything burned, and I started seeing things. I had hallucinations of people I'd hurt before, or people who had hurt me. My biggest fears—" Pete shut his eyes for a few seconds. "It was hell. Like being trapped in a nightmare. I could feel every bit of pain, but I couldn't get out of it. My parents thought I'd snapped, and when my body started shifting, they got so scared that they took my little brother and ran."

My bottom lip quivered. "They left? Did they come back?"

Pete's eyes fell, an old agony shining in them, breaking my heart into pieces. "I never saw them again. When I woke up, I was in my backyard. The house was a wreck, and the police were there. I guess the neighbors called about noise. Luckily, one of the officers who showed up was a member of the Shadow pack."

As glad as I was that a pack member found Pete, I couldn't take my mind off his family leaving. It tore me up. "I'm so sorry," I whispered.

He didn't say anything, but his creased expression turned blank before he smiled softly. "I only came out stronger, I guess."

He did, but I could see through the downshift of his eyes. His experience still broke him.

Would mine break me, too?

"You know," Aiden said, sensing my building anxiety, "you could talk to Sasha, too. Everyone's story is different. From what I hear, she chose to turn."

I twisted to face him. "She wanted to get bitten? Even though she knew she could die?"

"That doesn't surprise me," Pete said. "She's pretty hardcore."

"Yeah. I gathered that from the other night."

"She'll be at the meeting later," Aiden said. "You should talk to her after."

I reached for the cookie dough and took a massive chunk from the roll. "I think I will."

22

I followed Aiden through Ryan's and Tabitha's house. It was almost time for the meeting and I was a bundle of nerves.

Aiden led me down the hardwood hallway, past the same family portraits I'd noticed the night I met him. This time, I took a longer look at Aiden's younger self—a baby faced, scrawnier version, with braces and more prominent freckles. "Aww. How adorable."

He turned around and followed my line of sight to the picture. His cheeks flushed. "I'll have you know I was a total badass at ten. That's the year my parents let me watch my first rated R movie."

"Oh, *total* badass." I snickered and moved on to the next picture where he sat in the grass with a guitar. His face was a little fuller, and his smile was like the one I knew—perfect, with the dimple on the side. "You were so cute. I just want to reach through the frame and pinch your cheeks."

"Okay, that's enough pictures for now." He grabbed my hand and pulled me down the hallway.

"But I'm not done."

"I'm sure my mom would be more than happy to show you albums sometime and tell you all about how much of a dork I was."

"You say it like you aren't anymore," I teased.

He turned around so fast, I would have bumped into him if I hadn't had better reflexes. "You're calling me a dork now?"

My smirk matched his. "Maybe."

"And let me guess…" He crossed his arms, his black t-shirt tightening around his shoulders. "You were the girl with lots of friends, who had no idea how beautiful she was, and your guy friends were in love with you but could never have you."

"Did you just use the premise of every 80's rom-com?" I crinkled my nose up.

"Hey, 80's movies are awesome."

I laughed. "Yeah, but I think you know I was the wall-flower who hid behind books. Liv was the popular one."

He shook his head. "You didn't hide. You danced."

"Yeah, but nobody at my school knew about it unless they did too. Except Liv. She knew everything about me. She even came to my recitals." A small seed of sadness rooted in my stomach. "But I guess that doesn't matter anymore. Sorry. I don't know why I brought her up."

Aiden tipped his head down to look at me. "Because you miss her."

I shrugged. "I guess. In a way."

"It's okay to miss what you had." He reached for my hand. "It's okay to forgive her, too."

Forgive her? I lowered my voice to a whisper. "You want me to forgive the person who used me to try to kill you?"

"I didn't say that. It's not my call if you do or don't, but in the spirit of conquering your demons before the full moon,

I'm saying you don't have to hold on to your anger. I'm alive, and she apologized. It doesn't make what she did okay, but it's a start."

"I mean, I don't want to rip her face off anymore, but I don't really know how to forgive her yet."

"I get it. I just don't want you to feel like you're betraying me if you decide to bury the hatchet."

A short silence fell between us.

I hadn't thought of it that way, but I think I *was* worried moving on would be betraying Aiden.

Still, it was too soon to do that. She may have apologized, but saying sorry wouldn't mend a shattered friendship.

"Come on," he said, tugging me toward the back of the house again. "We need to get to the meeting."

We passed the living room and the bathroom, moving straight ahead to the cracked door all the way at the end of the hall.

Ryan's secret meeting room.

I'd imagined a huge round table with maps and control panels, complete with a warning button to alert the masses for war, but when Aiden pushed the door open, it was a big game room with a pool table, dart board, and giant TV.

"Oh, good. You're here," Ryan said. He held a pool-stick and moved around the table, strategizing his next move for the eightball. "We can get started as soon as the others arrive."

Aiden nodded and found a spot against the wall, leaning back with his arms folded. I took the place beside him, watching Ryan crack the white ball against another.

He stood up, maintaining a stony expression, but he gave me a nod.

Baffled, I blinked. Was Ryan acknowledging my existence without hostility?

I guess miracles happened once in a while.

I smiled back at him and quickly glanced away to keep things from getting too awkward.

"Sorry, but why are you here?" Manny's voice trailed over the pool table.

After a second, I looked up and realized he was talking to me.

"She's supposed to be here," Aiden said, standing taller against the wall.

The lines around Manny's mouth deepened as he looked over at Ryan, waiting for some kind of back-up.

Ryan stuck his hands in his pockets. "She's part of whatever they're sharing this evening."

"But she's not one of us. She hasn't transitioned yet. These meetings are for those relevant to our cause."

I froze, unsure how to respond to that.

"She is relevant," Aiden argued. "She's saved more lives in this pack in the last month than you have in the last year."

Manny's jaw squared off like marble. "I don't believe that for a second."

"Manny," Ryan cut in. "She has made more sacrifices for our pack than you know."

"We've talked about this. They can't—"

"Another time," Aiden snapped. "We're not talking about this here. This is my meeting, not yours."

My stomach twisted as I studied Aiden from the corner of my eye. His chest expanded angrily, like he was working hard to keep it together.

What was Manny about to say that made him so mad?

"All right." Manny's glare snaked over Aiden. "Please accept my apology."

Small bumps scattered over my skin at Manny's icy tone. His apology sounded more like a threat, and Aiden clearly felt the same way. He narrowed his eyes at Manny, and the only thing that ended their stare-off was Tabitha's and Theresa's entrance.

They sauntered in together, both smiling at Aiden and me, seeming completely unaware of the exchange seconds ago.

I waved to them, relaxing some as they took a seat on the couch. Not too long after, Pete waltzed in, followed by Sasha and Omar.

Sasha's eyes glimmered at me and she flipped her pink locks back. Did she and Omar know what Liv was? Would they say anything?

Aiden suggested I talked to her after the meeting about her transition. Maybe I could figure out if they suspected anything.

Aiden took charge of the meeting. As he filled everyone in on the details, Ryan's face changed from calm to *what-the-hell* at least five times.

When Aiden finished talking, I clenched my hands, waiting for Ryan and Manny to disown everyone or throw us out. Instead, they stood with red-raged expressions.

I could hear Aiden's heart beat like a sledgehammer on concrete. I wanted to reach out and touch his arm for reassurance, but I pinned my hands behind my back.

Ryan unfolded his arms. "What you all did was reckless."

Aiden cringed, but said nothing.

"However, there is something to be said for putting the safety of the pack first. I'm sure none of you were forced into going." We all shook our heads.

"The safety of the pack?" Manny's voice was steady but rigid. "If the Ancient had gotten Aiden, none of us would have been safe!"

"Not necessarily," Ryan said. "Aiden may have Alpha

blood, but he doesn't have full authority of the pack yet. The pack would not have been under the Ancient's control."

Ryan's words silenced Manny, but his skin deepened a shade of red.

"All right," Ryan sighed, his massive chest deflating. "Aiden, I need you to stay to discuss more details. Everyone else can go, but do not discuss this with anyone else in the pack. No need to cause panic until I address it at the next meeting. Until then, gather resources. We need to find this Eye of the Moon as quickly—and discretely—as possible."

As we began filing out, Aiden tugged my hand and pulled me into a hug. "Try to talk to Sasha," he said in my ear.

I nodded, closing my eyes as he kissed my forehead. "I'll meet you back home."

"Hmm." He tucked a strand of hair behind my ear, trailing his index finger down to my shoulder. "I like how you called it home."

"Oh. I guess I did." And I liked it, too. I reached up to his forehead and slid a strand back that always fell out of place. "I'll see you soon."

I sped out of the meeting to track Sasha down and found her chatting with Omar in Ryan's driveway. When they saw me coming, they hushed and plastered on fake smiles.

"Am I interrupting something?" I asked cautiously.

"No," Omar said quickly.

I watched how he scratched his arm and shifted to the other foot, and then Sasha looked off at the trees before smiling at me again. My pulse fluttered with unease. "What's going on?"

They both looked at each other again before Sasha finally caved. "We know your girl was a hunter."

The flutters inside me turned to heavy stones. "Did you tell anyone yet?"

Sasha shook her head. "No. We were going to talk to Aiden about it first. We're a little concerned."

"Concerned, how?"

"It would have been nice to know that someone like her was tagging along on the trip," Omar said, raising his graying brows. "We don't want to disrespect Aiden. He obviously knew what he was doing, and I trust him, but to expose us to an enemy like that—"

"I get it. But we're working with her. We made a pact. She agreed not to try to hurt any of us."

Omar nodded. "I know he's still learning how to step into the Alpha role. That comes with unexpected pacts sometimes, but if he makes one wrong step with the wrong person, it could be disastrous. Some people can't be trusted. Period."

My insides shuddered. He sounded so sure, like something was already on the horizon. "How do you know that?"

"Okay. Here's the thing..." Sasha threw both hands up like she was surrendering. "Becca talks. A lot. She can't keep a secret, and her dad isn't good at hiding his feelings. I'm sure you've noticed."

I rolled my eyes. Her dad, being Manny. He did seem intense.

"You need to be careful with him," Omar said. "Ryan trusts Manny. They've led this pack together for decades now. I used to work with them a lot and was always amazed at how they had everything down to a science, but lately things have been rocky. Just by watching how they interact, I can see Manny's attitude is geared toward control more than before."

"But when Aiden's Alpha, everything with Manny should calm down, right?"

Sasha tilted her head back with a short burst of laughter.

"In a perfect world, sure. Just because someone's born to be Alpha doesn't mean they can't be overthrown."

"Meaning…"

"*Ugh*, Sydney—hasn't Aiden told you anything?" Sasha shook her head. "Once he's Alpha, someone could challenge him. He'd have to accept it and fight to the death to keep his role."

The air left my lungs. "Seriously?"

"Seriously. And if he didn't accept the challenge, he'd be stripped of his leadership and get kicked out of the pack."

"Really?"

"It's rare. Most pack members don't want that kind of responsibility," Omar said. "But keep an eye on Manny."

"Thanks," I said shakily. "I'll let Aiden know." Although, I was pretty sure he already did.

"All right. I have to go." Omar took a few steps toward his blue car in the driveway. "I'll see you ladies at Aiden's birthday party."

When he got in his car and pulled away, Sasha gave me a tight smile. "Well, I guess I'll see you later."

"Wait." I caught her by the elbow, but quickly let go when her eyes shifted down to my hand defensively. "Can I talk to you for a minute? About your transition?"

Her face relaxed. "Sure. Let's take a walk. I need some movement." We started walking down the driveway toward the gravel road. For a moment, the only sounds were our footsteps and chirping birds among the trees. "What do you want to know? I'm mostly an open book."

"Um, everything, I guess. Aiden said you *chose* to become a wolf." I didn't know how not to be blunt.

Sasha flicked her eyebrows up. "Sure did."

"But why? You knew what could happen, right?"

"Yeah. I knew. I was desperate to get out of the foster system." Her nose ring caught a glint of sunlight as she stared ahead at the trees. "My parents weren't cut out for the job and gave me up when I turned one. I went from one house to the next—from one boring family to another abusive one." She shook her head. "I got so sick of it. When I was sixteen, one of my friends got me to join their gang. They told me they'd do anything for me if I did anything for them. Stupid me thought I'd found a new family. Turns out, they were lowlifes with a dark agenda. We had to do horrible things to prove we belonged..." She let out a harsh breath. "Who would have guessed, right?"

My heart clenched as she closed her eyes tight.

"I'm not saying I'm a saint, but I couldn't handle it. I started looking for a way out, and then I met Leo, who was in Omar's pack. He's not anymore. Turns out he wasn't who I thought he was, but I still owe him for offering me an escape. He told me all the outcomes, but if I lived, I'd have a real family. So I did what I had to."

"Wow. That's so brave."

"Brave," she scoffed. "I cheated."

"How?"

"I got a witch to help me."

"You made a deal?"

She nodded and scooped a strand of pink hair behind her diamond studded ear. "I'm all about survival. I did something for her, and in exchange, she siphoned some of Leo's were-wolf magic into me at the hardest point in my transition."

"That sounds..."

"Impossible? Crazy?"

"Smart." I admired her tenacity, but I wasn't sure I could ever make a deal. I'd gotten so mad at Aiden for making one with Fran before.

Then again...survival was key.

"What kind of witch did you work with?"

"Don't know," Sasha said. "Leo found them. I wasn't too

savvy back then. I did learn most witches don't get involved in transitions, but if you're looking for someone shady enough to help, maybe it's closer than you think." She tossed her gaze back in the direction of Ryan's house.

"The Seer? He tried to kill me. I don't think he'd be up for helping."

Sasha raised a dark brow. "Then make him an offer he can't say no to."

23

*A*iden reluctantly agreed to sneak me in to talk to the Seer. I didn't tell him the advice Sasha gave me about a deal, but that I wanted to ask about my necklace or see if he knew anything regarding my transition.

"Don't expect him to help," Aiden said, jingling the keys in the lock at his parents' back door.

"I have to try. I only have two days left."

He nodded and let me in through the kitchen. His footsteps tapped the tile floor behind me around the island. "Keep it short, if you can," he reminded me. "I don't know when my parents will be back."

"Got it. I brought reinforcements," I said, patting my purse on my hip.

He tilted his head with a smirk. "Reinforcements?"

"I baked him some cookies."

"You sacrificed some of your cookie dough for the guy who tried to kill you?"

"Blasphemy, I know." I opened the basement door and flipped the light on at the top of the stairs. The mustiness instantly brought me back to the night I woke up in this basement after my car accident. I shoved back the oncoming chill and looked at Aiden one more time.

He stared down at me from the doorway the same way he'd looked at me that night—lips tight, eyes fierce, and jaw squared—like I was someone to protect. "I'll be here when you're done."

I nodded.

The stairs gave like cushions under my feet. When I got to the concrete hallway, a cool draft kissed my skin. I traced my fingers along the deep scratch marks grooved into the walls, following the light guiding me from the room ahead.

I stopped when I reached the doorway, peering around the doorframe at the Seer.

He lay on the cot in the cell, with the chains draping down from his arms to the bedframe, which was also bolted to the floor. He had his feet propped up on the bars, and his eyes were closed.

"I knew you'd come find me," he said, cracking one eye open.

I pulled up a nearby chair that sat behind a desk in the corner. "We need to talk," I said, taking a seat a few feet back from the cell bars.

"I admire your persistence, but based on the questions you plan on asking, you won't get much from me." He sat up, the dark lines of his tattoos coming into full view again in the light. "But I will take those cookies. And a cigarette. You got one?"

I frowned and folded my arms. If he was going to make this difficult, then I would too. "No answers—no cookies. And I don't have any cigarettes."

He shrugged. "It was worth a shot."

"Do you see everything that happens in the future?"

He settled back and cupped his hands behind his head. "Not everything. Things change, too."

"Has anything with my future changed?" I asked impatiently. "Does Dorian win?"

He slit his eyes in my direction, the pierced corner of his lips turning up. "For Dorian, I can't see that far. For you, I still see the two equal possibilities." The way he said it made it sound like it was a bad thing, and a knot formed in my stomach.

But I decided to reward him to keep the conversation going. I reached in my purse and pulled out the crinkling bag of cookies.

He sat up and leaned forward on the cot, the clunky chains shifting with his movement. "I thought you weren't going to give me any."

"I thought you weren't going to answer any of my questions."

"Touché. Evidence that the future changes within a second." He smiled and watched my every move as I opened the bag and pulled out a cookie. Its fresh doughy scent wafted into the room, and the Seer held his hand out.

Reluctantly, I leaned forward and stuck the cookie through the cell bars. He snatched it from my hand and scarfed it down with one bite.

"When was the last time you ate?"

"I don't know." He wiped the crumbs from the stubble around his mouth, rattling the chains loudly. "How long have I been in here?"

I shook my head and looked at the floor. He'd been in there almost two weeks and acted like he hadn't had a real meal. I made a note to myself to ask Aiden to make sure he was better fed. Why I cared, I didn't know.

Holding up another cookie for him to see, I moved on to my next question. "Do you know anything about the Eye of the Moon?"

He crinkled his square brows. "Not much. The legend is

the Moon Goddess hid her most beloved possession on earth, but no one has ever found it."

"And what possession is that?"

He shrugged. "Some kind of crystal. But a legend is only as accurate as a rumor."

"What does it do? Why would Dorian want that?"

"Don't know." He scowled and folded his arms. "But in the past, Ancients' goals were usually power, strength, money… it's a long list."

"How could a crystal give an Ancient any of that?"

"How can werewolves exist?" he countered.

"Is that a trick question?" I waited for him to answer, but his drawn-out silence grated my nerves. "Magic?"

"Bingo." He stood up and moved to the cell door, resting his hands on the bars. "When in doubt, the answer is magic."

I handed him another cookie. "Speaking of that, can a siphon witch transfer werewolf magic into someone else during a transition?"

He broke the cookie in half, examining a chocolate chip in the center. "It depends."

"On what?"

"Lots of things."

"Like what?" I seethed, my patience wearing out.

"How many consequences they're willing to face." He shoved the cookie in his mouth and proceeded to talk between massive chews. "Are these homemade? You'll have to give me the recipe."

I rolled my eyes. "No. Store bought. What kind of consequences?"

"Everything comes at a price. For a witch to aid a wolf in a transition like that, they accept they might unbalance nature."

"What do you mean?"

"Things happen because they're supposed to. Deals can be

made and different sides help each other out, but nature always needs a balance. If someone's supposed to survive their transition, that's what the Moon Goddess and nature have in store. There might be some loopholes, but someone always has to pay for it."

My pulse escalated, and the plastic bag crinkled in my clenched fingers as I mulled his words through my brain.

There had to be a balance...so that meant the Seer accepted the consequences when he decided to try and kill me. Maybe he'd be willing to accept one more.

Maybe Sasha's advice was the only way out of this and he'd be willing to make a deal...

"Can you tell me *anything* about how to survive my transition?"

He tipped his head back, his deep laughter jarring against the walls. "Why would I help you? If Dorian got ahold of you, that could be it for everyone."

I shook my head. "But I'm just me."

"In the wrong hands, you are more than you think."

"What does that mean? Dorian doesn't know I exist. And if you say I'm more than I think I am, wouldn't it be possible for me to kill him if I survive?"

His eyes darkened, like swirling black holes looking down at me, but he didn't answer. Did he know something about that?

"Listen. If you tell me how to make it through the full moon, I *will* find a way to kill Dorian. I'll do whatever it takes." I leaned forward, willing him to agree.

He traced his finger up his chin and over to the hoop ring in his lip. "Seers are forbidden to strike deals if it means impacting the future."

"Please. You said there are loopholes. We could find one." I stood up, still grasping the bag of cookies as I reached for the bars.

The Seer watched me from the other side of the cell, standing less than a foot from me. "No."

All the air deflated from my lungs. This was pointless, just like Aiden said it would be.

I had to figure something else out—then Sasha's words popped in my head.

Make him an offer he can't say no to.

"Fine." I forced a smile and let my hands fall from the steel bars. As I headed toward the doorway, I jammed the bag of cookies into my purse. "I was going to offer to get you out of here, but I've changed my mind."

"Wait. Could you really get me out of here?"

I paused at the doorway. "If you made the deal."

He folded his arms, and the chains slinked along the floor toward the bed behind him. "How do I know you're not lying?"

"Wouldn't you be able to see me freeing you?"

He gave a harsh laugh. "Ironically, I can't see my own future."

"Oh. That sucks. Well, good luck. Hopefully they won't kill you, but some wolves here love tearing people apart." I turned away, stepping one foot in the hallway, when he called back out to me.

"I'll make the deal."

My stomach lurched in a victoriously nauseating flip and I turned around. "Part of the deal is you can't come back here or try to kill me again later."

He grimaced, but he nodded. "I, Ethan Sullivan, swear to tell you how to survive the full moon. I swear to bring no harm to you, in exchange for my freedom within three days after your first shift, and your hand in Dorian's death. Done. Now, your turn."

I raised a brow at him. "That's it? You just want my word?"

"That's all we need, since we both have witch blood. Our word is more sacred than a mere promise from one human to another."

"How did you know I have witch blood?"

His lips slid into a creepy grin. "I can't tell you. Now let's go. It's too late to back out."

I took in a breath of cold, damp air. Aiden would flip if he knew what I was doing, but this was for him, so I could still be there for him. He'd already done something like this for me, too. We could call it even.

"I, Sydney Cline, swear to free you within three days of my first shift, and…" I had to force myself to breathe again, "…kill Dorian, in exchange for *full disclosure* on how to survive the full moon." Two heartbeats passed. A sudden hair-raising tingle slid over my body all the way to my toes, and I knew it was done.

The Seer smiled. "I think you know I got the better end of the deal, right?"

I cast a glare his way. "Just tell me how to survive."

He sat back on his cot with a cool expression. "Look within yourself."

"Please tell me you have more to offer than that." I crossed my arms. "I'm looking. I'm doing peace spells and crap. Nothing is working."

"That's one way to approach it, but if you have *that* attitude, you're probably not digging deep enough. Get to a place where you feel connected to yourself."

"That sounds like a freaking cop out." My anger rekindled, and my skin ran hot. Had I made this deal for nothing?

"It's not," he insisted. "You have to harness everything from the *inside* out. I swear. That's it."

"That sounds too simple."

"That's magic. Complex, but the answer is simple."

My lungs shook with fury. "You cheated. That doesn't help me at all!"

"It's the truth, but if you choose not to take the advice, it's your loss."

"Then it's your loss too, because if I don't survive, you don't get your freedom."

"I'm well aware of that." His angled cheekbones hollowed a little as he pursed his lips. "That's why I told you the truth."

His words lingered in the air, filling the corners of the desolate, dark room. The walls seemed to creep in, leaning over me and threatening to bury me in the cement. I had to get out of here. I turned toward the doorway again, leaving the dirtbag behind.

"Good luck, Sydney," he called after me. "If you make it, you have one year to complete our deal in its entirety. That means you have one year to kill Dorian."

Everything in my body came to a halt, and I swiveled my gaze back at him. "What do you mean?"

"Unless specified otherwise, a witch's verbal agreement stands for one year. Both must uphold the deal within that time frame."

"A year…" I reached for the doorframe to steady myself. "Or what? What are the consequences if I can't kill him in a year?"

Ethan raised his chin and watched me like I should have known the answer to that. "You'll die anyway."

I couldn't sleep. I lay there with Aiden, listening to him breathe. The clock across the room displayed two in the morning like a red neon sign.

The full moon was in less than forty-eight hours, and I wasn't much closer to figuring things out than I was before.

Sure, I'd made peace with some things...mostly. I didn't want to rip Liv's throat out every time she texted me, and I'd partially forgiven my father.

But things with Mom still bothered me a lot. I missed her so much. She'd texted me every day, asking me to call her, but I couldn't do it. I'd said goodbye, and I didn't want to open that wound again until I made it past my shift.

And then there was the Seer.

Jerkface.

He'd freaking tricked me, locking me into an Ancient's death, all while ensuring he'd get his freedom.

What had I been thinking? I barely had one foot in this world, and I was already vowing to kill one of the oldest werewolves ever.

Nausea rolled through me, and I couldn't stop myself from whispering the first curse that popped into my head.

"You're still awake?" Aiden asked sleepily. He turned over and curled his arm around me, pulling me against his chest. "Or are you cursing in your sleep now? Did you dream about that car accident again?"

His piney scent filled my space, and the weight of his arm around me relaxed me a little. He made me feel safe, and I didn't want to leave this spot or face the threats outside this cabin.

"I haven't had that in a while," I said. Mostly because I couldn't sleep anymore.

"Then what is it?"

"Just nerves."

"About the full moon?" He lifted a strand of hair away from my cheek, looping it around his finger before drawing me close and burying his face in my curls.

"Everything. I think I focused so much on getting stronger physically and memorizing those spells that I didn't

207

really try to make peace with things. Pete told me to do that in the beginning, and I didn't really listen."

Aiden sighed, his chest expanding into my back. "What was it the Seer said again?"

"That I needed to connect with myself, or whatever." Plus a few other things, like that stupid deal, but Aiden didn't need to know that yet. Or maybe ever.

"Well…" Aiden brushed his lips over my cheek. "I have an idea. Get your dance shoes."

He sat up, tossing the covers off and crossing the room to his dresser.

"My pointe shoes?" I propped up on my elbows, watching him pull his t-shirt on over his bare chest. "Now?"

"Yup. Right now." He slid his shoes on and grabbed the keys from the nightstand. "Chop-chop."

"Wow. Somebody's bossy."

"Time is of the essence," he said, moving toward me and yanking the covers back.

"Aiden!" The blast of cool air sent goosebumps all over my arms and legs. "You're serious? We're actually going somewhere?"

"Mm-hm." He leaned over and gave me a peck on the nose. "Let's go."

I got up and grabbed my ballet bag, which I hadn't really touched since my car accident. The charred edges were frayed, but tossing it over my shoulder still felt like old times.

We got in the truck and headed into the city limits of Shadow Grove. The town was deader and creepier than I'd ever seen it. More businesses had closed down in the last couple months and even the streetlights were off.

But my heart skipped when Aiden turned into the parking lot of Ms. Felicity's studio. It was like coming home, and I couldn't believe I'd stayed away this long.

"Come on," he said, getting out of the truck and taking my bag for me.

I followed him through the empty lot to the dark glass doors. The moonlight flooded in through the windows, like a spotlight on the glossy floors. "You're not going to break in, are you?"

"Nope." He grinned, and that adorable dimple popped in his cheek again. "I have a key."

"How?" I asked, watching him pull a shiny set out of his pocket and open the door.

"I worked something out with Ms. Felicity." He held the door open and let me in.

I clasped both hands to my chest as soon as I smelled the citrus floor cleaner. Just stepping into the open room made the tears rush to the surface.

When I turned to face Aiden, he held out a silver key to me. It had the same pink pom-pom key-ring I'd seen Ms. Felicity hold before. "This is yours."

"Mine?" I tried to keep my voice steady.

Aiden flipped on the light switch by the doors. "I reserved the studio for you on Tuesday and Thursday nights after classes. I figured since you're probably not going to school in the fall, you can get back in here and start practicing for auditions again."

I couldn't fight the tears anymore. One slipped out and rolled down my right cheek. "How?"

"I had some extra cash coming in from guitar orders, and I had to convince Ms. Felicity to take the little bit I offered. She was ready to just let you have the space for free. She really loves you." He stuck his hands in his pockets and looked down at his feet. "It was supposed to be a surprise for after this week—a celebration for getting through everything, but I think you needed it a little sooner."

My heart squeezed like it was about to explode in my

chest. I ran forward and threw my arms around him, holding on like he was my lifeline. "Aiden, thank you. This is amazing."

He wrapped his arms down and around me, suspending me there in the moment. "I love you."

"I love you, too." As I held on to him, a peace came over me I hadn't felt in a while, and a small buzzing came from my chest. At first, I thought it was the bond filling me again, but it was more. Pulling away, the soft glow of my necklace pulsed, spilling a red tint over Aiden's face.

"I think this plan is working," he said with relief. "Too bad you can't transition here in the studio."

I grasped the pendant in my hand, still holding on to him with the other arm. "If you're with me, I think I have all I need to make it work."

*D*ancing in the studio again had been soul-rejuvenating. I felt so energized, I couldn't go back to bed when Aiden and I got back to the cabin. Instead, I put Gigi's spell books in my backpack and headed out to the lake to practice.

Spreading everything out on the end of the dock, I recited the spells Dad taught me until the sunlight trickled through the surrounding trees and my butt grew numb from sitting so long.

I thought through every pirouette, every sway my body remembered on the dance floor and the freedom that came with doing what I loved.

I thought about Aiden...how his eyes flickered whenever he looked at me, and how his skin warmed when he touched me. I went back to the second he gave me the studio key, like he was unlocking me from shackles all over again.

My heartbeat bounded with the freedom he gave me, spreading a deep tranquility to every cell of my body. Even the air around me and the ripples in the lake seemed to still with the peace I imagined exuding from inside me.

But nothing happened.

No glowing or humming, no matter how long I stared at my necklace.

None of this added up, and it was driving me crazy. The stone only seemed to activate with emotional extremes, where I was on the verge of explosion or feeling incredibly safe.

I'd hoped I could get back in touch with how I felt when Aiden was there and see if that would work, but nope. Everything pointed to him needing to be there with me, which was okay, but it meant I seriously messed up when I made that deal with the Seer.

I let the necklace fall against my chest and snapped the book shut so loudly, it echoed across the water. My exhale simmered through my teeth and I shoved the book in my bag.

I stood up and slung the bag over my shoulder, taking in a deep breath to calm myself.

Everything would be okay. Aiden would be with me. And then, after, we had a year to figure things out.

I made my way off the dock, heading back to the cabin. When I got halfway through the grass, a shiver coasted down my spine. I turned and scanned the perimeter of the woods, but there was nothing there.

My senses still sent off alarms through my body. Prickles erupted along my fingertips, and I fought the urge to round my back as my muscles spasmed with warning.

A buzzing on my sternum startled me, giving off light like a red flare. I grabbed my necklace, covering it up in case someone was watching me, which wasn't likely, but my intuition was hardly ever wrong.

I hoped I was being paranoid. This place was off-limits to the pack since it backed Aiden's cabin, but if a werewolf saw me with spell books and glowing jewelry, I could only imagine the drama that would unfold.

The feeling didn't go away, but I didn't see or hear anything else. I willed my feet to take me back to the cabin as fast as possible.

The branches swished as I passed them, my feet hardly making a sound as I ran through the woods. When I made it to the backyard, I slowed down, calming the burning in my lungs as I walked in through the front door.

"Hey." Aiden stood in the kitchen, sliding a buttered knife across a piece of toast, but stopped when he saw I was out of breath. "Are you okay?"

"Yeah. Great," I panted, shutting the door and taking a wobbly step toward the couch. I let my bag fall off my shoulders and land on the floor with a *thunk*, not even caring if the spell book disintegrated with the impact. "I was practicing at the lake."

"How did it go?"

It took me a few seconds to answer, debating telling him about that freak-out I'd just had, but it was probably nothing. "It went."

He quirked his mouth like he'd sucked a lemon. "That bad, huh?"

"Like I said last night, I think if you're there, I'll be okay." I kicked my shoes off and inched my way around the couch, throwing myself onto the middle cushion. It welcomed me with a softness that stole the tension creeping into my shoulders.

"Speaking of, I've been scoping out where we should go tomorrow night. I was thinking we should move the jackass witch in my parents' basement somewhere else and have you hang out in the cell."

My stomach tumbled, and I sat up straighter. "You want to put me in jail?"

"No. I don't want to, but it's the safest place for you and everyone else. I can't have you running off and getting hurt because of the tricks your mind plays." He put the toast on a plate and stuck the butter back in the fridge.

"Oh. Yeah. Okay. That's fine."

"I *will* be there," he said. "I'll get you whatever you need, and when it's over, you'll be free of this whole thing."

"Freedom. That sounds nice." Even being tied to his pack sounded more freeing than tomorrow night.

"Yeah." One side of his mouth slid up. "It does."

He turned and grabbed a small brown bottle from the countertop and twisted the lid off. Holding up a dropper, he let two beads of liquid fall into his mouth.

A small twinge made its way through me. It was the stuff Cora gave him to keep the poison in his wound from spreading.

Aiden casually set the bottle back on the counter and took a bite of toast. Then in a flash, he was on the couch right next to me. His leg pressed against mine as he propped his feet on the coffee table and hung his arms along the back of the couch. His gray t-shirt rippled down his abs, and he waggled his eyebrows at me, so carefree.

I twisted to face him, unable to hide my smile. "Happy birthday."

"Thanks." His eyes lit up, and he extended his wrist, looping one of my curls around his finger.

"Sorry I didn't get you anything."

"I can't believe you," he said, shaking his head.

I shoved my fist into his shoulder, and he laughed.

"You know I don't care about that. I've got everything I want right here."

"Cheesy line, but okay."

"I meant my house." He grinned, clearly trying to get another rise out of me. I whopped him in the shoulder again, and he rubbed his arm. "Ouch. That one actually hurt."

"Good." I smirked and leaned forward, running my thumb down the smooth cut of his jaw. He clasped his fingers over my hand, the moment taking a tender turn. I wished so badly we could stay here today, like this. In our pajamas, nowhere to go, nothing life-threatening ahead.

"Let's spend the day together tomorrow," he said, holding my hand against his face and leaning into my palm. "You deserve to enjoy your last day as a human. No studying, no stressing."

I perked up, my pulse fluttering. "What would we do?"

"I was thinking…" He smoothed his palm down my arm, leaving pleasant chills behind on my skin. "We could sleep in, go get lunch, see a movie. The possibilities are endless."

Even though I knew I'd still stress, all those things were distractions I needed. "I honestly can't think of a better day."

"Really?" Aiden leaned forward until our faces were inches apart, stirring up the whirlpool of heat inside my chest. "It's not too overwhelmingly ordinary?"

I laughed, my heart skipping at the phantom smile on his full lips. "I love ordinary sometimes. I'll even take boring occasionally."

"Then I'll do my best to give you the most boring, mediocre day of your life." He sank his lips into mine, pouring a warm, euphoric freedom through my veins.

Aiden could try, but there was a snowball's chance in hell he'd ever be able to give me boring or mediocre. It wasn't possible, and that was fine by me.

Aiden's birthday party was already underway when we arrived. String lights sparkled along the tree line, and music boomed from the speakers that catty cornered the field. We found Pete tossing another piece of wood into the bonfire, sending firefly embers up into the star-studded sky. "Hey! Happy birthday."

"Thanks." Aiden's cheeks tinted pink in the fire's glow.

"I think we have about three packs here." Pete dusted his hands off and looked around at the crowd mingling in the field and on the bridge. They had cups, and the sweet smell of punch and beer perfumed the air. "Your dad went all out to make sure everyone made it, and we had Cora put up some protective wards."

"Fun," Aiden said sarcastically, taking a seat on the bench. He looked at me and tugged on my hand. "Here, sit next to me so no one talks to me."

"Why?" I laughed and sat down, arching my brows at him.

"He doesn't like being the center of attention," Pete answered for him, taking a seat on the other side.

"Oh. I can totally see that," I observed, watching Aiden as he looked at the fire. The flames flickered, their light sparking against his smooth face.

"So," Pete said, "have you guys figured anything else out about the Eye? Or the other thing?" He looked at my necklace.

"Not really." I shrugged, leaning my shoulder against Aiden's side. "What about you?"

He shook his head. "I asked Naomi if I could look through her library again. She's checking to see if anyone else has any old texts and journals." He lowered his voice even further. "We might have to go to the Solstice Guardians."

"But wouldn't they already know about it?" I asked. "It seems they would look for the thing Dorian wants most." I made sure I lowered my voice when I said his name.

"Hopefully, but you never know." Pete shrugged one

shoulder. "Anyway, enough business talk. I'm gonna grab something to drink. And I'm going to get you your first *legal* drink." He gave Aiden a hardy pat on the back and disappeared into the chattering crowd.

"Your birthday party reminds me of the high school parties Liv would drag me to," I told Aiden.

He snorted. "I hope that's not a bad thing. We're all home-schooled here, so I don't know the difference."

"Well, hopefully no one will do any naked keg stands or anything."

His eyes widened. "Your friends did that?"

"No," I snickered. "You're so gullible. One time Trevor tried to do it, with clothes on, thankfully, but he ended up a human bowling ball and falling into everyone." A smile pulled on my lips. "I didn't know him super well, but I kinda miss him."

Aiden scooped his arm around my hip and rested his chin on my shoulder. "Maybe after this, you should see some of your old friends. Get back in touch with your old life."

"Yeah—"

Prickles broke out on the back of my neck. I sat up straighter and looked around the crowd of people, but nobody was looking straight at me. Nobody I could see, anyway.

Aiden glanced around. "What's wrong?"

"Uh—" I rolled my shoulders, trying to rid myself of the icy finger sliding up and down my back. "I feel like someone's watching me."

We turned, and under the torch lights, Manny's bulky shadow pushed through the crowd, coming face-to-face with us. His arctic eyes pierced through me, knocking the wind from my throat for a split-second. In the fire's glow, his scar made him even fiercer than normal, and my nerves ricocheted through my body.

Becca appeared right behind him. She folded her arms and brushed her hair back off her shoulder, staring me down like she was ready to take me on.

"What's going on?" Aiden stood up and stepped over the bench, shielding me from their glares.

"You." Manny's gravelly voice raked over me, and he pointed his stubby finger at me. "You had everyone else fooled, but not me."

"Dad, what's going on—" Pete came back through the crowd with a beer bottle in each hand. "Becs?"

"She's been lying to us the whole time," Becca sneered. "I saw her this morning by the lake. She was chanting, summoning magic. Probably hexing all of us."

The chit-chat from the other pack members died down to nothing, and even the music got cut off. Everything grew so silent, weighing me down until I almost collapsed. I stood up, my stomach roiling as Aiden's arm moved out in front of me.

Then my necklace glowed, humming forcefully against my chest. Gasps filled the field.

Great. Perfect timing.

"See?" Manny erupted. "Tell me, Aiden, did you know she was a witch? Or were you so blinded by your feelings for her that you didn't care about putting this pack at risk?"

Aiden's features steeled like armor. "You don't know what you're talking about."

"I don't?" Manny took a step forward until he could see me again over Aiden's shoulder. "Why don't we let her explain?"

"There's nothing to explain." Aiden's tone remained level, but I could feel the anger, like a hot fist, ready to reach out and grab Manny by the throat.

"Then how about explaining to the pack why you'd waste our potential in a time like this."

"Enough," Aiden growled, lurching forward a few inches,

but Manny stood up taller, broadening his shoulders like a brick wall.

"No. We need to know what our future Alpha has decided —*who* our future Alpha has chosen as his mate."

Mate?

Chatter swept through the crowd and my skin crawled with more pairs of eyes on me than I could count. A few feet away, Pete entered my peripheral vision, tossing the beers he'd retrieved down into the dirt and taking his place beside us.

The voices only grew louder, and the stares only intensified as Manny waited for a response. I looked up at Aiden, hot lava pumping through my veins. "What's he talking about?"

He didn't answer me. He stared ahead at Manny, his jaw working like a boulder rolling down a steep hill. "I'm tired of our Alpha line being pressured to mate right away, and with someone with full-blood. Who I choose has to choose me too, and it's going to be someone who makes me a better leader. It won't be based on anything as ridiculous as the difference between born and bitten."

His words only confused me. What was he talking about?

"So be it, but I want to appeal to the people." Manny turned around, casting his rigid gaze over the crowd, who had formed a wide circle around us. "Did you hear that? This Alpha not only refuses to follow our customs—customs that will protect and strengthen our pack—but might choose someone with dirty blood as his mate—"

Pete inhaled sharply beside us, his eyes glinting like the bonfire behind us.

"Is that what we want?" Manny continued, booming his voice over the crowd. "Don't we deserve someone who will follow our ways and choose someone who can strengthen our pack?"

"That's enough!" Aiden stepped forward, stopping only three feet in front of Manny. His shoulders coiled up, hands clenched at his sides.

Straight ahead, Ryan broke through the crowd, but he didn't step in for Aiden. A dull fire swelled in my stomach. Why wasn't he standing up for his son?

"I will lay down my life for this pack," Aiden yelled louder than I'd ever heard him before. "It's my choice. Many of you have met Sydney. You know she cares about us. She's risked her life to protect us. She stepped in for Nat, our only healer, who we all need. She saved my life, and she's put her neck out there to help us find out about this Ancient when she didn't have to do anything."

My heart battered against my ribcage, threatening to break the bones into tiny shards. Sweat slicked my skin, and I wanted so badly to run away, but I refused to leave Aiden like this, even though I didn't fully understand what was happening.

"You can't tell me that she won't make sacrifices for our pack after she turns," Aiden said, his tone softening as he looked at the sea of faces. Then he turned, eyes landing on me. "And if I follow the rules and mate within the first year of my leadership, I choose Sydney, if she'll choose me, too."

The air vacuumed around me, sucking all the oxygen from my lungs. Was mating...marriage?

Was Aiden saying he would choose me *forever*?

25

*A*iden and I stared at each other in the middle of a murmuring crowd.

I couldn't believe what was happening. I couldn't believe what he just said.

He wanted me as his mate if I chose him, too. His words had such finality to them, and I didn't even know how to unpack that statement. Even the way he looked at me, with that unreadable expression I came to adore, had a sense of finality.

He chose me.

My mouth opened, but no sound came out, and it wasn't like I could answer him here with all these people watching.

Manny whirled around to face the crowd again, pointing at me like he was about to grab a pitchfork and haul me off to Dead Man's Trail. "She's a witch! We can't trust her."

A few boos erupted around us, and angry, indiscernible shouts followed.

Becca folded her arms, her eyes glinting at me as perfect curls swayed over her shoulder. "I always knew there was something off about you."

"It's not what you think."

"Save it for someone who cares. Pretty soon, everyone will see that you've only brought more danger to this pack."

"No! I would never hurt this pack," I pleaded.

"Look around. You already have," she sneered. "I should have drowned you in the lake this morning when I had the chance."

That was it. I'd had enough of Becca. I curled my fist and took one step toward her, but Pete's hand caught my forearm.

"Don't," he said. "I'm not just saying that because she's my sister, but because she wants you to pick a fight. She wants to make you look bad." He looked over at Becca and shook his head. "You don't know what you're doing."

"I know what I saw," she said, giving me a judge-y once over again. I tried yanking away from Pete again, but his grip was like iron, bearing down on my skin with warning.

"You saw what you wanted to," he said to Becca. "Not what's really going on. You should have asked me before jumping to conclusions and feeding Dad's power trip. Now look at what you've done..." He nodded around to the shouts flaring around the circle. To our left, a couple people got shoved, almost causing a domino effect. "Whether you realize it or not, you've caused a split at one of the worst times possible."

As I looked around, people stepped out to the middle, holding their hands up as peacemakers. Nat and Theresa were the first, their faces contorting as they yelled something I couldn't hear over the noise.

Then Tabitha pushed her way out, shaking her head at Ryan, who stood there with his arms crossed like a pointless statue. Her red eyebrows pulled taut. She said something, giving him a fiery gaze just before holding her pale hand up.

The crowd slowly quieted down, and Aiden looked from

his father to his mother. Through the bond, a sinking weight dipped in my stomach.

"You've known our family for years," Tabitha said, her usually light voice carrying a hint of anger. "You know my son would never betray you. Please, listen to what he has to say. In the past, it was expected that the Alpha would mate in the first year to a full-blood, but times have changed. We shouldn't be so afraid of the future that we rely only on obtaining the abilities of the Alpha's Mate. We each have our own gifts. Let our alphas do what's best for themselves, so that they can do what's best for us."

Her words hung in the air, filling the gap in the center of the circle. She turned, her hair whipping around one side of her shoulder as she nodded at Aiden to speak again.

He turned away from Manny, his shoulders raising in a deep inhale. "The claims that Sydney is a witch are wrong. She has magic in her blood, but not enough to use it. We didn't find out until two weeks ago, and it doesn't matter. After tomorrow, she'll be one of us—"

"After tomorrow, she'll hopefully be dead," Manny countered.

In that second, I felt something snap inside Aiden as if it broke in my own chest. He lunged forward, landing his fist right into Manny's jaw with a loud crack.

Manny stumbled back, his features wide with pure shock and a front strand of hair ruffled out of place.

"You do not speak to *anyone* I care about like that." Aiden grabbed ahold of Manny's collar, getting in his face. "You've been trying to interfere with things outside your authority for years, and I'm done with it. When I'm Alpha, you're going on trial."

Manny thrust Aiden's hands off, and spit dark saliva off to the side. "When you're Alpha, I challenge you." He said his words slowly, shifting the air again to an eerie silence.

My heart stopped. All we could hear now was the fire popping. In the tiki lights, Aiden's eyes blazed, like aqua fire ready to blowtorch Manny's face off.

Finally, Ryan moved forward, a vein bulging down his forehead. "Manny, you're out of line."

"You're only saying that because you know I could win." Manny swiped his forearm over the blood trickling from the corner of his mouth.

Ryan grabbed him by the back of his shirt. "I think you proved your point. We're done here. Come with me."

Manny tried holding his ground at first, faltering his feet in the grass under Ryan's pull, but he gave in. He watched Aiden the entire way through the crowd. "You have to answer to this pack for your actions!"

Aiden dropped his gaze to the grass as the pack's voices picked up again. It seemed like the worst of everything was over, but by the way certain members approached Aiden—arms folded and brows furrowed—they wanted more of an explanation.

The circle began breaking apart, heads shaking and razor-sharp eyes pointed in my direction.

I'd done all I could to stay for Aiden, but now I couldn't handle it. I had to get out of here.

I took off running toward the cabin, praying no one would follow me.

"Sydney!" Aiden called after me, but I didn't look back. My skin burned with dozens of gazes, and I pushed my legs to go faster.

When I made it home, I slammed the door behind me and went straight for the bedroom. Heart pounding, I pulled out my suitcase and shoved anything in there that was mine and within arm's length.

This was crazy. How did I not see this coming?

Waiting to leave until the transition was over would have

been smarter. But how could I when Manny clearly wanted me dead, and now others might, too?

I smashed the suitcase shut and zipped it up, accidentally breaking off the zipper in the process. I tossed it off to the side and smashed my fist down into my luggage, denting the front of it.

This wasn't how it was supposed to be.

Aiden and I had plans. Not just for tomorrow, but from the way he talked, plans for a future. We'd defied the odds up to this point, and I pushed aside my fear of a brutal ending for us.

Maybe this was it…

The front door clicked, and the bond buzzed through me, alerting me to his presence behind me.

"Syd…what are you doing?" His tone was sharper than he'd ever used with me before.

"Leaving," I answered, the words wrenching through my heart. I dragged the suitcase off the bed and onto the floor. "I don't belong here. Everyone hates me, and they don't even know all the problems I've caused."

I turned to face him, and the desperate pleading in his eyes hollowed out my core. Tears rushed faster than I could keep up with. Within seconds, my cheeks were covered in water.

Could I really leave Aiden? I loved him, but I couldn't let him choose between his pack or me.

His hands reached up to my face, tilting my head back until I looked him in the eye. "Leaving isn't the answer. Not when you have to go through hell tomorrow night. Manny's crazy. His time to help lead the pack is ending, and he can't stand it."

"But he's turning everyone against us. Over something I don't even understand. What was he talking about? What's mating?"

Aiden froze. "It's like the werewolf version of marriage… they wanted me to mate with Becca within a year of rising to Alpha."

My stomach rolled, and I pulled away from him, almost tripping over my suitcase. He reached out for my hand, but I yanked it away in time to find my footing. "Then what is this? Why wouldn't you tell me that?"

"Because it doesn't matter."

"It does to them!"

"No." He moved up right in front of me and took my hand, clasping it against his chest. His heart beat like a hammer under my palm. "I tried it their way—I dated her. It went horribly, because I wasn't in it and neither was she. After that, I felt stuck. Then I met you, and I wanted us to have a *real* chance—without this pack bullshit. I wanted to have something normal."

"Sorry, but the *normal train* left a long time ago."

"I know." He hung his head down. "I didn't want to add to your list of worries, either. You've had so much to deal with, and I thought I was handling it. I never wanted to follow the tradition, and you gave me the confidence to stand up for what's right. You gave me the confidence to change things that could hurt the pack down the road. So, I don't care who they want me to be with. *You're* the one I want to be with, and that's all that matters."

Even if his words were true, the majority always ruled. "If I stay, I'll always have a target on my back. And so will you."

Aiden's eyes searched my face. "Then I'll go with you."

Floored, I stared up at him, taking in the raging storm in his turquoise eyes. I didn't doubt he meant what he said, but for him to leave his pack for me was insane. "That's ridiculous."

"No, it's not." His fingers clasped my hand tighter to his chest, and a brief tremor rippled down his arm. "I love you."

Another wave of water flooded my eyes. "But you can't leave your life behind for me."

"Why?"

"Because. They need you."

"I don't really know if that's true anymore." His tone fell, vanishing in a sadness that came through the bond.

A knock on the door startled me. I clenched my fingers into Aiden's t-shirt.

Had more of his pack come here for me?

Aiden glanced over his shoulder. "That's my dad. He wants to talk about what happened."

My pulse raced. "He was on Manny's side. Aiden—"

"I know. I have to fix that. Promise me you'll stay until I get back. Please."

I looked up into his eyes, grasping his waist as anxiety bubbled up. "I can't."

"I'll be gone thirty minutes, tops. That's it. If I can't fix it and you still want to leave after that, we'll go together. Just *please* wait for me."

I didn't want to leave, especially facing tomorrow, but so many things could go wrong between now and then. I felt stuck, but the way he held on to me, like he needed me as much as I needed him, nearly broke me. "Okay. I'll wait for you."

A spark of hope glimmered on his face. "I'll send Pete over here to make sure you're okay while I'm gone. No one will bother you."

"Okay." I nodded, partial relief settling in my shoulders.

Aiden leaned down and kissed me like it would be his last. He clasped his fingers around the back of my neck, the pressure of his lips lingering heavily on mine. "I'll be back soon," he said roughly. "I promise."

Then he was gone. He moved so fast to the front door; I didn't even get to look at him again. The door opened and shut, and the vibration of the bond faded as the distance grew between us.

Torn, I sat down on the edge of the bed. I promised him I wouldn't go anywhere, but I was scared of being alone until Pete arrived.

The French doors revealed the pitch-black sky outside. I could still see everything with my new wolf-vision, but it freaked me out. I got up and pulled the curtains down over the doors and moved back to the bed, hugging a pillow to my chest.

At least ten minutes passed before someone came through the front door again. The soft click echoed, pumping my blood until Pete's voice rang through the cabin.

"Sydney?"

"I'm here," I called back, jumping to my feet. I ran down the hall and turned the corner at the open living room.

"I'm so sorry for my family's behavior." He shook his head and sat down heavily on the couch. "I knew he was a jerk sometimes, but I didn't know he'd get Becca to do his dirty work." He raked his hand down the back of his neck, pausing with wild eyes. "And that he would challenge Aiden."

I moved across the room to the other side of the couch, my fingers digging into the edge of the cushion as I sat down. If that happened, Pete would lose either his father or his best friend, and if we lost Aiden—

"We have to convince my dad not to follow through with it, but I'm not so sure that will work."

Maybe Aiden leaving the pack wouldn't be such a bad thing if he kept his life for it.

"I'm so sorry, Sydney," Pete said again, leaning down and cupping his forehead in his hands.

"It's not your fault."

"Sometimes I feel like, just because he adopted me, he thinks he's protected."

"What do you mean?"

Pete let his hands drop from his face. "Because I have *dirty blood*. He thinks he's immune to being questioned about his own prejudices because he calls me his son. But he made it clear what he thinks about wolves like me... like us."

I reached my hand out toward Pete. I understood now what he meant before when he said his family reminded him he wasn't full-blooded. He deserved better than that.

A bang on the door made both of us jump, and Pete shot to his feet.

"What was that?" I asked, leaning on the edge of the couch cushion.

"I don't know." He moved to the door, but as he reached for the handle, the door blew off its hinges. Pete flew back against the wall, knocking over the bookcase and the guitar and hitting the floor.

My heart thundered and I stood up. When a red-hooded figure appeared in the doorway, I backed away around the coffee table. A small, freckled hand rose from underneath wide sleeves, and sparks of light jumped from their fingertips.

I didn't have time to react. With the turn of their palm, they sent the sparks at me, colliding with my chest. Fire burned through my core to the tips of my toes as I flew backward into the kitchen. I slammed into the cabinets, my head splitting as I hit the cabinets.

Plates crashed down around me, shattering and ricocheting porcelain everywhere. I sat up, reaching for my throbbing head. Blood ran down my palm where I pulled it away.

The red-hooded intruder slowly approached me, their cape swishing, giving the illusion of floating. Or maybe they really *were* floating. Then they pulled their hood back, gracefully revealing the familiar fiery red hair and chilly hazel eyes.

"Anika," I hissed.

She shrugged her cloak off her shoulders, letting it pool on the floor like velvet blood. Propping her hand up on her hip, she smoothed down the other side of her short black dress and thigh high boots, smiling at me through thin lips.

When her eyes flicked down to my necklace and back to my face, I knew exactly what she was here for.

Me.

26

ear seized my throat, stalling the air in my lungs as I pushed up onto my side. My necklace glowed and my muscles spasmed, ready to defend myself no matter what it took. I was stronger now than when I saw Anika days ago, and I would show her just how much had changed.

Pete climbed to his feet on the other side of the room, kicking away a piece of the door. Another shard stuck straight out of his arm. He grimaced, gripping the splintery wood and yanked it out of his bicep with a grunt. Then he shifted, taking up half the living room and charging at Anika.

She turned and waved her hand, stopping him mid-air. He yelped and crumpled down to the floor in a furry heap, panting on his side and clenching his eyes shut.

"Stop hurting him," I growled at her. Shoving to my feet, I jumped on her back, taking her down to the floor with a sharp collide.

She turned over, mumbling a chain of unrecognizable words and grabbing my hand. A scorching heat blistered me from the inside out. My skin broke out in beads of sweat instantly, and I couldn't breathe.

"Do you feel that?" she sneered. "I'm boiling your insides, and I'll do it again as soon as you've healed. But if you make this easy, I won't have to."

Somehow, I conjured enough strength to thrust myself away from her and break contact. My body cooled, but when I moved, it was like a hundred knives jabbing through me. She sat up right behind me and I sent my elbow back, hitting her in the temple. Her head jerked off to the side, smashing into the coffee table. I climbed on top of her and sent my fist across her cheek. The contact made a satisfying smack of flesh and I reared my other fist back.

She screamed like an angry banshee and grabbed my throat, inflicting an arctic brain-freeze through my skull. I couldn't move, and it was only for a second, but it felt like an eternity. Her lip curled in one of the most evil grins I'd ever seen. I had to think fast.

I closed my eyes and sent my head forward, ramming it into the bridge of her nose with a crack. She fell back, and I caught the glimmer of a ring on her finger. Then I remembered when Liv took the Seer's ring, effectively removing his ability to do magic.

It was worth a shot.

I grabbed her hand and tore the ring from her bony finger, tossing it across the room. It dinged against the wall and fell somewhere among the mess of books on the floor. But she laughed and chanted again. Her eyes lit with stark white light before she threw me off of her.

I rolled back, landing on my hands and knees beside Pete. He lay on his side, panting rapidly, his eyes wide open.

"What did you do to him?" I asked, my face flaming with anger.

She climbed slowly to her feet, grinning smugly. "Relax.

He might not ever walk again, but at least I left him alive. For now."

I sucked in a sharp breath. Something fractured inside me, erupting in a fury I'd never felt before. My skin tingled and my arms tensed with this primal need to tear her flesh apart.

I sprinted at her, introducing her supple skin to my fingernails. She didn't even have time to start a spell before I got her in the eyes and scraped down her face. We plowed over the coffee table, breaking it into pieces as we hit the floor again. My bones rattled at the impact, but we both shot up to our feet. I swung at her, my knuckles smashing against her cheekbone in the most satisfying hit. Her head swung back, and I came at her over and over, backing her up into the window with my blows.

She thrust her palm out, jolting me back with a bolt of electricity again. I toppled over the couch and landed face-down on the mess of what used to be the coffee table. Swiping up one of the legs, I swung it around as I turned over. The jarring through my weapon told me I'd hit her, and then she crashed onto her side a few feet away.

I scrambled on top of her and pressed the table leg against her throat. Guttural sounds strained from her mouth as she pried at my hands, but I was stronger. Her face shaded to a deep red, and her hands frantically searched the floor around her. I leaned in harder as a vein bulged down her temple. This would soon be over for her.

My blood pumped. Guilt and satisfaction poured through me. I'd never killed anyone, but she wouldn't stop unless I did what I had to.

Suddenly, an immobilizing searing pressure split into my side.

I screamed and lost my grip on the coffee table leg. It

rolled to the floor as I looked down at a red glowing knife in my stomach.

I collapsed, a sharp pain bursting through my shoulder as I hit the floor. My side burned white hot, and Anika leaned over me, jamming the blade deeper until I felt pinned to the floor.

She leaned further, closing the space between our faces a little more. Crimson red welts ran down her cheeks from when I scratched her face before, and all I wanted was to gouge her eyes out. She was so close. But my arms refused to move.

"You're a fighter. Too bad you couldn't have made it easier for yourself." She tsked. "Now you're weakened for the full moon tomorrow."

I tried to speak, but all I could get out were inaudible whispers. Black spots invaded my sight, tunneling the room behind Anika.

I fought to keep my eyes open, to hold out hope that Aiden would feel my struggle through the bond, but every second became harder to get through.

"Just give in," she said softly. "You can't fight this for too long. Nobody can."

I tried...for how many seconds, I didn't know.

The heat stemming from the knife scorched hotter. I let out a weak scream, inhaling shallow gasps.

Then everything around me went dark.

When I opened my eyes again, I looked up at a wooden ceiling. Strips of daylight peeked through wherever I was, and it smelled like...farm.

I turned over despite my insides rubbing together like

sandpaper. My side was sore from where Anika stabbed me, but I lifted my shirt to see a pink line.

Dirt covered my arms, and I searched my surroundings. I was in a barn. There was hay piled in a far corner, and blinding daylight pouring through wide double doors to my left. And they were open.

Freedom.

My muscles jumped with the need to run. I climbed to my feet, but when I took my third step, my body jarred back head first, like I'd hit a glass wall.

"What the hell?" I pressed my palms out in front, hitting a barrier I couldn't see. Then I looked down and saw the white sand circling me.

I scraped my bare foot along the sand, but as soon as my flesh touched it, it sizzled. I yanked back with a curse.

"I'm surprised you don't know that much about salt barriers," came a familiar voice from the barn doors.

I looked over, speechless to see Lucille in the doorway.

Her long braids cascaded down one shoulder in a low ponytail, and she wore the same all-knowing grin as the last time I saw her.

"I really thought somebody would have taught you more about your own bloodline," she said, sauntering over to me. Her boots treaded lightly on the dirt floor, kicking up dust clouds around her tight jeans and tunic shirt.

Still too shocked to speak, I stared at her with my fingers resting against the invisible wall between us.

"It's okay, love," she goaded. "I'm not here to hurt you. Anika wasn't *supposed* to hurt you, either. I guess she misjudged how strong you are. We both did." Her dark eyes slinked up and down me like I was a meal ready to be eaten, and I wanted to shrink away from her stare. "You'll do very well, I think."

"I don't get it," I stammered. "You went missing...we looked for you."

"No. I made it *look* like I went missing."

"But why? And your reading? I thought you were helping me." Bitterness saturated my words. I hardly knew this woman, but I felt so betrayed.

"That's actually quite a story," Lucille said, wandering over to a table lined with goopy candles. She picked up a matchbox and shifted it from one hand to the other. Her stars and moon tattoo danced down her shoulder with the movement. "I needed you. And now I have you."

"For what?"

"For myself." She elegantly flicked a match across the box, watching the red flame sizzle. "And for Dorian."

Every moving cell in my body halted just before exploding into a sprint. I heard him say her name at that meeting, but it was still just as shocking to hear her admit it. "What?"

She lit the candles on the altar one at a time, watching each one like it was a pet she loved and cared for. "The moment I saw you, I saw what you could be. I saw all the things you could do—all the power you could hold. When you came strolling into my Sight, I had to seize that opportunity." She turned toward me and tossed the charred match in the dirt. "You have no idea how long I've waited for someone like you."

"But what did you see? Why does everyone keep saying I'll be powerful? I don't even know what they're talking about."

She tilted her head, her brown eyes and full smile radiating a smug confidence I'd only seen a glimmer of before. "A hybrid. Wolf *and* witch. Incredibly strong, and very rare. So rare, you may be the only one in existence when this is over."

My knees felt like they were rubber bands. "But I thought witches couldn't be wolves?"

"Also true. Over the years, I tried creating one of you. I tried from every angle I could think of—witches, hunters, wolves—but venom and earth magic just don't mix. What a waste." She frowned and tossed a few braids over her shoulder. "When I gave you your reading, I still didn't understand *how* you could turn, but then Anika saw your necklace, and I knew that was the key."

"How?"

"You're wearing the Maiden's Stone, and guess what kind of bloodline it's attached to?"

I waited, raising my brows expectantly. "I don't know."

"*Solstice Guardians.*"

My mouth fell open, and I reached for the pendant, smoothing my fingers over the sleek stone.

"Most of us believed the Maiden's Stone was just a legend —a symbol of sacrifice. We'd heard about it, seen drawings of it throughout the years, but didn't really know it was real until Anika felt it a few nights ago. As Solstice Guardians, it calls to us, but it can only be used by its intended bloodline."

I blinked, forcing myself to follow what she was saying. "I'm barely a witch. How can I be a Solstice Guardian?"

Lucille chuckled like I'd asked a dumb question. "You're not directly a Guardian, but you possess the pendant, which makes you a descendant. That means you're wearing an enormous amount of power. Power that can defy the rules of magic itself, and I'm betting it'll help you in your transition."

"But wouldn't my dad have known this? Why wouldn't he have told me?"

She sighed. "Goodness, I really thought he would have. Maybe he didn't, but I'm sure you've heard the story about the witch at Dead Man's Trail back home?"

I nodded. "The coven there was attacked and the leader was hung from the tree."

"Bingo. Bravo, love. It seems you're finally catching on." Lucille's emphatic claps echoed through the barn. "They hung your distant relative."

"But the story said there weren't any survivors," I argued.

"There was one. The witch's daughter. She saved her and placed her magic in that stone for her bloodline to use when they needed it most."

I leaned into my hands against the wall of air, steadying my balance. "This is freaking crazy. This can't be possible."

"And yet, it is." She shrugged one shoulder up and let it drop. "When I saw you outside my shop, I didn't know you had the Stone, I only knew you were facing two paths...one where you'd continue in ignorance, never knowing who you really were, and one where you could be a hybrid. So I read you, hoping you'd take the bait and go running to Aiden Daniels."

My face ran hot with a burst of anger. "And my path now? What is it?"

"Oddly enough, you still have two. Hybrid, or death."

My heart sank, roiling my anger into confusion.

The Seer had been truthful about my two paths, at least. He kept saying Dorian couldn't get his hands on me when he first found me—

And then I remembered what Dorian said at the meeting. Whatever he was planning, he needed an eclipse...unless he had a hybrid.

If he had me in his possession, he wouldn't have to wait.

I clenched my hands so tightly, my fingers went numb. "Why are you helping Dorian?" I demanded. "What's he trying to do?"

Lucille raised her chin. "My reasons are my own secrets to keep. The less you know, the better." She strode back toward the barn doors. "You have about six hours before night falls. I hope you're ready, love. It would be a huge waste if you didn't make it."

"Wait. No," I called out, hands shaking, and my gut rolling. "I can't go through this *alone*."

Her face held its somber expression. "You'll have to. Nobody's coming for you. Aiden will try, but he'll never see past the cloaking candle." With one last pitying look at me, she turned back around and gracefully waltzed out the door.

"Wait!" I banged my palms against the shield again. "No! I can't do this here!"

But she wasn't coming back.

I sank to my knees in the dirt as hot tears welled in my eyes. Clutching my fingers around the red pendant, I looked at the afternoon sky outside. Terror knit its way through every part of me.

What was I going to do? The only peace of mind I'd had lately was knowing Aiden would be with me. He was *supposed* to be with me the whole time.

He was probably looking for me. I knew he would be—

And then I remembered Pete, and the guilt of not thinking of him sooner was so heavy. My mind flashed through how we left him...on the floor, helpless and unable to move.

I hoped Aiden found him in time. I hoped Nat could work a miracle for him.

I hoped for so many things right now.

My heart pounded against my ribs, and I curled my knees to my chest. It wasn't even dark outside, and I was already falling apart.

How was I supposed to survive this alone?

27

I huddled on the floor, clenching my side. My throat was parched and my body drained from too many panic attacks to count. I wished I could remember the things my counselor had gone over to remedy those, but that seemed like years ago already.

The sky was already darkening through the barn doors, and another surge of fear bubbled up. Soon, the worst night of my life would ensue...one I still wasn't sure I could survive.

How was I supposed to *connect to myself* when I was a freaking prisoner, waiting to be handed over to Dorian for who *knows* what?

I bit down on my lip until I felt the pinch and tasted tinny blood. Suddenly, I couldn't fault the Seer for trying to kill me before. He was only doing what he could to stop Dorian and protect everyone else. It wasn't anything personal.

Now, I almost wished he'd succeeded.

"It's almost time." Anika's light voice traveled through the barn. She carried a bottle of water in one hand and a plate in the other. "Are you excited? I am."

"Go to hell," I mumbled.

She laughed and set the water and plate inside the circle. "Eat up. You need as much strength for tonight as you can manage."

I sat up warily and reached for the plate, but instead of taking her advice, I threw the porcelain saucer at her. It only hit the salt barrier wall and fell back into the dirt.

"Oh," she pouted. "Poor little hybrid. Throwing a fit because you can't get your way."

"You know what?" I clenched my teeth. "I hope I die, just to piss you off."

Anika frowned. "We'll see. When it comes down to the moment where someone chooses to live or die, everyone chooses life. And judging by your survival instincts, I know you'll come through."

"But it's not my *choice*, is it?"

Her lips pursed, and she folded her arms, staring at me wordlessly. I knew I had her there. She didn't even know how all this worked.

"That's what I thought," I said with a spiteful smirk, determined to make her regret ever taking me.

Anika huffed and walked out, throwing me an icy glare before she tugged the double doors shut, leaving me completely alone in the wide-open space.

I dug my fingers into the grainy dirt, contemplating trying to dig a hole straight to the other side of the earth. But even then, I wouldn't be able to get out of the salt ring. They were pretty much unbreakable, except by the hand of the witch that created it.

Inhaling a sharp breath, I sat back on my heels. Worst possible case, I could give up. Death might not be so bad compared to being in Dorian's captivity.

But deep down, I knew I wouldn't do that. And Aiden would want me to fight through, even if he knew I could get passed over to an Ancient. Because he would still try to come for me. Still try to save me.

The breeze outside picked up, rustling the trees around and drifting through the creaky wooden walls. It swirled past me, kicking the ends of my hair over my sweaty shoulders and taking some pieces of hay with it.

I rubbed my hands over my arms, trying to calm the hairs standing on end, but something felt...different. The air had changed somehow. It was thicker...mustier.

A rush of heat flooded under my skin, like I stood directly in the sun's rays, and sweat beaded over my arms and my face. I wiped my hand down my neck as a tingle traveled from the top of my head down to the ends of my toes. Everything tensed.

I needed to move.

I got up, even though I was trapped inside this circle that could only fit about two of me. But a sudden pain snapped up through my back, and I fell to my knees with a scream. Within a second, another jolt shot from my neck to my tailbone, like someone was trying to pry my spine from my body.

My palms slammed into the dirt, and my arms shook as I leaned on them. The ground tilted, and the stale air scraped like gravel down my esophagus.

Oh, no.

My transition was starting, and if this was only the beginning, I didn't know how I'd get through without help. It was already a level of agony I'd never experienced before.

Drawing in as many deep breaths as I could, I tried concentrating on the spells Dad taught me to calm my pulse, but another sharp, stabbing pain wrenched through my arms. They gave out, plummeting my face into the ground.

My cheek throbbed. I rolled onto my side, clenching up into a ball. The edges of the barn doors fuzzed in my vision. I closed my eyes, pretending to be back in the cabin beside Aiden. Pretending nothing like this was going on, and that I was still completely, wonderfully human.

I pictured myself back in school with my classmates, and at my rehearsals with Ms. Felicity.

Then I thought about Mom. An ache clawed through me, like a fist gripping my sternum.

My thoughts went back to when she took me to the beach the weekend after Dad left. She said we needed an escape from reality, and that it was okay to do that sometimes.

Despite our family officially falling apart that week, that was one of the best trips we'd ever had. We cried together, watched movies, ate more than we should have, and we found a small bit of healing together.

"Honey?"

Mom's voice startled me, like I heard it audibly with my own ears. I opened my eyes—or thought I did, anyway. Everything still seemed blurry, but Mom stood there, right outside my salt circle.

My heart jolted, and I reached for her. "Mom? How are you here?"

She smiled faintly, but her skin was sallow, her brown eyes shadowed with sadness. She knelt down out of my reach. "Why did you leave me, Sydney?"

"What?" I stared at her. Was she really here? The person in front of me looked like her, down to the frown lines and beauty mark on her cheek, but Mom wouldn't ask me that. Would she? "Mom, I need help. I need to get out of here."

"That's what you said before you left. That you needed space. You needed to get out. And you did. Now look where you are."

"Mom," I choked out. "I told you, I had a good reason. I did it for you—"

"You did it for you." She shook her head, her eyes turning

down. They seemed so much darker than before. "You left me alone."

My heart pinballed down to my stomach. "I didn't want to."

"Don't lie to me. You resented me for pushing you toward college, and now you're making me pay for it. You left me, just like your father did. I hope you're happy." She glared at me like she could see into my soul.

But Mom would never talk to me like that. If she were really here, she'd help me. She'd put me first, like I did for her when I left.

"I kept you safe," I whispered, letting my hand drop to the ground. "I can't—I *won't*—feel guilty for that. It was the right thing to do."

"She'll never see it that way."

I forced my head to turn to see who was behind me. Dad stood there, hands in pockets. He looked at Mom, and then down at me.

"Dad?" I looked back and forth between them, my pulse rushing in my temples.

"You hurt her," he said. "You told her you were with me, and then never called her. Now you'll never get to tell her why, and I'll have to pick up the pieces."

Mom nodded, sitting down and folding her arms around her knees. "You were so selfish."

My lip quivered uncontrollably. "I wasn't!" Was I?

I looked at Dad again. "You told me to leave."

"I told you to stay with me. Not Aiden. Maybe if you had, you wouldn't be stuck here, waiting for death. Maybe we could have mended things, and you could have been there for your mother." Dad knelt down onto his knees, resting back on his heels. "You failed us."

"I tried to do what was best!" A cold ache dug through my chest as a hot tear rolled from my eye. "Please, help me."

"You can only help yourself now," Mom said.

"How—" Another angry burst of pain bolted through me, whipping my head back. My skin pulled tight against my muscles, and I breathed heavily, gritting my teeth through another wave until it was over.

I looked up at Dad, extending my hand out to him, but the invisible wall stood in my way. It was as if not being able to reach either of them gave me clarity. They weren't really here. They were the pieces of my guilt and resentment coming to life, and I couldn't let them take over.

I wasn't selfish. And as I stared at Dad, I guess I understood a little about why he left. Not the part about his affair, and his absence—that was totally worthy of the Worst Dad Ever award—but if he was keeping us from the supernatural world, it made a little more sense.

Mom and Dad were quiet, watching me like they were waiting for something.

I let myself collapse back onto the ground, my body already shaking with fatigue, but my pulse softened. "Dad, I forgive you. I'm still totally bitter about Cindy and you not being there, but I know you're trying now. And Mom...I know I hurt you. I'm so sorry, but I did it for you. I did it for myself, too, and there's nothing wrong with that."

The exhaustion pulled on my eyelids, and I closed my eyes for a few seconds, or maybe hours. But when I opened them, Mom and Dad were gone, and all I could do now was wait for the next round of torture.

And it delivered.

At some point, I passed out from the pain and dizziness.

When I opened my eyes, I pounded my fist weakly against the ground. Nothing about my body had changed yet, and the sky was still oily black through the slits in the barn walls.

What was all this pain for if nothing was changing?

So far, I'd gone through a nightmare where I was drowning, and another where I fought off a hundred nonexistent rats so hard, my arms burned with red welts from my own nails.

I let out a groan, my eyes registering over the curls of smoke dissipating from the candles.

Then a shadow moved from the far corner of the barn. I sucked in a sharp gasp, frantically searching over the pile of straw billowing against the wall, but there was nothing there.

"It's all in your head," I muttered to myself. I had to remember that. But then I saw it again. A flash of something, like a ghost.

I whipped my head to the right, the tendons in my neck screaming against the movement. My eyes snapped open wide, and my chest jolted with horror.

Dorian.

He stood beside the candle-lit table, in the form of the first hologram from the meeting. He took a step forward, wearing big black boots that pounded heavily into the dirt. His white shirt reflected an ethereal glow, and his blonde hair hung down to his collarbones, surrounding sharp cheeks and even sharper eyes. They held no kindness, but cooled to a polar blue.

How could he be here? Had Lucille brought him? Was he going to take me?

I couldn't let him. But I could hardly move.

I fought against the excruciating throbbing and rolled back, trying to distance myself from him. My fingernails raked the ground, and my pulse rammed hot blood through my veins like a roaring train going full speed.

I had to run. For my life. For Aiden's life.

He kept moving closer, examining me like I was a pathetic pawn in his game.

"Stay away from me," I stammered. I closed my eyes tight and opened them, but he was still there. His eyes traipsed down my body, and he lowered himself to one knee.

"I'm pleased with your progress," he said smoothly.

"Please. Don't." I didn't know what else to say. All I knew was I didn't want him anywhere near me.

"Your begging has no effect," he said. "You're wasting precious oxygen that you need to survive this." He carefully stretched his long fingers out toward me, and my eyes followed his reach as panic burst in my lungs. "Don't touch me!"

He stopped abruptly at the salt circle, pausing for a moment before letting his wrist fall. "You're *terrified*."

Dizziness clouded my head. Black dots stamped the edges of my vision. Was he even real?

A small frown line crinkled by his mouth. "I find it fascinating—poetic, even—that you'll be aiding in my ritual, considering I'm using your Alpha mate as well."

A sudden, fiery wave washed through me, adding to the tremors in my shoulders. "I swear, if you touch him—"

"What?" Dorian tilted his head, his hair sweeping down his shoulder. "There's nothing you can do. You know that." His words came out gently, like someone consoling a child. "I'll have you in my possession already, and just before the ritual, I'll find him again. My army will be stronger. He won't be able to fight us off. Or maybe he'll make it easy and give himself up, hoping I'll let you live." His long lips curled up into a subtle, wicked smile. "Hm. My money is on that last one."

The violent anger built inside me like a volcano about to explode. "Stay away from him," I spat, clumsily turning onto my side to face him.

"Your mate will die a slow, agonizing death."

"Shut up!" I let my rage take hold of me. Ignoring the pain and weakness consuming my body, I struck my fist toward him, but it cracked against the shield. My hand went limp, and a pulsing blaze traveled up my arm. I folded in on myself, clinging to my immovable bones.

Dorian clicked his tongue. "Now look what you did. That's probably shattered."

"Screw you," I growled, baring my teeth like a wild animal. "I swear, I will kill you."

"You may try. But I'm an Ancient. I'm untouchable."

But that wasn't what the Seer had said. I hoped with everything in me he was right when he said I could be powerful enough to kill Dorian. Only time would tell.

"You won't be," Dorian said, as if he'd heard my thoughts.

Was he really here? Or was my mind playing tricks on me?

I was about to respond when my insides snapped again, like an axe pummeling into my midsection. This time, multiple things crackled, the pain unbearable. My vessels pumped, pounding in my head, and my insides churned with a vengeance.

I leaned onto my hand and knees, retching against the acid coming up my throat. When I opened my eyes, the dirt was wet with crimson spatters underneath me.

Blood. Was that supposed to happen?

I strangled out a gasp, wiping my forearm across my mouth. Red smears covered my skin, and I sank down onto my side again.

I reached for my necklace. It hadn't hummed or glowed since last night, and I wasn't sure it ever would again.

I was alone in this. My last bit of hope drained away as I stared ahead at Dorian.

"You're letting yourself die." His voice cut through the barn again.

"Maybe that's a good thing," I whispered.

"But if you die, you can't protect him. Remember? I'll still use him. I'll just have to wait for the eclipse."

Another surge of hopelessness filled every inch of my body. Aiden wouldn't be safe, no matter what, and there was a growing chance I couldn't be there for him.

It was all too much.

"I can't do this," I whispered raggedly.

Dorian's outline flickered as he stared at me, like the corners of my mind trying to rid him from where he knelt.

"Wait…you're not real."

"I'm as real as your mind will let me be. And right now, your mind is winning."

"You know, if you'd just let me kill your boy-toy, none of this would have happened to you," said a sparkly voice I'd recognize anywhere.

Liv's sandaled and perfectly pedicured feet stepped into my line of sight. She looked down at me, wearing shorts and a pink crop top. "Babe, you look awful."

I let out a weak gasp, unsure if I was relieved or afraid of her being here. But she couldn't be. The Liv I knew wouldn't let me suffer here, waiting to die.

She wasn't real.

"Are you sure?" she asked.

"No," I whispered. Time seemed to blur, making everything fuzzy.

"You blame me," Liv said, sitting crisscross in the dirt and resting her chin in her palm. "But if you'd let Aiden die—"

"Stop." My anger spiraled through me again. "This isn't Aiden's fault. You were the one who betrayed me. You ruined our friendship over this, and your family was the link to Dorian."

I glanced around to see if he was still here, but it was just me and the figment of Liv.

"I told you I didn't know," she argued. "I told you I was protecting you. Why can't you get that through your head?"

"Because you were going to kill him. You didn't even know him. He saved me, and he was there for me while you led us into this huge trap."

She twisted her bright red lips. "It's just like you to hold grudges."

I jerked, digging my fingers into the dirt. "Can you blame me?"

"I guess not, but you carry these hatchets around, and eventually they're going to get too heavy."

I inhaled shakily. That was probably the truest thing I'd heard all day. "I know."

"Do you? It's already too much. Look at you. You're a mess." She shook her head, her green eyes softening with pity. "You need to forgive—and not just me."

"Who else?" My voice came out thick and raspy. "I forgave Dad. I'm working on it with you. You apologized, and I got you a place to stay. Why would I do that if I haven't forgiven you at least a little?"

She didn't answer, and I wasn't sure how long we stared at each other. I swore she blinked in and out at one point.

Then something slammed behind me, wafting fresh air over my face and jarring me from my swimmy vision. I forced myself to turn over, my arms and legs going limp like they weren't attached to my body anymore.

I got a glimpse of the obsidian sky before Anika and Lucille shut the doors with a bang. Their eyes were wide, and they jerked the wooden beam down across the doors, locking us in.

"I'll keep the candle going," Anika shouted, running to the table.

"It doesn't matter anymore," Lucille snapped. "Just make sure they don't take her."

They?

Who was she talking about?

"How did they even find us? I did the cloaking spell, and I always do them right." Lucille glanced over at Anika, who moved over to where I lay, crumpled on the floor.

She staggered her feet in a defensive stance and shook her head. "Wait." She paused, her face flushing with shock. A curse flew from her mouth as she stared down at her hand. "My ring. She took my ring off and—"

"And you didn't remember to take it with you?" Lucille's face tightened, fire lighting her eyes. "Idiot."

A low growl drifted around somewhere outside the barn, and Anika flicked her fingers out, shooting small sparks of light again.

Then a white wolf burst through the barn siding, splintering the beams into a broken mess that clattered to the floor.

28

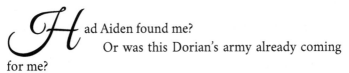

ad Aiden found me?

Or was this Dorian's army already coming for me?

I didn't have time to process the chaos around us as an explosion of anguish poured through me again. My spine straightened with a jolt, throwing me onto my back. Screams erupted through the barn, and it took several echoes for me to figure out they were my own.

I clenched my fingers into the ground, holding on to anything I could to keep my body anchored through the pain.

"You should give up," a voice said right by my ear. Startled, I turned my head. My eyes widened, and even through the blast of magical lights against the ceiling and the yelling around me, I could only see who was with me in the circle.

She stared at me with the same brown eyes I saw every day in the mirror. The same golden tones reflected in her light brown skin, and her hair fell down her shoulders in soft curls. Just like mine.

She matched me. She *was* me.

"You're weak, and you know it," she said.

Even her voice was the same.

My mouth opened, but I couldn't speak as I stared at her.

"Do you really want to be a burden to everyone around you? Especially to Aiden?"

"No," I finally managed to get out. "I'm not."

"But you are." She leaned over and touched her finger to the middle of my forehead, sending a splitting ache through my skull. I cried out above the crashing and snarling around me.

Somewhere in the distance, I heard Liv's voice yelling above the din.

Anika screamed from a few feet away, throwing her arms in wide circles and smashing the white wolf into the ground. The wolf yelped, but rolled up to its feet. It looked over at me, and as soon as those gold eyes flashed, I recognized her as Sasha. She turned back to Anika and swerved just in time to dodge another burst of lethal magic.

"You know, Becca might be better for him," my clone said, like there was nothing else happening around us. "She's gorgeous. A full-blooded wolf." Her soft voice drifted over my face. "She was born for this life. You weren't. Why would he want you when you're such a mess?" Still leaning over me, she pursed her lips tightly, indenting the same dimple in her temple that I'd had since I was a child. Her hair canopied down from her face, dangling over me, close enough to touch.

I reached up, trying to grasp a piece of her hair, just to make sure she wasn't real. Maybe I'd already died, and now I could see myself out of my body.

Without a warning, her hand shot down to my ribs, cracking them visibly underneath my tank top. Horror filled me as the bones splintered, taking shape into something gruesome through my skin. I screamed through the breaking, my body going limp until she stood up and kicked me in the side. Each rib cracked, one by one, and I thrust over, sucking dry air down my throat.

"You'll never be enough for him." Her footsteps slowly moved around me, stopping at my feet. "He just hasn't had enough time to realize what a mistake he made when he saved you from that car."

She knelt down and touched my kneecap, wrenching it backward and ricocheting lightning up my leg. I screamed, twisting again onto my stomach, unable to control my joints. They snapped back and forth, splintering like they were trying to spring from my body.

A thud and cloud of dirt brushed past me, clearing to show the glint of red hair that had crossed over the circle, scattering the salt. Anika sprawled face-up, her eyes blank and blood soaking through her shirt.

Liv and Aiden stood over her, scratched and smeared with their own blood, but they didn't hesitate to kick back into action.

"I'll help track Lucille," Liv said, sparing me a quick, horrified glance before running through the open side of the barn.

Aiden dove to my side, skidding in the dirt. I felt his hand gently land on my back, but was it really him? Or was this another trick my mind was playing?

I didn't have time to figure it out. A crushing pain erupted through my back again, and I screamed. It was the only sound in the barn now, besides Aiden's voice.

"Fight through it," he said.

"Or don't," my twin said.

"Stop," I cried out, breathing hot, shallow breaths.

Everything went quiet, and I felt tender hands roll me onto my back.

"Sydney." Aiden's voice loomed over me. It was clear and

filled my head like he was really with me. "Open your eyes. Look at me."

My hand was raised from the ground, shooting new pain up my arm, but it was nothing compared to what I'd gone through so far.

"Sydney!" Something about the raw desperation in his voice made me pry my eyes open.

Aiden's turquoise eyes hovered over me, glowing and pulsing like a steady heartbeat. His hands reached for mine. They were so warm, but I still couldn't be sure if I was imagining him being with me.

"You're not really here, are you?" My voice scratched my throat like tiny razor blades.

"I'm here. I'm right here. Don't you feel the bond?" Still holding my hand, he touched my cheek. For a few seconds, the pain subsided, letting the soft hum of the bond through.

"Is she...?" Omar asked from somewhere nearby.

"I don't know." Aiden held his eyes on me as he answered. "It's like her body's rejecting the change, but I can't tell."

My heart sank at his words.

"I'm sorry, Aiden," Omar spoke again. After a few seconds, he added, "Witches can't be wolves."

Aiden ignored him, clasping his hands tighter over mine. "Syd, please fight it."

I thought I *was* fighting it. I'd been fighting through the guilt. I'd even tried some of those spells Dad taught me. What more was there to do?

"Told you. You're weak," my moving reflection taunted again from beside me. "Weak and worthless."

"Stop," I said, looking up at the other me.

"You never thought you had that much worth either," she said. "After all, I'm you. I can't tell you anything you don't already know."

Aiden tracked my line of sight up to my duplicate and

255

then back down to my face. "Syd, listen to me. There's no one there. Whatever you're seeing is part of the shift. You can't let it win. Fight for yourself."

My reflection's features softened as she studied Aiden, but she pinned me with her stony expression once again. "He might love you now, but he'll realize what you really are, eventually. He can't love you like this. You're broken."

Wasn't everyone?

Her words rattled through my head.

Maybe I was broken—I had been for a long time, in so many ways—but I still had a purpose. I still had worth. My failures and fractured relationships couldn't define me the way I let them before.

It wouldn't work to rely on anyone else for strength and purpose. I needed to rely on myself. And I could.

I *would.*

Everything went quiet, except for Aiden's ragged breaths over me.

When I opened my eyes again, my evil alter-ego was gone, and the only ones there were Aiden and Omar.

Aiden looked over me with pale cheeks and pooling tears in his eyes. I thought my heart might rip through my chest. I hated seeing him in pain, and as much as I wanted to win this for him, I wanted it more for myself.

A burst of red light flooded over Aiden and draped over the ceiling. My pendant vibrated against me, and I almost couldn't breathe from how much relief sank in my bones.

Aiden glanced over me, a hopeful smile tracing his lips as he frantically curled his hand under my neck. "You're going to be fine. You're going to—"

My body convulsed, jerking my arms and legs with sickening cracks. But the movements weren't painful anymore. They were like a release.

"Aiden, get back," Omar yelled, pulling him away from me. "She needs space."

Aiden's hands dragged down my arm, unwilling to let go. My body turned with his pull until his hands lost their grip on my fingertips.

I lay on my side. The pain was gone, my body either numb or healing.

My heartbeat picked up. The air suddenly slid into my chest easily.

A cool pressure balled in my core, spreading out to my limbs. It was potent and powerful. Everything buzzed with a current of new energy. My eyes snapped open wider; the world now covered in a tinted purple hue.

I turned onto my stomach and pushed up on my hands. Rich bronze fur covered my arms. My fingers shortened and thin claws grew at the tips where my nails should have been.

My clothes snapped and tore until they fell in strips on the ground.

By instinct, I stood up on shaky legs, but steadied within a few seconds on four paws. Then I let a howl rip through the air that had been dying to release since the day I was marked.

Dust stirred around me, and I glanced at Omar and Aiden. Pure shock settled on both their faces. I wanted to stay there and bask in it, but something outside called to me.

Without hesitation, my legs burst into a run. The wind whipped against me, ruffling my fur as I broke free from the confines of the barn. I dodged through the trees, not sure where I was going—all I knew was I had to get there.

I passed an old cottage with a lush garden that filled the entire yard. My senses exploded with the smells of herbs and cinnamon, and something else...*magic*. I wasn't sure how I knew that, but I did. That must have been where Anika and Lucille had been staying. Or maybe where they lived.

Pushing myself to get away from there faster, I savored

the full extension of my muscles, powering forward with an agility I'd never known before. The dirt around me kicked up, and I could smell and see every individual fleck. I could hear everything within miles.

Something sped behind me. Four other paws pounded the dirt until Aiden appeared beside me. Even though he blended in with the night, I saw him in vivid shades of black and purple. He glanced at me with those familiar aqua eyes I adored and closed the space between us, bounding fluidly beside me.

The bond fluttered in my chest, and for a second, I thought my heart would crack open from how happy I was to feel this freedom with him. It was unlike anything else. I never wanted it to end.

I wasn't sure how long we ran for, but it was enough distance to pass by a couple towns and into Shadow Grove. We dodged through the trees along the mountain, and then I veered off toward Havenport.

The closer I came to the city limits, the more something pulled at me, leading me down a path only I could see. I darted down a gravel road, hurtling over a dip in the metal fence surrounding thick woods.

I sped faster, raking dirt back with every strike against the ground. Aiden kept pace with me the whole time. His breaths were strong and even, but his muscles probably burned pleasantly like mine did.

Whatever pulled me loosened its grip. My sprint turned to a jog, and I continued to slow until I came to the Weeping Witch's Tree at Dead Man's Trail.

The charred bark on the tree stood out against the shadows, and its ugly branches contorted down and out, almost like they reached for me. As I approached the tree, a heaviness and a newfound gratitude settled in my chest.

I had no idea when Trevor told us that story a month ago

that it was true, and that it was about *my* ancestors. A tear filled in each eye, and I leaned against the tree, letting a droplet fall.

My racing heart slowed, seeming to trigger another change in my body. The fur shortened, almost itching, until it disappeared under smooth skin. I grabbed the tree to steady myself, suddenly aware of how naked I was.

Aiden's paws softly trod the ground behind me, but he stopped abruptly when a hazy glow evaporated off my necklace.

The sparkling smoke drifted around me like fireflies spreading out and funneling into my fingertips. Soft light soaked into my pores until my body gleamed like sunshine. A mix of warmth and elation stirred inside me. Then everything was peaceful.

And I was exhausted.

My legs buckled, and I let the fatigue take me down to my knees. Warmth continued spreading through me, like the magic from the necklace wound itself through my DNA.

I fell forward on my hands, and then my arms gave way, but I didn't hit the dirt hard. It was as if something laid me down gently, lulling me into a deep sleep.

*T*he bumpiness of a gravel driveway jolted me awake. A soft blanket was wrapped around me, and the pressure of a sturdy hand rested on my shoulder. My pillow was incredibly warm, and when I opened my eyes, I realized it was Aiden's leg—covered in wrinkled denim, thankfully. As I turned my head to search for his face, he smiled down at me warily, a small wrinkle forming between his brows. He cupped my shoulder with his hand. "Hey."

"Hi," I replied hoarsely.

"You're awake?" Omar asked brightly from the driver's seat. He stopped the car and twisted around, grinning so wide I could see all of his pearly teeth. But his smile quickly faltered into a flat line. "Whoa."

"What?" I asked, sitting up with ease, and realizing I was totally naked under the blanket. I clasped it tightly beneath my armpits and glanced between Aiden and Omar. "What's wrong?"

"Nothing's wrong." Aiden shot Omar a sharp look. "We have a lot to catch up on."

"Right." Omar waved his hand and looked ahead at a

secluded two-story house with a faded green door and dark-ened siding from years of weather damage. The gutter hung off the left side of the roof, and jagged cracks filled most of the windows. The porch could have used some new boards, too. "This is your stop."

"Where are we?" I asked, tilting my head down to get a better look through the windshield.

"Home," Aiden said, getting out of the car and holding his hand out to me.

"Home?" I eyed him suspiciously as I slid my fingers into his palm. When I climbed out of the car, my foot landed on the bottom of the tent-sized blanket, and I shrieked at almost giving Aiden and Omar a peep show. After a few more seconds of struggling, Aiden scooped me up in his bare arms.

I draped my arm around his shoulders. "I can walk myself."

He smirked. "I know."

"I'll see you kids later," Omar said over the top of the rolled-down window. He switched the car into drive, looping it around the vast gravel that spread out to the surrounding trees.

Aiden walked us past a few cars and his truck, taking his time up the squeaky porch steps. I had so many questions about where we were and who else was here, but at the moment, all I really cared about was being with him again and knowing he was safe.

I leaned my head against his shoulder, concentrating on all the emotions flowing between us. They built until I thought I'd combust, all of them amounting to a quiet desperation.

He glanced down at me when we reached the door. "Before we go in, I want you to keep an open mind, okay?"

I cupped my fingers around the back of his neck. "I honestly don't care where we are, as long we're together."

261

A relieved smile crossed his lips. "Keep that in mind."

He pushed the door open and stepped in, and a pungent, earthy smell rushed at me. The room was big, but there was a massive hole in the drywall straight ahead where pipes and wires hung down. Yellow stains covered the corners of the ceiling, and I didn't even want to know what made the carpet visibly crusty.

"Wow," I gasped. "You weren't kidding."

"Nope." Aiden kicked the door shut, scattering down grains of drywall with the impact. "We'll have help fixing it up. I was thinking for that wall over there we could install a built-in bookshelf. We'll have to go get the rest of your books though. I didn't have time to grab them. We can rip up that carpet and expose the hardwoods. They'll need some work but it will look a lot better."

He rambled on about his plans for the dining room and kitchen, which I was terrified to see. As he kept talking, I got the feeling he was avoiding telling me what was going on.

"Aiden," I interrupted as soon as he started talking about recessed lighting. I reached up and turned his face toward mine. "Why are we here? If it's because I ruined your house, I'm so—"

"Don't even think about apologizing," he said, voice gravelly. "I would gladly let the entire house burn to the ground if it meant you were safe."

"But your furniture...your *guitar*. You loved that guitar."

"I love *you*. I can always build a new guitar, but I can't build a new you."

He held my stare as I trailed my finger down his smooth jaw, sinking into his arms a little more.

After a moment, he took me through the massive room, turning left up the staircase. "I'll show you our room."

The stairs squeaked under his feet and the wallpaper peeled up around the edges of the hallway. We got to the second floor, and a soft, musty draft swept down my arms as we passed five bedrooms.

Aiden took us into the last one on the right. The drywall was cracked in spidery lines in the far corner, but the way the afternoon light spilled through the window made it feel more open.

Our bed sat against the wall, facing out to the middle of the room. To my surprise, our sheets and disheveled navy comforter were still on it.

He set me down on the edge of the mattress, and I squeezed my fingers into the silky fabric. I desperately wanted to climb under and sleep, but I wanted answers first...and a shower.

I opened my mouth to ask another question, but Aiden's stormy eyes stopped me. Their blue depths pooled as he studied my face. The wrinkle between his brows pinched the way it always did when something was wrong.

The bed dipped under his weight as he sat down to face me, and his hand softly met my cheek. He leaned in and tilted his forehead against mine.

My heart clenched, needing to be closer. I was halfway unsure if he was really here or if I was still a victim of my own mind. Clasping my fingers around his wrists, I took in the humming bond wherever we touched.

I was still alive. He was real. And I could feel every drop of guilt and relief rolling through him.

"I thought I lost you," he said shakily. "I'm so sorry. I'm sorry I didn't get there in time. I'm sorry I didn't listen when you wanted to leave."

"You can't blame yourself for what happened," I whispered.

He blinked, clearing his eyes before they welled again. "Your blood was on the floor. I went crazy not knowing where you were or if you were even alive. And Pete was so bad off."

My stomach turned, picturing Pete laying on the floor, panting. Unable to move. "How is he now? Please tell me he's okay."

"He will be. Nat's been healing him. He can already walk with some help."

"Good." I sighed, my shoulders melting back down. "Will we get to see him soon?"

"At the meeting tonight, with the others." He paused, leaning back but staying close enough that I could feel his uneven breaths skate down my neck. "When you were taken, I called Liv first."

"*You* called Liv?"

He nodded, his face stone serious. "I had to find you, and I *knew* she and your dad would want to find you as much as I did. We got Omar, and then Sasha, when she wasn't helping Pete. I couldn't trust my pack anymore after that stunt Manny pulled. It split everyone up."

I glanced around the airy room. "Is that why we're here?"

He paused, raking his teeth over his bottom lip. "Yeah. I left the pack."

My pulse sped. "You left?"

"I had to. I'll never stand with a pack who treats someone I care about like that."

"But you were supposed to be Alpha. How do you just leave that?"

"The pack bond is strong, but fragile, too. I severed it when I renounced my dad as my Alpha."

My brain reeled. I couldn't believe what I was hearing.

"Manny and Becca made such a mess. Some of the pack members stayed behind, but a few followed me out. There are some others who haven't left yet after renouncing my dad, too."

"How did you get this house so fast? And where will the others stay?"

"Your dad has some investment properties. This was one of them. He said he'd planned on flipping it."

That sounded like Dad. Always looking for business opportunities.

"You should know...the pack members that left with me are staying here too."

"Oh." What would that even look like to have so many people staying under one roof? "Where are they now?"

"Theresa and Nat are at Pete's. They'll be back and forth until he's well enough to move over here. Then we have Sierra, Kyle, and Quon. They helped move our bed here. Figured you'd need some rest."

I smiled. Theresa and Nat were probably my favorites, besides Pete. The others, I didn't know, but I was glad to have on our side. "What does this mean for your Alpha role?"

Aiden's hands draped down to my shoulders. "I won't be taking over the Shadow Pack anymore. I severed that tie when I left. But I'll be Alpha on the Blood Moon to this crew."

"But your family—"

"My family will be fine without me." His tone hardened. "Mom was on my side, but she's staying with Dad. She said she'd try to get through to him, but it doesn't matter. He's not going to change, and the wolves staying with him won't either." He slid his hands down to mine, grasping them tightly. "We're right where we're supposed to be."

"Okay." I laced our fingers together until we were both holding onto each other like we were about to fall off the edge of a cliff. How could everything change so quickly in a matter of one day? "This is a lot to process."

Aiden smiled faintly, his features shifting to the unreadable expression he used to give me all the time. His smile fell away and his eyes filled with unspoken thoughts.

By now, I'd learned this look meant he wanted to talk about something, but didn't know how.

"What is it?" I asked.

He squeezed my hand like a reflex. "You don't look like we expected. You still look like you, but your eyes are...different."

"Different how? They're not gold like Pete's or Sasha's?"

Aiden shook his head slowly. "Do you want to see?"

Not really. I probably looked like a hot mess, just based on the tangy smell of blood and salt on my skin, but I needed to suck it up and face the new me, whoever that was now.

Aiden leaned in and brushed his lips across mine, lingering at the corner of my mouth for a few seconds. "Come on."

He led me across the room to another door that opened into a bathroom. It had a wide mirror and a yellowed sink, with faded green wallpaper surrounding the walls.

Aiden shifted out of the way, nudging me up to the counter. My gaze started at the white blanket around me, working up to the smears of blood and dirt on my cheeks. Then I stopped at my eyes.

My breath hitched. "Holy crap."

My eyes were a deep, astonishing violet, like two galactic explosions held inside my irises. There was no way people wouldn't notice how unique they were at first glance.

"They're *purple*?" My voice carried up an octave, realizing that's what Omar gasped at in the car. "I look like a freak."

"No. You're beautiful. I loved your brown eyes, but I love these too." Aiden brushed back a few tangled curls from my shoulder and looped his finger under my necklace chain, which had somehow stayed on, even during my shift. "I think it has something to do with this, and whatever happened at the tree. Why did you go to Dead Man's Trail? Do you remember?"

"It seems familiar." I rested my palms on the countertop, peeling my gaze away from myself and staring at my dirt-caked fingernails. Somewhere in the back of my mind, I caught pictures of the trail. The charred tree. The exhaustion that came over me. But what else? "It's a little fuzzy. I just remember wanting to sleep."

"You touched the tree, and then I swear the air sparkled around you," Aiden said. "We need to figure out what's happening before too many people ask questions. I need to know what to tell the pack members staying here. They're going to notice."

There was only one explanation for what happened at the tree and my purple eyes. Lucille's Sight had been right, and I was pretty sure that was the same thing the Seer saw, too.

"I think I already know what it all means." I looked up at Aiden's reflection. He stood beside me, raising his brows expectantly. "I'm a hybrid."

30

"*A* hybrid." Aiden's voice remained completely level, like he was in some sort of trance. The color in his complexion slowly drained down his neck as he processed my words.

I was a hybrid now, having fully shifted as a werewolf, and I had ancestral magic from the pendant Gigi gave me.

"Are you sure?"

I turned to face Aiden. "That's what Lucille said. I wasn't sure I believed her before, but I do now." I went on to explain my connection to the trail and Lucille's reading. By the time I finished, Aiden was sitting on the edge of the tub in shock.

He cursed under his breath. "No way. What are the chances that *that* witch is your ancestor?"

"Does it matter?"

He shook his head. "Not really. I just can't believe it. Your family goes back to Dead Man's Trail and that coven leader."

Now that he said it out loud, things started clicking. "The last time I went there, I had this really strange feeling. I was hot, but felt this cold draft down my skin the whole time. You don't think…"

"What? Ghosts?"

"I don't know. Maybe. There was something about that place, and at first, when you gave me my memories back, I thought it was because of the werewolf evidence left behind. But it was more than that."

Aiden dropped his hands and looked at the tiled floor. "When a witch that powerful dies violently and sacrificially, there's a lot of darkness left over. Sometimes, if most of a coven is taken out, that earth holds onto that magic. That might have been what you were feeling. The magic called to your Solstice blood."

"How do you know?"

"Because werewolves are tied to Dead Man's Trail, too. It backs up to the mountain my pack—my *dad's* pack—lives on. We had to know some of the history to stay there, and we decided to keep humans off the trail."

"Oh. Trevor did say the legend is a werewolf comes back every full moon to haunt the trail, but that's not true, is it? Those wolves spotted there were your pack members."

He nodded. "We aren't connected to the legend, but you know how people love a good ghost story." A long moment passed. "Syd, if you're a hybrid, that is...incredibly dangerous."

"Shocker." At this point, going out for ice cream was dangerous.

"No, I mean *dangerous*. Take how dangerous you think it is, and multiply that by a hundred."

Knots twisted in my stomach, and I leaned back against the wall. "Thinking like that doesn't help my anxiety."

"Shit...Syd...I'm so sorry." Using his max speed, he moved right in front of me and held me close. "I'm sorry for everything. I'm sorry I dragged you into this entire world. Over and over, I've thought back to that night where I failed to chase that hunter to the bridge. If I'd done what I was told, he never would have made it to the highway. He never would have gotten in your car. You could have gone home. You could still be safe. Away from me. Away from all of this."

I couldn't believe he was saying that. *Away from me?*

"No." My tone came out more forceful than intended, but I needed him to stop blaming himself.

Yes, my summer would have gone very differently if that accident never happened, but how long could I have had a normal life?

"My Gigi was a witch. Without knowing it, I was around magic every single day because of my necklace. She told me to wear it, and she had a reason. She knew something would happen. If it hadn't that night, then probably another time, and who knows if someone like you would have been there to help me? You might blame yourself, but you've been there for me. I will never regret you or blame you for any of this."

"You should."

I tilted my head up, bringing my hands up to his face. "I won't."

He didn't say anything for a long time.

When his arms finally let go of me, I wanted them back right away. The cold air rushed at my arms, and I knew he was about to leave me alone.

He cleared his throat and moved to the doorway. "I'm going to call Omar. We'll fill everyone in tonight. It's not for a few hours, so you can get cleaned up and rest."

"And eat some food?"

"I'll see if anyone brought some groceries over." He smiled weakly, but he didn't move.

I took a step toward him, wanting to ask him to stay. Last night may have taught me I was strong, and yeah, I might be a hybrid now, but I was kind of afraid of being alone.

"Are you okay?" he asked, turning the doorknob absently.

Clinging to the blanket, I ignored the anxiety-induced hammering in my chest. "Yeah. It's just a shower."

"Right." A hint of doubt settled in his features. Then he stepped out, leaving me alone with my fears and swaying emotions.

I got out of the shower to find my suitcase in the closet and a sandwich on the corner dresser, but no Aiden.

I paused, holding my towel around myself in the eerie quiet.

It was too quiet. Just like the barn had been when I saw everything that haunted me. My guilt with my parents, with Liv, and then Dorian...

We would never be safe until he was gone.

My pulse escalated as my mind started down dark roads I didn't want to go, and my hair dripped cold lines down my skin that unsettled me even more.

I threw my black shirt and leggings on, yanking the hem of my shirt down as I headed through the hallway. I needed to find Aiden. He had to still be here. He wouldn't have left me alone, would he?

No...he'd never do that. Not when we'd just gotten here.

Unless someone had already come for him.

"Aiden?" I called out, checking the vacant bedrooms. My palms were clammy and my stomach churned as I ran down the stairs.

My feet hit the tattered carpet at the bottom of the steps, and I scanned the empty room. I was probably being super irrational, but the air grew suffocatingly silent.

"Aiden?" I lunged to the front door, and as I reached for the handle, he came around the corner from the dining room. He stopped right beside a pile of tile and broken wood, wearing a black t-shirt and shorts.

"What's wrong?" he asked urgently. "I was out back and I felt you panicking just now."

My chest heaved in dusty air, and I dropped my hand from the door. "I didn't know where you were."

"I'm right here." He moved across the room until he stood right in front of me, pressing his hands around both of mine. "Syd, you're shaking."

"Sorry." I tried to keep my voice steady, but the burning in my throat made that impossible. "I'm still freaked out, I guess."

"It's okay. I'm sorry. I should have at least been in the house for you. I didn't realize..." He pulled me into him, securing his arms around my waist, and squeezing until I was completely against him. His chest was warm and his heart beat strong under my ear.

I closed my eyes, telling myself over and over he was really here. After several minutes, my heart slowed to a steady thump.

"Syd, can I tell you something?" Aiden stared down at me, and a strand of his hair fell over his forehead.

I reached up, sliding it back. "Sure."

"What happened at the party the other night—when you found out about the whole mating thing—I meant what I said about choosing you."

I paused, and I was pretty sure I forgot to breathe.

"I know I said later I wanted us to have time without dealing with that stuff, and I stand by that, if that's what you want, too. But I love you. You're the only one I'll ever want. If that means I'm waiting for years for you to choose me, I don't care. I just want you, and I need you to know that."

Flutters bounced around inside me, like a family of

butterflies trying to escape a cage all at once. "Is this a were-wolf proposal or something?"

His eyes flashed at me. "You could say that. If you need to think about it—"

I didn't. I loved him.

He'd be crazy to think I wouldn't choose him, and after everything we'd been through, being apart would never be an option for me.

I was completely his until my last breath.

I stretched up onto my toes and pressed my lips against his as hard as I could. His shoulders tensed at first, then he pulled me closer. The hum of static and elation erupted from his skin to mine as he kissed me like he was making up for lost time.

"I love you," I said.

He brushed his lips against mine one more time. "Are you saying yes?"

"Yes."

His face lit up, all tension leaving with his smile. "We can take as much time as you need if you—"

"I don't need time. Tell me how it works. Is there a ceremony or something?"

He tilted his chin down, looking at me like I should have guessed what *mating* was.

"Wait," I said, my cheeks flushing. "Oh…"

"A lot of wolves have a ceremony at some point, but that's a formality. You don't *need* to do that to claim your other half. But when you do claim them, it's binding. Until death. There's no going back, even if you fall out of love. Wolves believe you stick with your partner."

I paused. It wasn't the whole thing about till death do you part that stumped me, but finally putting together why we hadn't gone further with each other before. "That's why you shut me down?"

He nodded. "I wanted you to know what you were getting into. I've never been with anyone because of that."

A wave of relief settled over me, and I couldn't fight the small smile filling up my face. "Glad to know there aren't any women out there who I might want to fight someday."

Except Becca. Because she's Becca.

Aiden laughed. "You've had your wolf for less than a day and you're already getting violent."

"To be fair, I got kind of violent before the full moon."

He grinned and bent down toward me, pressing his mouth to mine again. My lips parted to meet his, and I threw my arms around his shoulders as he lifted my feet off the floor. My legs encircled his hips, and he held me against him, never breaking our kiss as he took us over to the stairs.

Through his skin, the gust of everything we both felt for each other collided. The bond whirred stronger, and I felt my wolf rising to the surface, trying to break free now that I'd chosen Aiden and he'd chosen me. Trying to control that part of me only made things more intense. More electrifying.

Aiden carried me up to the bedroom. Within seconds, we fell on the mattress, completely lost in the moment. He followed me, nipping at my lips as I shifted back toward the pillows. His hands touched my face, eventually working their way down to my hips. When he pulled mine against his, heat flooded my entire body.

I closed my eyes, inhaling his piney scent. That was something I thought I'd never experience again. Now it was so strong, it spiked my blood with exhilaration.

I skimmed my hands up his back, gliding over taut muscles and finding immense satisfaction in the way they shuddered under my fingers. Then I pulled on the edge of his shirt, and together we slid it up over his head.

He brushed his mouth across mine. It was feather light,

moving to my cheek, then carefully trailing down my jaw. Chills followed where his lips left their heated memory.

His hand curled around my waist again, his thumb skating under the hem of my shirt. I pulled in a sharp breath as the fabric slid up my skin.

And then his eyes met mine. They were like deep, glimmering pools I wanted to get lost in forever. I reached up, trailing my fingers through his soft strands and listening to his breaths as his chest expanded against mine.

"I love you, Sydney," he said, outlining my cheekbone with his thumb. "Forever."

I reached up and kissed him again. "I love you. Forever."

31

"Where's the meeting?" I clasped Aiden's hand and leaned on the console, batting my eyes at him. "*Please* tell me where we're going."

The corner of Aiden's mouth tipped up slightly, and he looked down at the clock. "All right. I guess we're far enough, I can tell you. It's at your dad's house."

"*My* dad's house?" I stammered, sitting up straight. "No way."

Aiden shifted his eyes toward me, his mouth quirking. He had guilt written all over his face, and if I hadn't just had the best moments of my life with him, I would have punched him.

"Please don't freak out," he hurried. "I didn't tell you when we left because I knew you'd refuse to come."

I scoffed. "I *might* have agreed to come."

He squeezed my hand gently. "I love you, but you're a terrible liar."

With a sigh, I sat back against the seat. I'd never been to my dad's house before. I was always too angry with him for leaving. That, and he'd never really invited me.

"Why? How—" I stammered. "How do you know where he lives and I don't?"

Aiden's thumb traced over the side of my wrist. "This was where we all met to figure out where you were. We couldn't do it in Shadow Grove, and we couldn't risk Anika or Lucille finding us."

We passed through a neighborhood of newer homes and finally pulled up to a one-story brick house with two white pillars on either side of the front door. The landscape was clean and cut, matching the neighboring homes perfectly, and I frowned. Its tidiness definitely reflected my dad's yard-work, and Liv's piece-of-junk car clashed entirely with it.

Aiden started to get out of the truck, but I gripped his hand tighter.

"Wait," I said. "Is…she here?"

His brows furrowed, and after a few seconds, he seemed to figure out who I meant. He nodded. "Cindy? Yes. She's here. And she goes by Cece."

"So much for her not existing," I murmured. My stomach clenched up like a fist. "Is she nice?"

He nodded again, giving me a sympathetic smile. "Yeah. She's really nice. You're gonna hate it."

"Ugh. How nice are we talking here? Like, just a little and I can still find a valid reason to punch her in the face? Or…"

"Well, she's how we found you."

"What?" My voice blasted through the truck. That would be my luck, that one of the people I never wanted to come face to face with would be the one who saved me.

"Your dad was so rusty with his magic, she stepped in to help. She was the one who came up with a solution, including looking for anything Anika left behind. When we found that, she did a locator spell on it and found the location."

"In exchange for what?"

He shrugged. "Nothing. No deals. No tricks."

"Are you serious?" I let out a harsh breath. "The universe hates me."

Aiden laughed. "Syd. You literally just went through an unimaginable night of hell and you think meeting Cece means the universe hates you?"

"Yes! Because now I have to like her or that makes me a jerk."

I guess being a jerk wasn't the worst thing in the world.

"You don't have to like her," Aiden said, eyes flashing with amusement. "But I know you will whenever you're ready to give her a chance. You two have a lot in common. She used to be a ballerina, you know."

"*No.*" I shot him a sharp glare. "Now you're just messing with me."

The silence told me he really wasn't messing with me.

"Couldn't you have told me something I wanted to hear?"

He chuckled. "I'll keep that in mind for next time."

I threw the truck door open and followed Aiden to the front door, closing in the distance as slowly as I could. His fist beat against the door four times, and my heart beat faster with each passing second.

Was I ready to meet the elusive Cindy?

Right when I thought about stealing the keys and taking the truck, Liv opened the front door and rushed out. "Holy crap, Syd. You're freaking alive," she gushed, her arms around me like a vice.

"Hey, Liv," I said, patting her back lightly.

"I'll give you two a minute," Aiden said, moving inside the door.

"Thanks, Fur Face," Liv sang as she let go of me. She threw him a mischievous grin, at which he rolled his eyes, though it was nothing like the animosity they'd shown until now. When she looked back at my face, her eyes widened.

"Wow. Your eyes really are purple. Like, a super bright, glam purple."

"Yeah. I guess I'll need contacts to go out in public again."

"I don't know. They're kind of freaky, in a really cool, sexy way. You should totally rock it all the time."

I laughed softly. "Thanks. So how are you? How's staying here?"

"Oh. I'm okay. Your dad's cool. And Cece cooks all the time. It's been weird not having to survive on frozen dinners." She giggled, but it faded quickly. As she looked down, she plastered a sad smile on her face. That was so Liv to cover things up.

"But really. How are you? Have you heard from your family at all?"

She shrugged one shoulder. "Yeah. I mean, Donnie and Dad have called and texted, but I haven't answered. Donnie sends me updates about Chris' recovery, though. They moved him out of the ICU, and he'll go home soon. I think they're hoping I'll come back to see him." A dark shadow drifted through her eyes. "Dad keeps saying that what we saw wasn't what it seemed, but I don't know what to think."

"I know. I'm glad you're safe." And I really meant that.

Liv's red-stained lips broadened into a bright smile. "Thanks. Me too." A few seconds passed. She cocked her head, examining me with narrowed eyes. "Hold on."

"What? Is there something on my face?"

"No." But she wouldn't stop staring at me.

"Then what are you looking at?"

"You smell different." She leaned forward and sniffed me, and I jumped back. She wrinkled her nose. "More like a dog now, for obvious reasons—"

"Jerk," I muttered. "Aiden told you, though. Right?"

"That you might be a hybrid? Yeah. Crazy. I guess you *would* smell different because of that, but I don't think that's what I'm picking up on. This is more…" Her eyes widened, and she grabbed my shoulders. "You mated!" She exclaimed it like she'd won the lottery.

"Liv!" Eyes wide, I put my finger to my lips to shush her, but she didn't get the hint.

"You had—"

"Don't!" I pressed my palm over her mouth this time. "My dad might hear you, and that's a thousand levels of awkward I don't want to deal with."

Her face lit up. "So, I'm right! You and Fur Face…*bow chicka bow*—ouch!" She yelped when my fist met her side.

"Stop it! Seriously. How can you even tell?"

"It's one of my superpowers." She flipped her hair off her shoulder. "Okay, fine. I've come in contact with a pair of mated wolves before and they had a slightly different smell. My hunter instinct picked up on it. The other wolves might pick up on it, too."

My stomach tightened. "Good to know."

She folded her arms. "So, how was it?"

My cheeks heated, but she got me to laugh, mostly in disbelief that we were having this conversation.

"Hey, are you guys coming inside or what?" Sasha leaned against the doorframe, her pink bob slightly curled at the ends today. "We need to strategize."

I followed Liv and Sasha inside, walking through this immaculate living room that looked more like a staged home than one someone actually lived in. Leather furniture surrounded a wide coffee table, complete with fake flowers, and stock photos of tropical islands hung on the white walls.

Voices carried through the house, growing louder as we slipped through the dining room and into the kitchen. It was huge, probably half the size of the house, and Dad was the first person I saw. He leaned against the counter, listening to the conversation from everyone sitting around the wide table, but jumped at attention when I walked in.

"Sydney," he said, taking long strides to me and pulling me into a tight hug.

The room grew quiet around us, and I didn't really know what to do or say without feeling like a spectacle. But I was the new hybrid in town, and this was probably how it was going to be for a while.

Dad didn't seem to mind my silence, and he didn't seem to have any intention of loosening his grip, either. My blood warmed, and I finally wrapped my arms around him for the first time since he left Mom and I. Tears threatened again, but I squeezed my eyes shut. I refused to cry in front of everyone.

Dad stepped back a little, reluctantly letting go of me before resting his hands on my shoulders. "I can't tell you how relieved I am that you're safe now. And how proud I am of you. Only the strongest survive."

"Thanks, Dad." I appreciated his words, but glanced down, too embarrassed to look at him now.

Dad stepped to the side, and when I looked up again, my eyes landed on a woman I'd never met before. A spike of dread nailed through me, especially at the way my father beamed at her. She had short blonde hair with silver high-lights, translucent blushing cheeks, and soft hazel eyes.

"Sydney, this is Cindy," Dad said, opening his arm out to her.

"Oh, Ezra, please, for the last time, it's Cece."

"I don't see why you don't like Cindy. It's a nice name," Dad argued.

She gave him a gentle shove as she approached and smiled warmly at me, running her palms down her denim button-up shirt. "It's so nice to meet you, Sydney. Your father never stops talking about you."

He didn't? I stared at her blankly, and then finally noticed her hand extended out to me. Hesitantly, I took it in a loose handshake, but I still couldn't find my voice.

How was one supposed to act when meeting the home-wrecker who broke up their parents' relationship? Rip her hair out one strand at a time? That's what I wanted to do, but she was also the one who found me in my darkest hour. The one who saved my life. And for that, I had to let her keep her hair.

Aiden pushed his chair out from where he sat at the table, probably sensing my rising pulse. He stood up, waiting and watching, like he was ready to come to my rescue—or maybe to Cece's rescue.

"Hi," I finally replied, letting go of her hand.

"Can I get you anything? Tea? Coffee?" She smiled again, her smooth skin wrinkling a little at the corners of her eyes.

"No, thanks." My voice came out a little cold, but that was the best I could do until Aiden came over and put his arm around me.

"Why don't you come sit down?" He led me over to the table where Liv, Omar, and Sasha sat, and as soon as I peeled my gaze away from Cece, I saw Pete.

"Pete!" Suddenly forgetting having met Dad's girlfriend, I lunged at him and threw my arms around his shoulders, knocking down a cane propped on his chair. "You're okay."

He reached over and gave me a one-armed hug. "And you are too. I'm so sorry. I let them take you—"

"Stop it. You didn't let them do anything. If anyone's sorry, it's me," I said, fighting back another rush of tears. When would I ever get my emotions in check?

"It's okay. Um, you are choking me, though," Pete strained out.

"Oh, sorry." I let go of him and stood back as Aiden pulled out a chair from the table for me. I took a seat, scooting in closer to Aiden while still facing Pete. "How are you feeling?"

He swiped his cane back off the floor and hooked it over his chair. "Pretty good. Tabitha's been taking care of me, and—"

Sasha fake-coughed from the other side of the table, raising her eyebrows at him.

"And Sasha. Thanks for the reminder, although I didn't really need it." He smiled at her, holding her gaze for a few seconds longer before turning back to Aiden and me. "I could walk across the room today, but I get tired really fast. Almost *jet-legged*."

I stifled a laugh, and Aiden shook his head. "Dude, that was *not* funny."

"For the love of everything holy, please stop with the leg puns," Omar said from a couple seats down. "I had no idea there were so many possible leg jokes until the drive over here."

"Come on. They're funny," Pete argued.

"No, they're not," Sasha said with a grin, patting his hand on the table.

"Fine. I'll cut back a little." Pete shrugged. "So, how does it feel to be a wolf now?"

The room fell quiet again, and my skin tingled with everyone's stares. "Uh... pretty good, I guess. I'm still getting used to it."

"Getting to know your wolf side is a process," Omar said. "You move differently. Your temper can be different, too. And from what I hear, hybrids are stronger than wolves. Or everything else."

"Everything?"

Pete nodded. "From what I've read in the past, that's true."

"Which means," Liv said, leaning her elbows on the table, "if people find out, she'll be a target."

283

My breath caught. I knew Dorian would want me, but others?

Aiden put his arm around me protectively. "And just so we're clear, we can't afford for this information to leave this room just yet. If word gets out, people will be afraid, and people do crazy things when they're afraid."

"Even more of a reason to find Little Miss Bitch Witch," Liv sneered.

"Liv," Dad said sharply, making his way around the table and taking a seat between her and Omar.

"Mr. C, I'm just calling her what she is. We have to find her. If she only wanted to turn Sydney over to Dorian, she doesn't have to personally deliver her now. All she has to do is tell others, and then he'll catch wind and come looking for her. Along with everyone else who's afraid." She glanced at Aiden, and he nodded, clenching his jaw.

"We need to find out what she's getting out of this, too," he said.

Dad sat back in his seat. "Why would a Solstice Guardian be helping an Ancient? Guardians keep them locked up."

"What if she was the one who woke him up?" Cindy —*Cece*—asked from behind us. I didn't turn around to acknowledge her like everyone else did, but she had a point. "Only the Solstice Guardians knew their whereabouts."

My muscles tensed as I went back to my conversation with Lucille in the barn. She said she needed me, and she was helping him for her own reasons.

"She had to have been the one to wake him up," I mumbled. "I'd bet anything that's what happened."

"We should let the other Guardians know. They can help us find her," Dad said. "If she's getting something from Dorian, then there's a bigger plan we don't know about."

The silence that followed was like a soaked blanket

draped around me. What kind of bigger plan could they be working on? How big?

"Is no one going to even mention the bounties on Sydney's head?" Sasha looked at us individually, saving me for last.

I sat up straighter, my mouth drying up like a desert. "What do you mean?"

"Everyone will be afraid," she said. "Seers will come out of the woodwork with their covens. And don't even get me started on how valuable your parts would be on the black market."

"Parts?" A wave of nausea washed down my face, and Aiden clutched his hand tighter around my arm.

Sasha shrugged. "Witches are always looking for rare things for spells."

"Sasha," Omar clipped. "Maybe not the right thing to say right now."

"We need to acknowledge *everything* we're up against," she argued. "This is more dangerous than anything we've ever faced."

My palms grew clammy. I heard what she was saying, but I couldn't accept it.

"She's right, and I hate to bring this up too, but…" Liv tapped her finger on the table. "If Dorian or Lucille have that knife, and he finds out you two are the dynamic duo…" She glanced between Aiden and me, and she didn't need to finish her sentence for us to piece it all together.

All Dorian would have to do is trace Aiden's blood to find both of us. It'd be the two-for-one deal of the century.

"We can't waste time then," Dad said. "Until we find Lucille or the knife, we'll figure out protective barriers…" He kept talking, discussing safety and procedures, but I couldn't listen. All I could think about were the odds stacking against us.

Covens. Black markets. Dorian. Lucille. A bigger plan.

Heat swept through me. I gripped the edge of the table to keep myself from bolting.

Was this what life would be like now? Always on the run? Never able to *live*? Not until Dorian was dead...

And I had to be the one to kill him. I had a year.

Was it really possible for me to kill him? Did I have what it took?

This was all too much.

I was way over the line when I made that deal. I'd been too trusting with the Seer's words. I let my desperation get the best of me. And now, if I failed, I would die. I wouldn't be able to keep Aiden safe in the end.

I could lose him still. I could lose my life. *Everything*.

I was such an idiot.

My insides coiled, and the longer I sat in this room, the more I needed air. And trees. I needed freedom.

I jerked. My skin pulled taut around my shoulders, tingling all the way down my spine. The room cast in a purple haze, shading the staring faces in violet.

Aiden's gaze snapped to me, and he started to speak, but the cabinet doors tremored around us. He looked around the room, eyes as wide as everyone else's.

Plates tinged together. The lights flickered. Pete's cane toppled to the floor.

My breaths came faster and harder.

Aiden reached for me. "Syd, are you doing that?"

When he touched me, it was like a zap of electricity bolting through my blood. I couldn't answer him. I just sat there, on the brink of hyperventilating and staring at my hands.

"We have to go," he said. "Before you lose it."

He tugged on my arm, barely snapping me out of my

stupor. I mechanically followed him through the house and out the front door.

The earthy smell was an instant rush of relief to my lungs, but my hands shook and the wind kicked up around us, rustling pieces of our hair around.

"Breathe." Aiden cupped my face. "You have to calm down."

"I can't." I blinked back tears, unsure how to calm the storm literally exploding out of me. With each passing second, my wolf tried to break free, but I kept pushing back, keeping her in this mental prison that only brought more grief. "We'll never be safe. And I'm not splitting up. We can't do that."

"We *are* safe," Aiden insisted. "We're with all these people who care about us, and I'll never let us get separated again. That's not going to happen."

"But Dorian is out there. He'll find me. And then he'll find you if I fail."

"Fail at what?" he asked over the roar of the wind.

My heart sank to my toes. I'd hoped to avoid having to tell him about the deal for a while longer. He would be so angry.

"Sydney, fail at *what*?" he asked again, squinting as the air swirled so much the leaves ripped off the tree behind him one by one.

"I'm supposed to kill him."

Aiden shook his head. "What makes you think you're supposed to kill him alone? He's an Ancient. We don't even know if he *can* be killed."

Panic rifted through me, threatening to shatter me from the inside out. What had I done? Tears leaked from my eyes, and Aiden looked up as the storm door banged open on its own behind me.

"Syd, tell me what's happening."

I reached up, curling my fingers around his wrists as he clasped the back of my neck. "I made a promise to kill Dorian. It has to be me, and I have a year to do it."

Aiden shook his head, his eyes fluttering over my face. "What are you talking about?"

"I made a deal with the Seer. I promised if he told me how to survive the transition, I'd let him go…and I'd kill Dorian."

"You did what?" Aiden lowered his chin, his shoulders stiffening. Through the bond, I felt his wave of anger and fear rolling through me like a tornado. "What were you *thinking* making a deal like that?"

On the verge of completely losing control, I stepped away from him. My muscles spasmed, and the fine hairs all over my arms and legs stood up. "You can't be mad at me for it," I yelled. "You did it for me before, and now I did it for you."

With that, the ball of emotions in my chest burst at the seams, unraveling beyond what I could handle. My back stiffened, painlessly cracking and sending me onto my hands and knees. I curled my fingers into the grass.

"Just shift," Aiden said over me. He raised his shirt up over his head and tossed it to the ground. "We'll talk about this, but right now, you need to free everything. I'll go with you."

I nodded, taking a breath to stop fighting the change. My body shook down to every cell, but when something flickered inside me, I knew Aiden had shifted behind me already.

That was new. I could always tell with the bond that he was near, but now I could sense what form he was in.

He stepped up into my peripheral vision, and seeing his bold blue irises among sleek black fur settled everything inside me. I let out a deep exhale, and when I opened my eyes, I looked down at fur and claws.

Aiden gave a nod and took off running toward the trees. He looked back at me and his voice rang through my head, almost startling me.

Come on, he said.

Without hesitation, I sprinted after him. *How can I hear you?*

We're mates, he answered. He bolted ahead into the woods, probably to give me some space, and I bounded up the hill behind him.

The wind instantly died down around me, giving me this sense of peace and release I desperately needed. I leapt through the tree line like crossing the finish line in a marathon.

My paws took me so fast between the trees, the air whisked through my fur like a gentle hand stroking over my skin. The woodsy scent circulated through my lungs, calming me like I was home.

Out here, I could finally breathe.

As I watched Aiden briskly move up ahead, my mind cleared from raw fear to a determination I'd never felt before.

With every second, it became clearer that my mission would not stop at killing Dorian. It would never be enough if I wanted to survive this life and keep my mate safe.

No. I had to be stronger and more powerful than anyone who would ever come for me…

I had to give in to whatever it meant to be a hybrid—no matter the cost.

Thank you for reading!

Sydney's story continues in Red Moon Rise, book 3 in the Wolves of Shadow Grove series.

ABOUT THE AUTHOR

Leah was born and raised in Virginia, and now resides in Northern VA with her hunky hubby, two kids, and German Shepherd.

By day she conquers tantrums and milk-spills, and by night she conquers the keyboard, delving into Paranormal and Urban Fantasy worlds with magic and high-stakes.

She loves to read and write stories with sassy heroines, a little humor, and sizzling [no spice] romances that will take you on an emotional roller coaster.

Leah's a huge fan of Friends, Wonder Woman, coffee, and buying books she makes no promises to read one day.

Visit https://leahcopeland.mailerpage.io/ for the latest news and updates.

Made in the USA
Columbia, SC
16 September 2024

41886452R00161